FALLEN ANGEL

Some angels never find their path to heaven...

DI Stacey Collins has seen the darker side of humanity all too often. A single mum brought up on the grim Blenheim estate, she knows only too well what terrors the world can hold, but even her jaded eyes have never witnessed a crime of such unspeakable horror. A body, broken and lifeless, is found in the gloom of a London church. Kidnapped and horrifically murdered, young Daniel Wright never knew his tormentor – and this is only the beginning. Soon Collins finds herself both haunted by the demons of her past and battling in the name of innocence itself...

Please note: *This book contains material which may not be suitable to all our readers.*

FALLEN ANGEL

FALLEN ANGEL

by

Kevin Lewis

Magna Large Print Books
Long Preston, North Yorkshire,
BD23 4ND, England.

British Library Cataloguing in Publication Data.

Lewis, Kevin
    Fallen angel.

    A catalogue record of this book is
    available from the British Library

    ISBN 978-0-7505-3054-5

    ⟋⟍⟋⟍

First published in Great Britain in 2008 by Penguin Group

Copyright © Kevin Lewis, 2007

Cover illustration © Elisa Lazo by arrangement with
Arcangel Images

The moral right of the author has been asserted

Published in Large Print 2009 by arrangement with
Penguin Books Ltd.

Magna Large Print is an imprint of Library Magna Books Ltd.

Printed and bound in Great Britain by
T.J. (International) Ltd., Cornwall, PL28 8RW

This book is dedicated to my sister Sharon for standing up for herself and having the courage to start a new life.

Proud of You, Buddy
Kx

Friday

Prologue

'He won't kill my little boy, will he?'

It was just before three on a sticky July afternoon, but, despite the stifling heat, all the windows in the small terraced house on the outskirts of Croydon were firmly closed, turning the living room into a makeshift sauna.

Christina Eliot's voice cracked as she spoke. Her eyes bloodshot, desperately looking for signs of reassurance, she searched the blank faces of the four men in the pastel-coloured living room, but there was none to be found. Beads of sweat ran down her forehead, her face was pale and drawn, and her usually immaculate shoulder-length brown hair had clumped into sticky strands behind her ears.

David sat beside his wife, his thick-set features struggling to cope with the heat. Dark wet patches had formed under his arms and at the base of his spine. The other men in the room were not faring much better. When one had tried to open the window, Christina had immediately asked him to close it. She couldn't bear to hear the happy sounds of the children – many of them Daniel's friends – playing outside.

It had been a little more than forty-eight hours since her eight-year-old son, Daniel, had gone missing. The sheer horror Christina and her husband David had experienced when they realized

11

their only son could not be found had subsequently been replaced by an absolute and all-consuming terror when they discovered he had been kidnapped.

The first contact had been through a text message to Christina's mobile phone – a number Daniel had long ago learned off by heart in case of an emergency. I HAVE YOUR SON. CALL THE POLICE AND HE DIES. The message went on to provide a user name and password for a Hotmail account. At first they thought it was some kind of sick joke, until they logged on and found two messages sitting in the draft email section. The first contained a short video clip of a terrified Daniel in a bare room pleading for his mother. The second laid out the kidnapper's demands.

The instructions had been crystal clear: if Daniel's parents ever wanted to see their son again, they would have to pay a ransom of £25,000 and follow the kidnapper's rules to the letter. The drop-off was to be made by David Eliot on Friday. The money was to be in used bills with random number sequences, and under no circumstances were the police to be involved. A single slip or deviation from any of these instructions, and Daniel would die.

Why on earth would anyone kidnap their son? She was a secretary on thirteen thousand a year, he a mechanic on not much more. Their home was partly owned by a housing association, and Daniel attended the local state school. How could they be expected to raise £25,000? What sick bastard would do something like this?

During the next few hours they had maxed out

12

their credit cards, borrowed from friends and family, and withdrawn their small savings before finally requesting an urgent meeting with their bank manager. Their desperation to get hold of such a large sum of money and their refusal to leave the manager's office led to the police being called and the Eliots being escorted out of the building. It was at this point that Christina broke down and told the officers of the kidnap demand. Shortly afterwards an unmarked car carrying two plain-clothes police officers posing as insurance salesmen arrived at the door of their home.

With little money to give the kidnapper and fearing for the safety of their son, the Eliots soon agreed to let the police take over the case. Detective Chief Inspector Colin Blackwell, one of the officers posing as a salesman, had sat down with the parents and explained that, while he was not able to make any promises, in the entire history of the Metropolitan Police's Kidnap and Extortion Unit they had never lost a single soul and that they were not about to start now.

As for the money, Blackwell had produced £5,000 and suggested handing this over, along with a handwritten note from the mother explaining that this was all they could afford in the short term. It was a technique the police had used in the past to draw the kidnappers out, force them to engage in negotiations and therefore buy them more time to track down the victim.

Neither Christina nor David had been convinced. If Blackwell had access to a special fund for these kind of cases, then why not simply pay all the money?

DCI Blackwell had been in the force for nearly thirty years and had spent the last seven as the head of the kidnapping unit. In his experience the whole thing stank of opportunism – the relatively small amount of cash being asked for pointed to someone desperate for money who had made the mistake of thinking this might be an easy way to get hold of it. Most of the cases Blackwell dealt with involved rival gangs kidnapping one another as part of their brutal turf wars. This was amateur hour. 'Whoever did this is completely out of their depth,' he reassured them. 'We're going to be ahead of him every step of the way.'

That had been on Wednesday. Since then a team of specialists from Blackwell's unit, officially known as SCD7 (Specialist Crime Directorate), had begun to monitor all communications in and out of the Eliots' house from the fifth floor of their high-tech base at New Scotland Yard. There had been daily emails containing more disturbing video images of Daniel and regular threats about what would happen to him if the kidnapper's demands were not met. All they were waiting for were the final details of the drop-off.

At 3.08 p.m. Christina's mobile rang. Everyone sat up as a charge of adrenalin shot through the room. They all looked at the phone as it vibrated on the glass coffee table. Christina turned to face Blackwell, who was already talking quietly down the phone to colleagues back at base. 'Are you ready?' he asked the person at the other end of the phone. When he received the acknowledgement he wanted, he nodded at Christina, doing his best to give a look of encouragement.

14

Christina picked up the phone and flipped it open.

'Hello?' Her voice was quiet, nervous.

At first the person on the other end of the line said nothing, and all she could hear was the sound of breathing – heavy, certainly, but slow, very slow. And then, at last: 'Do you have the money?' The man's voice was deep, controlled and measured. It sent the same chill down her spine as it had when she heard it on the videos.

'Yes.'

'Good. Now listen carefully. Embankment underground station. There is a line of three telephone boxes on the left of the news-stand. The middle phone will ring at precisely 5 p.m. Your husband better be there to answer it.'

'He will.'

'You understand what will happen if he doesn't make it.'

'Yes, I understand.'

DCI Blackwell was drawing letters in the air with his finger, signalling for Christina to ask the kidnapper a specific question, one she could only barely bring herself to say out loud.

'How do I know ... how do I know that you haven't...'

The kidnapper grunted, and Christina heard the sound of his hand closing around the bottom of the phone's handset. Suddenly the sound of breathing was gone, replaced by a new, lighter voice. A scared voice. The voice of a small child.

'Mummy?'

'Daniel? Daniel! I'm here, my darling...'

But the boy was gone, and the kidnapper was

15

back on the line. 'I'll be watching. If I see any sign of the police, any sign of a trap, if you deviate from my instructions in the smallest way, the next time you see your son, he'll be in a box.'

Christina felt her stomach twist. 'He's just a little boy,' she sobbed.

But there was no response. The line was already dead.

As Christina was being comforted by the family liaison officer, Blackwell was still on the line to New Scotland Yard.

'Do you have anything?'

He could hear the sound of fingers frantically tapping against a keyboard before he got his answer. 'Mast 2275. Elephant and Castle. Phone's a Sony Ericsson K75oi, unregistered.' Another pause, more finger tapping. 'The phone's moving south. Requesting CCTV coverage. Wait. The signal is gone. Battery's been taken out. I'm sorry, sir, we've lost him.'

There was something about the call that set Blackwell's mind racing. The kidnapping unit had the ability to trace phones even when they had been switched off – unless the battery was removed. Very few people knew about this, and yet the kidnapper had taken out his phone's battery, ensuring that this could not be done. The incident left Blackwell unsettled in a way he had never been throughout his whole career. Maybe this guy wasn't such an amateur after all.

Blackwell chased the thoughts out of his mind and refocused his attention on the delivery of the ransom money. Despite the kidnapper's demands, David Eliot would not be making the drop. Instead a member of Blackwell's team would go in his place. Earlier, DCI Blackwell had explained to the parents that in every case of this kind, the point at which the kidnapper attempted to collect the money was when he became the most vulnerable. It was their best chance of catching whoever was responsible.

David and Christina stood by the living-room window, neither touching the other, as they watched Blackwell and his team head off for the vicinity of the drop-off site. All that was left of the unit was the family liaison officer. Blackwell had seemed calm, confident and more than a match for whoever had taken their son.

They couldn't help but feel confident that Daniel would be home soon.

The waiting was the worst part. The agony and uncertainty seemed to go on for ever. At first Christina and David sat in silence, watching the hands of the cheap carriage clock that sat on their mantelpiece drift slowly around its face. When Christina could bear it no longer, she opened the laptop computer that had been sitting on the coffee table.

David stood up and looked down at her, the horror visible on his face. 'Jesus fucking Christ, not again,' he raged. 'Just leave it alone.'

'I want to see my son,' she said, her voice wavering dangerously. 'I need to see my son.'

Christina pressed a few keys, and the screen was suddenly filled with a dark, grainy video clip, along with the sound of a key unlocking a door.

17

The room was dimly lit by a bare bulb hanging from the centre of the ceiling. The camera shook as its operator walked in, but when it stopped, the screen was filled with the image of Daniel lying on a stained mattress that had been thrown into the far corner of the room. His eyes were red from crying, but the look of exhausted terror on his face made him almost unrecognizable, even to his mother.

It was the second of three videos the kidnapper had sent, a new one every day as stark proof that the boy was still alive, each one tormenting the parents further.

Christina didn't know how many times she had watched them, paused them and examined them closely in an attempt somehow to feel closer to her son. She had observed, even in the poor light, how dirty his face had been, how his lips, normally so pure and angelic, seemed red and raw. At first she could not work out why this should be, but then DCI Blackwell had gently explained that the marks were mostly caused by pulling off the tape that had been used to silence him. Her son gazed into the camera without saying anything, and it was almost as though he was looking directly at her. She stretched out her hand and touched her fingers to the screen, gently caressing the image of Daniel's cheek.

The man behind the camera spoke in a voice lacking in any emotion. 'Say something.' You could read nothing into it – God knows she had tried. And at New Scotland Yard they had tried even harder, listening for any outside noise – a bus, a plane, anything that would help to narrow down the search. Christina held her breath, knowing with such pain what was about to happen but unable to tear her eyes away.

'Say something, Daniel.' She whispered the words under her breath in an unconscious echo of Daniel's captor. She continued to watch as the camera moved closer to her son. His eyes winced as a hand appeared in front of him. It dealt him a quick but brutal blow on the side of the head, jolting the camera in the process. For a moment Daniel disappeared from the picture. There was a childish whimper, followed by the words that she had repeated so many times in her head: 'No. Don't hit me again. I want my mummy.'

She knew she was playing into the kidnapper's hands, yet Daniel's agonized words were her only source of comfort, her only contact with her missing son. This time, however, as they replayed yet again, her husband slammed his fist on the table. 'For fuck's sake,' he said through gritted teeth. 'Turn it off.' But it was too late. The video finished there, stuck on the final frame of Daniel lying face down on his bed.

David got up and stormed out of the room, leaving the family liaison officer to comfort his weeping wife. By the time he returned, clutching a glass of scotch, Christina was sitting rigid on the sofa, her pale, drawn features transfixed once more by the hands on the carriage clock. Her lips moved as she silently counted off each second. As she reached 5.03 and fourteen seconds, her phone rang. Instantly alert, her heart in her mouth, she snatched it off the table. 'Do you have him?' she said breathlessly, expecting to hear Blackwell's voice on the other end of the line.

She was coldly interrupted. 'Be quiet,' said the voice with its subdued authority. 'If you speak again, I will hang up.' The man paused to allow his ultimatum to sink in. 'You've failed to follow my instructions,' he said flatly.

Daniel's mother started to feel dizzy, as though her mind had suddenly been divorced from her body and she was experiencing the conversation from another place.

'I told you what would happen.'

A choked sob escaped Christina's lips. It was like no sound she had ever made before.

'You know exactly what this means.'

Christina's body started to bend over, almost as though there were physical pains in her abdomen that were making her do so. She knew, with a dreadful certainty, what she was about to hear.

'Daniel is going to die.'

The line clicked dead, Christina dropped her phone, and an awful, inhuman scream filled the room.

1

Father Patrick Connelly, the stooped and elderly incumbent of the church of St Andrew's in Peckham High Street, was uncomfortably warm as he hurried along the path towards his place of worship.

The last service of the day was never particularly well attended, this being a part of London where gods other than his were worshipped, especially by the young. Friday night Mass had long seemed – Lord help him – something of a chore after the rest of the day's ministry. It was therefore one of the shortest of the week.

He looked up at the church as he approached. The white stone walls, rendered black by the fumes and dirt of London living, always saddened him, and he found it a relief to get inside, where the rich colours of the Victorian interior and the quiet dignity of the altar would fill him with the inner warmth that had comforted him ever since he joined the Catholic Church. Outside all seemed chaotic; inside was a place of peace.

The key to the heavy front door of the church was pleasingly large and chunky. It was a shame that he had to keep the place locked when it was unattended. While the gangs of youths that roamed the streets were happy enough to let him pass through their territory unmolested – he had no mobile phone and never carried enough money to make him a worthwhile target – they would never be able to resist the temptation of the valuable ornaments within.

As Father Connelly inserted the key into the lock, the door swung open. His first reaction was one of horror. Had he really forgotten to lock up again? Eager to check whether his mistake had allowed in any vandals, he headed for the light switches, his footsteps echoing gently off the stone floor. As he flicked on the first switch, the church filled with a faint electric hum and its front section lit up, revealing the ornate splendour. Nothing seemed out of place but there was an unusual odour in the air. It was a strong, metallic smell like nothing he had ever known. Father Connelly took a large lungful and tried to make it out as he continued to turn on the lights.

Then something in the centre aisle caught his eye. As he moved closer, he could see that it was a puddle of dark liquid. In front of it was a piece of paper. He bent down to pick it up and immediately recognized it as a page from the Bible. One passage had been underlined in what looked like red ink.

By the disobedience of one man, many were made sinners.

The text only barely permeated his consciousness, for, as he read, a drop of liquid hit the side of his cheek. He instinctively reached up to wipe it away, then stared hard at the sticky red stain that covered his fingers.

As he raised his head, another drop of blood fell on to his face.

Something was above him.

Hanging from the rafters was a body. Apart from the bare feet, which pointed listlessly at the stone floor, it was fully clothed. The face had been horrifically disfigured with deep, diagonal slashes. One hand was missing, and the mouth hung open as if emitting a desperate, silent scream.

But it was none of these things that made Father Connelly turn to one side and retch over the wooden pews. It was not the death, or the blood, or the disfigurement that unsettled him so. It was the fact that the corpse hanging there so dreadfully above him was that of a child.

'Holy Mother of God,' he whispered to himself, making the sign of the cross with a trembling hand. He turned and ran as fast as his legs would carry him, stumbling occasionally in his robes as he tried to wipe the blood from his face, and screaming for help in a voice that echoed helplessly off the walls around him.

2

Stacey Collins could not remember how the argument had started – she was just desperate for it to end.

Her daughter, Sophie, was one of only three pupils from her school who had been selected to play at a gala concert later that evening at the Fairfield Halls in Croydon. Despite this, Sophie had not spoken to her mother since she had got home earlier that day, ignoring her in the way that only a twelve-year-old could.

They were sitting at the table in the kitchen eating pizza with Stacey's parents. Sophie had barely eaten a slice and was just playing with the rest. The silence grew more and more uncomfortable, until Stacey could bear it no longer.

She turned to face her daughter. 'What's wrong, Sophie?' Her voice, with its tinge of a South London accent, was calm.

Sophie continued to ignore her.

'Please, Sophie,' she persisted. We're trying to have a nice time together before the show starts.' But Sophie just shrugged without looking up at her mother and continued to play with her food.

'Are you ever going to talk to me?' The words came out a bit more fiercely than she had intended, yet Sophie continued to ignore her.

Sitting across the table, Stacey's own mother shot her a disapproving look. 'Just let her be. You're always nagging at her.'

'Thanks, Gran.' The young girl's voice was quiet and soft.

The four were cramped around the small kitchen table. Stacey's father, John, was in his wheelchair, as he had been for the past twenty-two years. Her mother, Penny, spent far more time with Sophie than Stacey was able to. She was grateful for that – of course she was – but sometimes it felt, with her parents always around, as if she had never left home.

Sophie got down from the table abruptly. Her pizza was hardly eaten, and she managed to look somewhat guilty as she caught her mother's eye. 'Where do you think you're going?' Stacey asked.

Sophie scuffed her way to the door before replying, 'My room.'

'What about the rest of your dinner?'

'Not hungry,' Sophie called back, already slamming the door to her bedroom.

The irony of the situation wasn't lost on Stacey. She was a detective inspector within the Met's murder squad whose work involved tracking down and capturing some of London's most dangerous criminals. She could square up to a drug-crazed killer any day of the week. So why couldn't she get a twelve-year-old kid – her own daughter no less – to do what she wanted?

As these thoughts ran through her head, her mother made her way upstairs to see Sophie, while her father manoeuvred his way uncomfortably around the kitchen until he was beside her. Something about his bulky wheelchair always made whatever room he was in seem smaller than it actually was. She always noticed the look of desperate concentration on his face as he tried to propel himself to wherever he wanted to be; she had to fight the urge to rush over and help him. That would never do. He hated not being able to do things for himself and was stubborn in his insistence on maintaining what independence he had.

As he drew the wheelchair alongside Stacey, the familiar fragrance of his cheap aftershave reached her nose. Ever since he had been confined to the wheelchair, he had taken the same care in his presentation as he had beforehand; he couldn't afford much, but, as he always said, when you lose your dignity, you lose your self-respect. And if he lost his respect, it would be the end of him. 'Watch how you talk to your mum,' he said softly. 'She's only trying to help.'

'I know, Dad. I'm sorry. It's just Sophie. She's like this all the time at the moment. I wish she could be a bit...' She struggled to find the word. 'Nicer,' she said, her voice barely masking her frustration.

'Like mother, like daughter,' he observed pointedly. 'Don't forget that when you were her age, you gave us just as much back-chat, if not more. Your mother and me thought you'd be spending your fifteenth birthday in borstal.'

Stacey smiled, even though she knew her dad wasn't joking. A silence fell between them again. 'Are you coming back to stay the night after the show?'

'No, love. We'll go home. I didn't bring my pills. Anyway, it'll be good for you and Sophie to spend some time together.'

'I'm sure she'll be thrilled.'

'You'd be surprised,' her father said, ignoring Stacey's sarcasm. 'You've hardly seen her for the last three weeks. She misses you. And I expect she's nervous. It's a big night for her.'

'Well, she's got a funny way of showing it...' she started to say, before being checked by her father's disapproving glance. 'All right, Dad,' she said with uncharacteristic humility. 'I'll go and see how she is.'

As her father moved aside to let Stacey through, they were distracted by a low buzzing sound. Stacey reached for the mobile on the kitchen worktop, flipped open the phone and answered it. 'DI Collins,' she said firmly.

She listened for a few moments. 'I can't. It's my daughter's gala concert tonight – surely there must be someone else?' She continued to listen. 'Okay,' she said in a resigned voice, 'I'll be there in ten minutes.' She turned to her father. 'I'm sorry, Dad, I have to go.'

John just sighed as Stacey knelt down to him. 'Please' – she placed her hand on his arm – 'please explain this for me – she'll take it better from you than from me. I'll try to get to the concert as quickly as I can.' Stacey got up and kissed her father on the head.

'Go and do what you have to do.'

'I love you, Dad.'

'I love you too, darling.'

3

The young PC in his fluorescent yellow waistcoat stood beside the tape marking the border of the crime scene and watched closely as the three series BMW pulled up close to where he stood. He only got as far as 'You can't park there, miss...' before Stacey Collins flashed her ID in his face.

'DI Collins, I'm the SIO for this case.' The young man immediately stepped aside and lifted the tape, allowing her to pass underneath. As she walked along the path towards the church, she secretly prayed that she'd been given the wrong information. But even in this house of God her prayers were not about to be answered.

The first thing that struck her was the smell: a mixture of blood, vomit and death. In seventeen years of policing she had never witnessed a scene like the one that now unfolded before her eyes. Up in the gloom of the rafters was a sight she knew she would never forget: the body of a young boy.

It wasn't just the poor child's youth; it was the look in his eyes – that of terror personified.

Perhaps it was the environs of the church and the mythological images on the stained-glass window that made the DI remember a book her parents had when she was a child. It had shown pictures of the nine circles of hell. The looks on the faces of the tortured souls had been so distressing to her that she used to insist on checking that the book was closed and safely hidden away before her lights were turned out at night. The same look was on this poor dead boy's face – exaggerated fear, a hideous caricature. She knew she would not be able to describe it to anyone who hadn't seen it, nor would she want to. Some things shouldn't be shared.

With her eyes, she followed the line of the rope that was attached around the boy's neck. From the ceiling rafters, it went down on a diagonal to the end of one of the heavy wooden pews on the left-hand side of the church, where it seemed to be tied in a firm knot.

The pews to her left were soiled with vomit, and the sound of a man's pitiful sobs, coming from a room adjacent to the altar, echoed around the church walls. She assumed both came from the priest who had found the body. She looked above the altar at an ornate statue of the Madonna, her hand held forward in a gesture of benediction, her gaze beatific. To Collins, it somehow seemed gruesome.

The fire brigade were quietly erecting a scaffolding tower around the body in preparation for lifting it down, but nothing could be done until the forensic scientist and his team of SOCOs, along with the pathologist, finished their initial examinations. There were still procedures to be followed, even in such difficult circumstances.

'DI Collins? What are you doing here?'

Collins turned around to see DCI Colin Blackwell moving towards her.

'I was on call.'

Blackwell's face fell a little. 'I was told Watson was on call.'

'He was supposed to be, but he's ill so I took his slot. Is there a problem?'

'No. Of course not. I need to give you some background on the victim.' His voice had a tone of disappointment in it that he couldn't hide.

'You know who this is?'

Blackwell nodded and began to relate the events of the last few days, doing his best to avoid eye contact with the junior officer.

Blackwell and Collins had run into each other a few times over the years, and there was little love lost between them. She was well known in certain circles of the Met but not well liked. Blackwell had first heard about her through an old colleague, DCI Sean Baxter, who had spilled the beans about her after a few pints. He was at his wits' end. She was insubordinate and a loose cannon without any thought for proper procedure or authority. But his hands had been tied: the DCS insisted that she should have a free hand, as long she continued to get results – which she did with astonishing regularity. Baxter knew that one day she would go too far, and that when she did, she would inevitably take good officers down with her.

They were three pints down when Baxter's tongue started to wag more freely than it should have done. There was one occasion, he said, when he had caught Collins attempting to falsify evidence in a child molestation case. Blackwell had listened and quietly absorbed the antics of this renegade officer. He would never have had her on his own team, and would never have wanted to work with her, especially on a case like this. But he knew that, although the Eliot case had started out with SCD7, it would now proceed as a regular murder case and therefore had to be passed over to homicide's murder investigation team.

'So. Who fucked up? You?' asked Collins once Blackwell had finished.

The DCI spoke through gritted teeth. 'Remember who's the senior officer here. This is my case.'

'You mean *was* your case,' she replied, turning to look directly at him. 'SCD7 is for kidnapping and extortion; once it turns into a murder, it comes under the jurisdiction of MIT. I'll be answering to DCS Higgins – which you know as well as I do. I've already called my team in, and they'll be here shortly.'

Blackwell frowned. He knew she was right, and it annoyed the hell out of him. 'But we have a relationship with the parents, we've been with them from the time the first call came in. And anyway, it's not down to you.'

'True, it's the Chief Super's call, but you guys don't have the manpower to run something like this. Something tells me we're going to have to learn to get along.'

Blackwell nodded slowly. 'I need to make a couple of...' He was interrupted by the ringing of his mobile. He glanced at the screen and saw displayed a number that filled him with dread: that of Daniel Eliot's parents. He had received more than a dozen hysterical calls from Christina ever since the kidnapper had told her he was going to kill her son. The family liaison officer was doing her best to try to calm the parents down but failing miserably. Blackwell knew he could not postpone the inevitable for much longer.

Blackwell excused himself from Collins, headed to a quiet corner of the church and hit the answer button.

'Do you have him yet?'

Blackwell knew he couldn't tell Christina over the phone that her son was hanging above him from the rafters of a church in Peckham. 'I'm going to be heading over to you very shortly, I promise.'

'What's going on? Something's happened. Something's happened to Daniel, hasn't it? Why won't you talk to me?'

'Christina, I promise I'll be with you soon.'

'Please bring my little boy back with you,' she sobbed. 'Please.'

Collins went over to the table the SOCOs were using to hold their evidence. A page from a Bible was inside an evidence bag next to a pile of gloves and swabs. She picked it up and read the words underlined in blood: *By the disobedience of one man, many were made sinners.*

The sound of a disapproving cough came from behind her.

'Didn't anyone ever teach you to keep your hands in your pockets at a crime scene?'

Collins turned to see Edward Larcombe, a veteran forensic scientist with whom she had worked many times, walking along the aisle towards her, two more evidence bags in his hands. They exchanged weak smiles.

Despite Larcombe's joke it was clear that they were both deeply affected by the horror of what they could see around them.

'I hope to God you catch the sick bastard that did this,' said Larcombe.

'I'll need everything you can find.'

'I'm already ahead of you. That's why I called in Jessica Matthews: she's the best forensic pathologist I know.'

Collins chewed slightly on her lower lip. She was always telling Sophie not to do this but sometimes did it herself without even noticing.

'Edward, are you religious?'

He looked confused by the question but shook his head. 'No,' he replied. 'Why do you ask?'

Collins glanced down at the page from the Bible. 'It doesn't matter. Have your guys found any sign of a forced entry?'

Larcombe shook his head. 'None.'

'Is the priest still here?'

Larcombe nodded and pointed to a door on the far right of the altar. 'The paramedics took him in there. He's in shock.'

The door to the side of the altar was slightly ajar. Collins pushed it open with her foot and stepped into the vestry. It was a small room, dimly lit by a single light bulb. A number of cassocks hung on the wall, and the air was filled with the musty smell of incense and old hymnals. There was a steel cabinet with a flimsy-looking lock on the front – probably where they kept the communion wine, she supposed.

Father Connelly sat on a wooden chair, his eyes staring blankly ahead of him, his deeply lined face grey and pallid. A female paramedic in bright-green overalls knelt beside him, gently stroking one of his hands. She looked up enquiringly at Collins.

'You're needed out front, one of the lads has fainted. You know what these probationers are like,' said Collins.

She shook her head. 'I can't leave him. I've just given him a sedative to calm him down.'

'I can watch him for you,' said Collins, smoothly interrupting.

The paramedic looked at her patient, then back up at the DI. 'He can't be left alone,' she warned.

Collins nodded, then knelt down on the other side of the priest and removed his hand from the woman's gentle grasp.

'I'll be back as quickly as I can,' the paramedic said before walking briskly away.

Collins had to move fast. It would only be a couple of minutes before the woman realized she had been sent out on a false errand – but there were a couple of questions that needed answering, and she knew from experience that it could be hours, or even days, before the doctors gave the all-clear to formally interview the old man. She took the priest's face in her hands and turned it towards her. 'I need to ask you some questions,' she said in a low but direct voice.

Father Connelly just started at her, his eyes seemingly focused within.

'Can you hear me?' she said, more firmly this time.

The priest seemed to nod his head, though in truth it was more of a tremble than a nod. Collins had so many things to ask him. Routine questions, ones that he was in no fit state to answer.

She ran through them in her mind. Does anyone beside you have keys to the front door? Do you know the parents of Daniel Eliot? Why would someone leave the body of a child in *your* church?

Then, in her mind's eye, she pictured the torn-out page from the Bible and the words marked out in red. She recited the line: *'By the disobedience of one man, many were made sinners.* What does it mean, Father Connelly? Why would someone underline it in blood?'

At first the priest just stared, as though he hadn't heard. But, at the mention of the word 'blood', his whole body suddenly started to shake, and Collins felt the rough skin of his face slip in her sweaty hand. He opened his mouth and took in a gulp of air, and then another. And another. In seconds he was hyperventilating, his lungs wheezing.

And then the paramedic returned. 'What the hell...' she started to say, before removing the officer's hand from around the priest's face. Collins stood up and let her attend to him.

'He's in no state to talk,' the medic barked over the sound of the priest's gasping. 'And you knew full well there was nobody in need of my attention outside. I've got a good mind to report you for this.'

The woman's voice boomed off the walls of the

small room, but Collins had already turned away. She wasn't going to get anything out of Father Connelly at the moment.

Back at the altar, Collins slowly absorbed the scene in front of her. She pictured the killer standing at the side of the pews, pulling on the rope as Daniel's body rose into the air. It must have taken some strength, especially as there would have been a good deal of friction between the rope and the wooden beam. Was it possible for one man to get Daniel in here without being noticed and then to hoist his struggling body up like that? Perhaps there was an accomplice, someone to help in his sinister night's work. There was no way of telling. All she knew was that she was dealing with a very dangerous person – or persons – capable of watching fear distort the face of a child, watching his legs flail around while the light of life slowly faded from his eyes.

Collins walked out of the front entrance, manoeuvring her way round a SOCO clad in a white boiler suit who was dusting the door and handle for prints. She made her way to the back of the church. She needed to see what was there. The answer, of course, was another cordon. The familiar blue-and-white tape cut off the road on either side of the back of the church, and two uniformed constables stood guard while a small crowd of onlookers wondered what was going on inside. Beyond the cordon the street itself was busy with Friday night traffic. A little further down was a pub with an abundant display of hanging baskets outside.

She looked up at the walls of the buildings

around the church until she found what she was looking for: a sleek grey rectangular CCTV camera trained on the street to record the drunken antics of trouble-makers who might cause damage to the pub or surrounding buildings. Collins made a mental note to ensure that her junior officers retrieved the footage as soon as possible and continued her walk.

Back at the front of the church, she saw a small laminated sign, held in a wood-and-glass frame, showing the weekly Mass times. Collins checked that day's services: there had been a morning Mass, a midday Mass and another scheduled for seven. The priest must have been arriving to prepare everything for the evening service. The phone call to Daniel's parents had been made at just after five o'clock. The killer must have known that he had a window of about two hours should the money not arrive or the drop-off turn out to be a set-up.

Larcombe appeared beside her. 'We're ready to bring the body down now,' he whispered. 'Unless you have any objection.'

Collins shook her head and followed Larcombe back into the main hall of the church. She stood beside Blackwell at the back of the pews as Larcombe walked up the aisle towards the scaffold tower that rose up directly beneath Daniel's body.

Collins was suddenly aware that everyone in the church had stopped to watch the operation in absolute silence. It was as though no one wanted to disturb Daniel from his sleep.

Two firemen climbed up to the top of the tower along with Larcombe and Jessica Matthews, the forensic pathologist. A stretcher was passed up and set in place, and the two firemen, with tears in their eyes, supported the dead weight of the child. The noose was gently lifted from around Daniel's neck and left hanging in mid-air as the boy's body was placed on the stretcher and secured ready to be lifted down. All eyes in the church were transfixed, and many of them also filled with tears as he was gently brought down to the ground.

Collins's mobile buzzed into life, alerting her to an incoming message. She retrieved it in time to see the name of the sender appear on the screen: Sophie. She hit the 'read' button and the full message appeared: THIS IS NOT FAIR!!!!!! YOU'RE NEVER AROUND. YOU PROMISED!!!!

Blackwell noticed how distracted she suddenly appeared to be. 'DI Collins, is there somewhere else you need to be?'

Collins snapped her phone shut. 'It's nothing. I'm fine,' she whispered.

Collins walked, over to where the firemen were gently laying the body down on a trolley close to the entrance. The boy's eyes were bloodshot and bulging. His mouth was wide open, as if emitting a silent scream. Up close the slash marks on his face were paler than expected, each one framed by congealed blood. His bare feet were a deep purple and horribly swollen where the blood had pooled. There were angry red rope burns around his neck, and the stump of his left arm had already been wrapped in an evidence bag.

Blackwell kept back. He felt strangely responsible for the boy's death. He hadn't been the one to hoist him up in this twisted way, of course, but the case had been his; the responsibility had been his. Damn it, it was only a few hours ago that he had promised Daniel's parents that he would bring their little boy back safely. Why had he said that?

Now he was going to have to tell them their son was dead.

They had called several times, and he had repeatedly put them off, knowing that he had to tell them face to face. Tell those poor people that their son was never coming home. Tell them that the worst thing that could happen to any parent had just happened to them. He looked across at Stacey Collins, who was still looking over the body. He knew that all the trust he had built up with the parents of Daniel Eliot had been shattered. The best he could do for them now was to reassure them that the police would do everything in their power to find the killer of their son.

'Collins,' he said, his voice much softer than before, 'I need to tell the parents. You'd better come along.'

4

He hadn't been watching from the kitchen window when it had started. He had wanted to, but there were things that needed to be done in the basement. It didn't matter, though; in his mind's eye be could picture exactly how it had all begun.

The cat would have been strolling aimlessy through

the back gardens, chasing a bird or perhaps looking for a mate. The scent of the tiny morsel of food would have hit its senses right away, and the animal would have pinpointed its source and wolfed it down. That would have put it in the perfect position to find the next scrap and the next and the next.

The trail he had laid led directly to the back door, where the especially loosened cat flap had been installed in order to encourage even the most timid of creatures to enter. It was the sound of the cat flap shutting that had alerted him, and he had hurried upstairs, panting with excitement.

The cat was in the centre of the kitchen, enjoying the veritable smorgasbord of delights that had been laid out for it. There were saucers of fresh, creamy milk, a selection of wet and dry foods as well as leftover chicken bones with a generous amount of meat clinging to them. It was this last treat that the cat had selected.

He looked down and took in the details of his new visitor. It was a smallish tom, tabby across the body, with white feet and a white tip to its tail. The cat lifted one eye lazily as he entered the room but soon returned its full attention to the feast in front of it.

He approached gently, with the manner of someone used to dealing with nature's most delicate creations. He kept his voice soft and low, avoided any loud noises or sudden movements. It was a technique he had perfected over the years, and one that had yet to let him down.

As he drew level with the cat, he began to lower his body into a kneeling position while at the same time stretching out his left hand, gently, oh so gently. When the hand was an inch or so above the cat's head, he began to lower it, until his fingers gently brushed the cat's upright ears and then made contact with the crown of its skull.

A soft, slow scratching motion on the head and behind the ears soon produced the desired effect – a deep, soft purr from within the cat's body. The cat was half sitting now, fully relaxed, eating to its heart's content and enjoying its scalp massage. Experience had taught the man that any second now the cat would give in to pleasure and roll on to its side, inviting the man to scratch its stomach.

He felt his breathing increase in pace, his lips turn dry, as he waited for the moment to arrive, that delicious moment, the one he had been dreaming of, the one he had been working towards for so long.

And then it happened: the cat's body seemed to lose all its stiffness, and first one front paw, and then the other, stretched out in front, and suddenly the cat was on its side, legs kicking uselessly in the air, its purr a gentle gurgle.

Then he struck. His heavily gloved right hand moved in as quick as a flash, grabbing one of the front legs hard, bracing it between his thumb and forefinger and squeezing harder and harder until … crack … the bone gave way, breaking clean in two.

He could feel the animal's pain, shock and surprise. The scream was almost human. The purr was gone, the cat was wailing like a police siren. The three remaining legs moved towards the hand, scratching, gouging, the head moved up to bite, but it was useless. The glove was too thick, the hand too strong.

He began to press harder and harder on the useless broken leg, forcing it down on top of the animal's throat. Somewhere in the body he felt another small snap, followed by another yelp of agony. A rib, perhaps, *an unexpected bonus.*

Down, down, slowly. The man moved to his knees and leaned forward. From here he could see the cat's eyes blinking wildly as it struggled against the impossible odds. Down and down. He looked deeper. He could see his own reflection; the eyes were like two deep dark pools. Then, slowly, its face seemed to go cloudy, the light behind the eyes seemed to fade. The struggles became slower and weaker, the breathing more shallow.

At the exact second when the last flicker of light ebbed away, his face was just inches away from the cat's. At that moment he felt an enormous shiver of excitement and sheer delight run down his spine.

He relaxed his hold on the animal's neck and moved to the other legs, breaking each in turn. He was getting better and better at this. Practice really did make perfect.

5

It was gone eleven o'clock when DCI Blackwell and DI Collins arrived at the Eliots' house. Blackwell had sent word ahead that he didn't want anyone to inform the parents that Daniel's body had been found. He had not only lost all credibility with the parents but had also lost the case, which is why Collins would be the one to break the terrible news.

The door was opened by David Eliot, and it was immediately obvious that he had been drinking heavily: Collins and Blackwell could smell the harsh odour on his breath. He led them unsteadily through to the living room, where Christina, her face wet with tears, was slumped in a corner of the sofa next to the family liaison officer.

Christina stood up immediately. Collins had done dozens of 'death knocks' in her time and knew only too well that no matter how well the parents had prepared themselves, confirmation would still come as a terrible shock.

Christina looked over at DCI Blackwell, who in turn looked at Collins, who took a deep breath.

'Mrs Eliot, Mr Eliot. I think you'd both better sit down.'

Usually when she said those words people had an inkling of what was coming, and Collins had expected that to be the case here. But for some reason Christina's eyes simply widened in expectation, as though she had not taken on board the negative implications of what Collins had just said. Her husband's emotional reactions had been flattened by the booze. The two sat down together on the sofa, Christina sitting straight and looking appealingly right into the detective's eyes.

'I'm afraid I have some awful news for you,' Collins began, as she sat in the armchair opposite. 'There's no easy way to say this. Daniel was found dead four hours ago.'

For a moment their faces did not change, as though the words were taking time to sink in. They just looked at Collins and Blackwell with a terrifying blankness.

Christina's reaction came first. It started as a whimper in which she breathlessly repeated the words 'No! Oh, God, no!' Gradually her voice became louder until she was wailing. Great racking movements surged through her, as she bent over double in grief and then sat up straight again to fill her lungs with air.

But the father's reaction surprised Collins more. He looked at his wife, helpless in the face of such despair, and all signs of drunkenness fell from him. 'Where?' he asked above the sound of his wife's crying.

'In a church. In Peckham. I'm so sorry, Mr and Mrs Eliot. I really am so–'

In an instant Christina was on her feet, her fists pounding into the chest of DCI Blackwell. 'You fucking bastard – you told us everything would be okay,' she screamed at the top of her lungs. 'You told us that our little boy would be okay.'

Blackwell made no move to defend himself against the attack. His arms remained by his side as guilty feelings overwhelmed him. 'I'm sorry, I'm so sorry...'

Christina stepped back. 'Sorry? Is that all you can fucking say? Sorry. Why didn't you pay the money? Why? You could have paid it all. He told us not to tell the police, but you said it would be okay. And now Daniel's dead. Now my little boy is dead. My son is dead because of you.'

Christina raised her hand to slap Blackwell's face, but Collins moved between them, grabbed hold of the woman's arm and hugged her. She hugged her so tightly that Christina eventually buried her head in the detective's shoulder, and her whole body became weak as she sobbed.

Collins turned to Blackwell. 'You'd better wait outside,' she whispered.

Blackwell left the house, still mumbling his apologies. He stood outside the front door, lit a cigarette and inhaled deeply, his mind churning over the events of the day. He had followed procedure to the letter, but now Daniel was dead. Where had he gone wrong? It was a question he couldn't answer.

In the Eliots' living room exhaustion had begun to take over from raw emotion as Collins continued to comfort Christina. The two women were on the sofa while David stood in the corner pouring himself yet another drink.

'At some stage we will need you to formally identify Daniel's body. But only when you feel up to it.'

David instantly stood up straight. 'Let's do it now,' he said gruffly.

Collins got to her feet and put one arm on David's shoulder. 'Really, Mr Eliot. You don't have to–'

But he quickly brushed her hand away. 'I'll do it now,' he said forcefully. 'Get it over with.' He looked down at his wife. 'She can stay here. She's in no state–'

Before he could finish, Christina was screaming again, this time louder than before. 'No!' she yelled. 'You're not going without me! I want to see my son! I won't believe he's dead until I've seen it for myself!' Her husband grabbed her by the arms, but she wriggled and writhed so violently that he soon took a step backwards. 'Get off me!' she shouted. 'Get off me! It's what you wanted, isn't it? It's what you wanted!'

David said nothing, seemingly in a state of shock. Whether it was shock at what his wife had said, or shock that she had said it in public, Collins could not tell. 'I'll take you both,' Collins told them in a consoling but unsure voice. 'Just as soon as you're both ready.'

David gave her a look filled with poison, then stormed out of the room.

Just then Collins felt the distinctive buzz in her back pocket. 'Please excuse me for a moment.' She went out into the corridor and retrieved the phone. Even without looking she knew it was Sophie. The guilt was already driving her crazy. Sophie had been rehearsing her clarinet solo for the gala concert for months. Stacey had insisted that she would be there, but once again her job got in the way of family life.

'Darling...' Stacey began. It was as far as she would get.

'Where the hell were you? You promised. You promised. I can't believe you. You just don't care about me at all, do you?'

'Darling, I had to work...'

'And that's all you ever do,' Sophie sobbed. Stacey could imagine her young face red and streaming with tears. It almost broke her heart. 'You're never around. You're never there for me. I'm the only one at school whose mother never turns up for stuff and I hate being the odd one out. You never come to anything. Your work is always more important than me.'

If there was something she could have done, anything she could have done at that moment to make it all better, she would have done it, but she

45

knew that life simply wasn't like that. Just then the sound of the kitchen door opening and David Eliot's heavy footsteps on the laminate flooring told her that her attention was needed elsewhere.

By now Stacey could hardly hear her daughter, whose words were being consumed by floods of tears. 'Darling, I'm really sorry, I promise I'll make it up to you this time. I really will, but right now I have to go, I really have to go. I love you, my darling, I really do.'

As she ended the call she heard a wail of protest from the other end of the line, followed by a stream of angry words she could not understand. She placed the phone in her pocket just as Christina and the family liaison officer joined David in the hallway.

'Okay, then,' Collins said with as much compassion as she could muster. 'Let's go.'

6

His stomach was full of butterflies – he could almost feel them moving. His large hands were clammy. There was a spring in his step. It had been a long time since he had been this excited about anything. He liked it. He liked it a lot.

He entered the lounge with its late-1970s decor. The light-brown corduroy sofa and armchair were slightly worn, but otherwise the room was in pristine condition. Someone had taken pride in this house. All the photographs on the ash-veneer sideboard and drinks cabinet were of him as a young child with his parents and grandparents. The walls were bare apart from a picture of the crucifixion of Christ. It sat pride of place above the dark-green tiled fire surround. The only modern items in the room were the large flat-screen TV with a Sky box and DVD player/recorder on a glass stand nestled in the corner.

As he sat down in the armchair, he noticed the remote controls were in the wrong order on the coffee table. He slapped his forehead hard and rearranged them – TV, DVD, Sky – then walked back out of the room, mumbling to himself. 'Everything must be right – stupid man – stupid man.' He counted to ten, as he always did, but this time much too quickly, as the excitement of what he was about to do engulfed him. He turned and re-entered the room.

He sat in the armchair the machine was all cued up and ready. He pressed the remote control, and the hum of the large TV came to life and then the DVD. He sat forward excitedly, but the first time he played it, he could barely watch himself. There was something about seeing his own body through the lens of the video camera, so new, so different. He couldn't get used to it at all. He didn't like it. So he had learned to block out the sight of it. Now, when he looked at the screen, he no longer saw himself, just whoever was in the picture with him.

The boy looked a lot younger than eight. He had been surprised when he saw him close up for the first time. He had long thought that with better nutrition and health care, that kids were bigger and stronger than ever. But not this one. Scrawny, stunted. A mass of bones. And he was so pale. But that might have been the fear. Yes, it was almost certainly the fear.

47

The boy's back appeared on the screen – which meant he didn't see him approaching from behind. That made him smile, the way he managed to sneak up on him like that. The boy was crying so loudly he didn't even hear the door open. And by the time he realized what was happening, by the time he tried to move into the safety of the corner, he was right on top of him. His body was sweating and he could feel the pounding of his heart as he continued to watch for what he knew was coming.

The light from the camera was shining directly in the boy's face, and he was frozen, like a rabbit caught in the headlights. A rabbit. He liked that.

Then came his favourite part. The part where he attacked him. He paused the DVD, then slowed the action down and ran it back and forth again and again.

When he had finished, which was much too soon for his liking, he set the disc back to the beginning. He sat there and watched the whole thing through again, beginning to end. The remote controls were by his hand, but he didn't need them. No fast-forward, no rewind, no pause. And of course it was even better the second time around. Not because he knew what was coming, not because he could move his lips in time to each and every one of the little cries and screams that escaped from the boy's lips, but because this time was special.

This time he was making a copy.

Saturday

7

Stacey Collins was woken by the summer sun streaming into her bedroom, casting the silhouette of the neutral curtains on to her cream bed linen. Her mind was foggy, the result of yet another night with an over-the-counter sleeping pill. Whenever she knew she wouldn't be able to sleep because of the stress of work or guilty feelings about Sophie, she would take a pill or two. As her thoughts cleared, she began to recall the events of the night before, and with these memories came the horrible realization of the task ahead of her.

Her mobile began to buzz on the bedside table, startling her from her troubled thoughts. She picked it up and saw the caller was identified simply as JS. She let it continue to ring and headed for the shower.

Stacey looked at her naked body in the mirror. She was thirty-five years old, with light-blue eyes and mousy-coloured, shoulder-length hair that had been gently highlighted and parted at the front. She had taken care of her body, and it showed. Her looks ensured she had no shortage of male admirers, but she remained single out of choice. Her relationships were always on her terms and rarely lasted more than one night.

As she entered the shower, her thoughts returned to the missed call. Only one contact on her mobile had been given initials instead of a full name. Jack Stanley. A blast from the past who had a habit of cropping up time and time again in the present. He was one of the few people outside the force who had her number, and it was the fifth time in as many days that he had tried to call her. She had ignored him every time. Whatever Jack Stanley wanted, he would simply have to go to hell.

It was just before eight o'clock, and her parents and Sophie were still asleep. Stacey poured herself breakfast – a bowl of good-quality muesli and a fresh vegetable juice. She would get her usual double espresso from the local Italian deli just around the corner from the station. No one had appeared by the time she finished, so she left a note for Sophie on the kitchen worktop:

Hi babe,

Sorry about last night
Will call you later

Love
Mum
xx

The investigation into the death of Daniel Eliot was to be headed by Detective Chief Superintendent Mark Higgins of the Homicide and Serious Crime Command. Higgins had been in the force since his early twenties. Now in his mid fifties, he had been involved in many cases that had exposed London's darker side and in the process had gained a great deal of respect from all the officers around him.

The media had learned of the case within an hour of Daniel's body being found. The front page of virtually every Saturday-morning paper carried a picture of a small body bag being wheeled out of the church and into a waiting ambulance. Earlier that morning Higgins had met with his superiors along with DCI Blackwell. The public outcry was going to be enormous, and the police would be under intense pressure to catch the killer quickly.

The incident room was set up on the first floor of Peckham police station, and, as Higgins made his way up the stairs with DCI Blackwell in tow, one concern was in the back of his mind – DI Stacey Collins. She and her team had been there for the crucial 'Golden Hour' and visited the parents. They had spoken several times on the phone, and she had done everything that he would have expected. He knew she was an outstanding detective, but in such a high-profile case the ability to liaise with the media and public was crucial. Collins had a reputation for being outspoken and arrogant. Was she the best lead officer for this investigation?

Higgins entered the incident room. His tall elegant posture, brown eyes, slicked-back grey hair and deeply lined face made him look ten years older. The whisper campaign had already started, and the talk in the room was all about SCD7 and how badly they'd fucked up. All eyes were fixed on Blackwell as he followed Higgins to the front of the room, where a white board with pictures of Daniel and the crime scene had been assembled.

Collins was sitting on a window ledge with her team – and chief amongst them was Detective Sergeant Tony Woods. Tall, black and twenty-seven, he had graduated from Cambridge University with a First in Psychology before joining the police force. A potential candidate for fast-track promotion, Woods had decided to remain at DS level for a couple of years because he enjoyed being at the sharp end of street work.

'The trouble with the police,' he had told her soon after they met, 'in fact the trouble with any profession is that as soon as you get good at a particular aspect of the job, they promote you so you have to start doing something else. Once you get good at that, they promote you all over again, until eventually you end up doing something you're crap at. For the time being at least, I'd like to stick with something I'm good at.'

And when it came to detective sergeants, Tony Woods was one of the best Collins had ever known. His knowledge of psychology gave him an uncanny ability to read people and situations. More than once he had asked the right question at just the right time to elicit a confession or produce a vital clue that helped bring a case to the right conclusion. Woods also had a reputation as something of a ladies' man, using his excellent knowledge of human nature to charm any attractive woman that he fancied. Under different circumstances, Collins might well have been tempted herself, but the fact that she was his superior officer seemed to have proved an incredibly effective deterrent so far as Tony making any moves was concerned.

Her team also included Natalie Cooper, a young detective constable who had caught Collins's eye during an earlier investigation. What appealed most about her was her attention to detail – careful almost to the point of obsession. In a world where people increasingly relied on a computer to draw out similarities between two seemingly unconnected cases, it was often forgotten that a computer is only as good as the information put into it. With Natalie, every entry on the computer was pure gold. If the clues were in the data, she would be sure to find them.

All three looked up at the Detective Chief Superintendent as he turned to face them. 'Settle down, please – settle down.' Higgins spoke in a deep Mancunian accent. It was a voice you didn't mess with.

'As I'm sure all of you already know, this case started out as a kidnapping. DCI Blackwell from SCD7 is joining the incident room to be our liaison from the original investigation.' Higgins had seen all eyes on Blackwell as they entered the room. 'Believe me when I say that the death of Daniel Eliot was in no way related to the pro- cedures that SCD7 followed. They did everything by the book. Do I make myself clear?' There was muted agreement in the room.

Despite what Higgins had said, Blackwell still felt uncomfortable. He knew what his fellow officers thought of him.

Collins looked around to see if there were any other familiar faces. One, a young Asian lad, caught her eye and gave her a weak smile. It was obvious from his expression that he was having trouble with the photos on the wall. Did she know him? Something about his face certainly looked familiar. And then it occurred to her. She had seen his face in the newspaper a few months earlier. This was Rajid Khan, a recent and highly controversial recruit to the civil support unit. Just nineteen, Khan had been a member of a notorious computer-hacking ring called the Sons of Eve, which was named after a popular computer game. Highly skilled, he dropped out of college to spend his days hacking into games and extracting 'cheat' codes to enable lesser gamers to proceed more quickly without having to spend months building up their skills. Charging a small fee for the service, Khan had soon found himself sitting on a nice little earner.

But his path to the inside of a police station had been a curious one. One of his cousins had been mugged on his way home, and, despite providing the police with a detailed description of his attacker, the officers at his local station had failed to make an arrest. A few hours later the cousin's house was burgled by someone using the keys that had been stolen during the mugging. When the police finally turned up, an officer explained that there was little chance of their finding the culprit and recovering the stolen goods. Furious, the cousin complained to Khan, who had promptly hacked into the website of the Metropolitan Police, changed all the faces of the senior staff into pigs and filled the 'Welcome' page with slogans advising the public that they were wasting their time asking for help and would be better off tracking down their local Mafia representative. The damage to the website had taken days to correct, thanks to a clever replication virus that had been hidden in the code. Each time the site was cleaned up, the modifications would return in a matter of minutes as if by magic.

Khan had been careful to cover his tracks, but his cousin had been so proud of what had been done on his behalf that he bragged to everyone who would listen. Within a week the story had made it into the papers, and the police were knocking on Khan's door. When the Assistant Commander in charge of the division found out what had happened, he proposed a novel solution: Khan could choose between criminal prosecution or working for the police. With only two options, it didn't take Khan a long time to decide. Since then he had helped to track down a gang of people traffickers through emails and mobile phone signals. He had also traced a paedophile ring to a computer hub on the south coast, which led to the arrest of more than fifty people.

Undisciplined, unruly and, to some degree, untrustworthy, Khan was nevertheless an asset. Whoever was responsible for Daniel's death had managed to send emails and video clips to the family without revealing anything about where he was. It was understandable why Higgins had brought Khan in on the case.

Collins focused back on Higgins, who was handing out assignments. 'Okay,' he said. 'Collins with her team are lead investigators. The civvy team are going to track down the emails that the kidnapper sent out to the parents. Up until now we've hit a brick wall with this. I'm hoping to get a breakthrough soon.' The four people in the team, including Khan, nodded silently.

Higgins turned to the team headed by Detective Inspector Yvonne Drabble, a CID high-flyer. 'You guys, I want you to pull in footage from every CCTV camera in the area around the church. And get every piece of film you can from the vicinity of the money-drop: there's a good chance that he was there before, in the past couple of weeks, so check it out. You know what we need. And I want to know the name of every sex offender and registered paedophile within a thirty-mile radius of this crime. I want to know what each and every one of them was doing from Wednesday to today.

'DCI Blackwell will be looking into other cases of kidnap for ransom, involving both children and adults, going back at least ten years. DC Cooper will be responsible for the HOLMES, so I want to make sure that every statement, every piece of evidence, every fact that we retrieve, is channelled through her.'

Higgins looked towards Collins and her team. 'We need to know more about the parents. How much do we have on them, on the father in particular? Remember that in seventy per cent of child murders one of the parents is to blame. I want to know everything about them, their background, their alibis. Be sensitive, yes, but don't feel you have to tread on eggshells. You might piss them off, but that's nowhere near as much as you're gonna piss me off if three months down the line you tell me the prime suspect was staring us in the face all along.' Collins nodded.

'Finally, I know this is a very emotional case, and we all want to catch the killer. But today's papers already have pictures of Daniel being removed from the church, and we don't want the sort of news coverage that will fuel public emotion further. We need to be at our best and most professional at all times – do I make myself clear?' Everyone nodded.

'Okay. Collins, come with me. They're ready to do the post-mortem. The rest of you know what you're doing, so let's get on with it.'

The people in the room began to disperse as Collins pulled Woods and Cooper to one side. 'Listen, guys, be discreet when you're doing the background checks. Don't let the parents know what you're up to.'

'Why?' asked Cooper.

'Because the last time they saw their son he was on a slab.' Cooper and Woods nodded. 'Tony, we'll go to see the parents when I get back from the PM.' Then she turned and followed Higgins out of the room.

8

DCS Higgins and DI Collins walked into Guy's Hospital. With a murder a day in London, both had been there many times before. Both knew their way to the mortuary and were moving quickly, ignoring the signs, pushing through doors, turning swiftly left and right, their footsteps clicking in the hollow antiseptic corridors. They entered the changing room and put on the disposable plastic gowns, overshoes and face masks that had been neatly set aside for them before making their way into the mortuary.

The room was stark and bright with white walls and a concrete floor that had been painted pale blue. Three large stainless-steel tables, each looking like a shallow bath sitting on a cylindrical pedestal, filled the centre of the room. The first was empty. The third was covered with a foamy mix of brown-black sludge and was being washed down by a pretty young mortuary assistant.

The centre table had been prepared for what was to follow. A video camera and microphone were suspended from the ceiling, ready to record the proceedings. Two trolleys, one loaded with surgical instruments, the other empty apart from a box of evidence bags, were in place on the far side.

As soon as she saw the officers, Jessica Matthews, the forensic pathologist, went over to greet them. 'Morning. We're just waiting for the Exhibits Officer to turn up, and then we'll be ready to start. He'll be here any minute, so I'll prepare the body.' Her educated voice held an aura of professionalism and authority. Matthews was thirty-nine, tall and slender with straight brown mousy hair, a few strands of which were poking out from under the bottom of her disposable cap.

All three headed towards the bank of square metal doors on the far wall where the refrigerated bodies were kept. Matthews stooped down to the door on the bottom left where D. ELIOT was written on a plastic tab beneath a small viewing window. She opened the door, releasing a blast of cold air that made Collins shiver involuntarily. She had been to plenty of autopsies, and they were never pleasant, but she knew she would find this one particularly difficult.

Matthews pulled out the metal shelf and the small black bag containing the body of Daniel Eliot came into view. The young assistant helped Matthews lift the body on to a trolley. As they were wheeling it over to the centre table, the Exhibits Officer arrived.

With everyone now in the room, Matthews switched on the camera and microphone and recorded the formalities of date, time, the name of the victim and persons present. She then unzipped the body bag to reveal the blue-tinged body within.

Matthews and her assistant lifted Daniel's body to the table and began to cut away his clothes.

'Oh my God,' gasped Collins. 'What have they done to you?'

Daniel's naked body revealed for the first time the full extent of his injuries, and even Matthews took a sharp intake of air as she saw the damage. There were deep slash marks on his chest and shoulders; his arms and legs were broken in several places, creating gentle unnatural lines in his body. Burn marks appeared at random intervals, and there was a deep puncture mark on his right-hand side just below the ribs.

Everyone in the room was shaken. To Collins it

seemed only yesterday that Sophie had been that small, that vulnerable. She had seen plenty of corpses before, of course she had, but this one was different. Usually a dead body had an aura of peace. Even those that had died violently seemed to carry with them a sense of relief that their suffering was at an end. But not this one.

'Are you okay?' Higgins whispered gently.

Collins turned to face him, wiping away the tears that were starting to fall from her eyes. 'I'm fine. Thanks,' she replied, quickly regaining her composure.

'Shall we begin?' asked Matthews.

Higgins and Collins nodded, and watched as she carefully inserted her scalpel into Daniel's left shoulder, cutting diagonally across his chest to the middle. She repeated the process on the other side, this time continuing down towards his genitals, forming the shape of a large Y on his small torso. As she began to peel back the loose flaps of skin to expose the ribcage, she looked across at her assistant. 'Please prepare the head.'

An hour later Higgins and Collins emerged from Guy's Hospital, back into the sunshine, and walked to the car.

'Fuck me, I thought I'd seen it all,' he said.

As Matthews carried out the autopsy, she gave Higgins and Collins her initial evaluation. Blue-tinged lips and fingernails, along with blood around the nose and severe bruising around the neck, supported a diagnosis of asphyxiation as the result of hanging. This was further confirmed by the internal examination, which revealed compression of the neck and burst blood vessels in the heart and lungs. Daniel's left hand had been chopped off with a heavy sharp instrument, most likely an axe, which had cut cleanly through the skin, sinew and bone. The body had lost so much blood that Matthews had to do further tests to determine whether this had been done pre- or post-mortem.

A definitive time of death also could not be arrived at until those further tests were conducted, but Matthews's initial findings suggested that Daniel had been killed around the time the kidnapper called the parents.

Collins, as lead investigator, then had to ask questions that might provide them with clues in their hunt for the murderer. She established that Daniel had not been sexually assaulted and that his stomach had been full of partially digested chips, which meant that he had been fed shortly before he died. Matthews sent several samples, including Daniel's clothes, scrapings from under his fingernails and various swabs from around the boy's body that might produce DNA evidence, to Edward Larcombe in Forensics.

'Why do you think he took the hand?' Higgins asked Collins as they got into the car.

'Trophy perhaps? Or might have held a clue.'

'Like what?'

'Maybe Daniel had scratched him and got his killer's skin and blood under his fingernails.'

Higgins nodded thoughtfully. 'Makes sense. What are your thoughts on the hanging? There are far easier ways to kill someone. He must have wanted to display the body like that for some other reason. But to get a struggling boy into the church in the middle of rush hour without being seen would be nigh on impossible. And he must have spent some considerable time in there breaking the bones and then stringing him up.'

Collins replied without answering him. 'There's also the question of why he tortured him. If he was going to kill him, why not just kill him and dump the body? It's like he wanted to punish the parents for going to the police.'

Higgins could sense growing anger and emotion in Collins's voice. It was clear to him that she was becoming increasingly distressed by what had happened to Daniel. It was a side of her he had never seen before.

'Stacey.' This was one of the rare occasions when he addressed her by her first name. 'I need to know if you are capable of dealing with this case.'

'Why are you asking me that? I'm just running through the possible scenarios.'

'I know. It's your emotional attachment to Daniel that's giving me cause for concern. I've never seen you like this before.'

'I'm fine, guv. Please. I'm on top of it.' Her voice was firm and assertive, and left no room for doubt. 'As soon as we get back, Woods and I are going to see the boy Daniel was with shortly before he went missing. I know it's pretty thin, but until the forensics get back, we've got nothing else to go on.'

9

Flowers had started to collect on the small front lawn of the Eliots' house soon after Daniel's picture first appeared in the morning papers. By early afternoon the entire garden was covered with offerings and still people were coming from miles around in order to pay their respects, some breaking down in tears as they left their tributes. Collins and Woods saw the flood of flowers as they passed the house, on the way to the home of Mr and Mrs Hardy, the parents of Sammy, Daniel's best friend.

An hour before Daniel had gone missing, he and Sammy had cycled to the local newsagent's shop to stock up on sweets with their weekly pocket money. Daniel had been abducted soon afterwards, but, if this was no random act, there was every chance that the person who took him had been quietly observing the boys earlier that day. Collins hoped the little boy might have seen or heard something that had been overlooked by Blackwell's team.

'Sammy's been interviewed before,' said Woods as they walked up the path to the door of the Hardy home. 'They didn't spend a lot of time with him, because at that point they were focusing on the kidnapping. Although Sammy was the last person to see Daniel, I don't know if we'll be able to get much out of him. And, from what I gather, the parents aren't keen on us having too much access.'

Collins noticed the curtains twitching, but there was no answer at the door, so she knocked again. 'Ever get the feeling you're not wanted?' she asked.

Eventually the door was opened but only a few inches. 'Yes?' a faceless voice said.

Collins introduced herself and Woods, waving her ID through the crack in the door. It opened wider to reveal a middle-aged woman in a plain skirt and blouse. She looked at the officers with suspicion. 'Mrs Hardy?' Collins asked.

The woman nodded.

'May we come in? We have a few questions.'

Mrs Hardy held the door open a little wider, and Collins and Woods walked in. The woman led them into an immaculate sitting room where her husband sat drinking a cup of tea. Collins made her introductions once more as Mr and Mrs Hardy eyed each other uneasily.

'We've already told the police everything we know,' said Mr Hardy.

'This must be a very difficult time for you,' Collins observed, without really addressing what she had just been told.

Mrs Hardy nodded her head. 'We're very shaken up. Daniel was a lovely boy.'

Mr Hardy spoke again. 'It could so easily have been Sammy. We don't usually let him go out by himself. It's only in the past few months...'

'Actually,' said Collins, grabbing her chance, 'it's Sammy I'd like to talk to. Is he here?'

Another glance between the two parents. 'He is

66

in, Miss, er...'

'Call me Stacey.'

'He's in his room. But is it really necessary to talk to him? He's a very sensitive little boy, and it's not good for him, having to go through all this. It was bad enough when Daniel went missing, but now...'

Mrs Hardy clenched her hands in front of her and looked appealingly at the two officers.

Collins walked over to the window. She pulled back the net curtain a little, then peered on to the street. There were surprisingly few children around, given that it was a beautiful hot summer's afternoon; but then maybe it wasn't surprising at all, given what had happened a few doors away. 'It's not the sort of thing you expect to happen in a place like this,' she said quietly.

Mr and Mrs Hardy shook their heads in agreement, and Collins let the curtain fall closed as she returned to the centre of the room.

'Having said that, it's not the sort of thing you expect to happen anywhere. Tell me, did Sammy and Daniel often play together?'

'They were best friends,' said Mrs Hardy, slightly avoiding the question.

'So Sammy spent a lot of time at the Eliots' house?' asked Woods.

Mrs Hardy seemed unwilling to answer, so her husband stepped in. 'Daniel was a sweet boy,' he explained, 'and we enjoyed having him over. But we didn't really like Sammy to spend time at that house. Have you met the Eliots?'

'I have, yes,' said Collins.

'Then you'll be aware that Mr Eliot is an

alcoholic.' He spoke rather primly, and said the word 'alcoholic' with a good deal of distaste.

Collins nodded but said nothing.

'A violent alcoholic,' Mr Hardy continued. 'There have been times when Mrs Eliot has had bruises on her face and arms. You can draw your own conclusions.'

'Have you ever personally witnessed any violent behaviour by Mr Eliot?' asked Collins.

Mr Hardy shook his head. 'We try to avoid him; it's not something we want Sammy to be exposed to. But he was insistent that he wanted to play round at Daniel's house on Wednesday. Mr Eliot wasn't around at the time, he was probably out drinking, knowing him, so we made an exception just so long as he came back nice and early.'

Stacey considered her next move. They were protective parents and justifiably so. If she wanted to get anything out of Sammy, she would have to get him on his own, and that meant winning over the parents.

She smiled at them. 'I wish all the parents we saw were as conscientious as you.' Woods took her lead and nodded his agreement. 'I used to run wild when I was his age,' he said. 'Of course it was a different world back then. You can't be too careful now. I think you play it just right.'

Mrs Hardy seemed almost to preen herself.

'Sammy must have gone through an awful ordeal,' Collins continued. 'It must have been very difficult for all of you.'

'It has been,' Mr Hardy agreed.

'I understand why you don't want to expose him to too much questioning. Police officers can be a little abrupt at times, especially when it's such an emotive case. They can be under a lot of stress.'

'I'm sure that's true,' said Mr Hardy.

'But I do need to speak to Sammy just one more time. He was the last person to be with Daniel...'

'But that was before Daniel went missing,' said Mrs Hardy. 'The boys were both home safely. It's his parents you should be talking to.'

'And we have,' said Collins firmly. 'But I need to make sure I've dotted every "i" and crossed every "t". If I'm going to find out who did this terrible thing, I just need fifteen minutes with Sammy. Please, Mr Hardy, I wouldn't be asking unless it was absolutely necessary.'

Another nervous look passed between the parents. 'Fifteen minutes, no more,' the father finally said with reluctance, and he nodded at his wife to fetch Sammy from upstairs.

He was a handsome little boy with ruffled light-brown hair and wide brown eyes.

'Hi, Sammy, I'm Stacey.' She held out her hand, and the boy took it to shake rather uncertainly. He wore a short-sleeved blue-and-white T-shirt, a pair of jeans and white trainers with a logo that Collins recognized instantly.

'K-Swiss! They're the best,' she said, crouching down so that her face was level with his. 'I've got a pair of those in black, Of course, mine are a little bit bigger than yours.'

The boy smiled.

'Have you got a bike, Sammy?'

The little boy nodded.

'Do you want to show it to me?'

Sammy smiled without looking at her. 'Okay,' he said.

Collins stood up again. 'Is that all right?' she asked Sammy's parents. They nodded their agreement. 'Tony, perhaps you could just run through Mr and Mrs Hardy's version of events one more time.' She knew Woods would not get anything new, but the parents needed to be kept out of the way.

She took hold of Sammy's hand. 'Come on, then,' she said, and he led her through the kitchen and into the small back garden.

Sammy's bike was lying on its side in the middle of the lawn. The blue paint was scuffed, and one of the pedals looked like it had recently been replaced, but he presented it proudly. 'Nice bike,' she noted. 'Did you and Daniel go out on your bikes a lot?'

Sammy's head fell. 'Sometimes,' he muttered.

She went over and picked up the bike. 'I bet you can go really fast on this.'

'Really fast,' Sammy agreed with the seriousness that only an eight-year-old talking about his bike could muster.

Collins pretended to examine the bike in more detail. 'Does it make you sad that you won't see Daniel again?' she asked obliquely.

Sammy nodded.

'Would you like to help me work out what happened to him?'

Again he nodded mutely.

'I bet you would. I've got a feeling you'll make a great policeman when you grow up.'

Sammy glowed at the compliment.

'The last time you were with Daniel, the two of you went to buy some sweets. Is that right?'

'Yes. He only had 90p, and I had two pounds, and so I gave him some of mine so we could have the same.' The words tumbled out of the little boy's mouth.

'That was really nice of you, Sammy. Do you want to show me where the sweet shop was?'

'Okay.'

They left the garden by a gate at the back that led to a narrow alleyway and, hand in hand, started to make their way down to the road. 'We came along here on our bikes.'

Collins bent down so that she was face to face with him. 'I want you to try to remember everything you can about the day you and Daniel went to the shops. Do you think you can do that for me?'

Sammy nodded in agreement, his little face serious.

They continued in silence as the alleyway joined the main road to the side of the terraced houses. They turned right and followed the road as it curved round towards a small parade of shops: a dry-cleaner's, an off-licence and a newsagent's with a red awning on which a Coca-Cola logo was emblazoned in big, swirling letters. Sammy pointed at it. 'That's where we went,' he explained.

'This is important, I really need you to think hard. Did anyone talk to you on the way to the shops?'

His brow crumpled in thought. 'No.' He

71

paused. 'But we heard a dog crying down there.' He pointed to a long alleyway at the side of the shop. 'There was this little puppy limping and crying. A little brown thing. It was a bit scary, really. Daniel went and stroked it, but I didn't in case it tried to bite me.'

'Do you like dogs?'

'Nah, not really. But Daniel always wanted one for his birthday.'

'Then what happened?'

'We went in and got a packet of crisps and a bag of sweets, then we stood outside and ate them.'

'So what happened when you finished your sweets?'

'Daniel wanted to go back and see the dog again, but it was gone.'

'Had it run off?'

'Couldn't have. It was tied to the white van.'

'What white van?'

Sammy looked at her as if she was being stupid. 'The one the dog was tied to!'

As they reached the entrance to the news-agent's, Sammy blurted out the one question he had been dying to ask. 'Do you have a gun?'

Collins smiled. 'Not today, Sammy. Come on, I'll treat you to something.'

Sammy's eyes lit up. He quickly selected his assortment of sweets and presented them on the counter. As the young Asian man counted them up, Collins tried to imagine the scene on Wednesday afternoon, the two boys on their summer holidays, deciding which treasures to spend their few pennies on. She remembered the feeling well from her own childhood.

'Ninety pence,' said the man behind, the counter. Collins reached into her bag to retrieve her purse.

'Do you own a dog?' she asked.

The man shook his head. 'Never much cared for pets. Don't see the point.'

'How about the other shopkeepers on the parade, any of them own dogs?'

The man shrugged. 'The bloke that owns the dry-cleaners, Ray, he used to have a pit bull, but it had to be put down. I don't think anyone else has one now.'

'Does anyone on the parade own a white van?'

'Well, I do, and Ray does, and the off-licence does. We all do.'

Collins and Sammy walked back outside, blinking in the bright sunshine after the dimness of the newsagent's. Sammy was totally absorbed in the process of consuming his sweets. Stacey allowed him to finish before asking her next question.

'What are Daniel's mum and dad like?'

'His mum's all right; his dad gets angry a lot.'

'What happens when his dad gets angry?'

'Daniel would sometimes sleep over.'

'Do you think he was scared of his dad?'

'Yes.'

'Was his dad there when he got home?'

'Dunno. I went to my house, and he went down the alley to his.'

'And that was the last time you saw him.'

Sammy's bottom lip quivered as the loss of his best friend started to hit home. 'Yes.'

She could see he was starting to become uncomfortable with her questions. 'Come on, Sammy,' she said, offering him her hand again. 'Let's go home.'

Mr and Mrs Hardy were waiting anxiously at the window; as soon as Collins and Sammy came into view, Mrs Hardy went to open the door. 'You didn't say you were taking him out of the garden,' she said accusingly.

We just went to get some sweets, didn't we, Sammy?' Collins replied. 'He's been very helpful indeed.'

'Stacey thinks I'll make a good policeman, Mum,' Sammy told his mother brightly.

'Come on,' she told her son, struggling not to seem cross. 'Inside.' She directed her conversation back to Collins. 'Is there anything else?' she asked rather coldly.

'No,' Collins replied. 'Nothing else. I've got everything I need. Thank you very much, Mrs Hardy. If there's anything else, I'll be in touch.'

But the woman made no acknowledgement and just slammed the door behind Woods and Collins.

'Christ, it's not much.'

Woods was driving north, back towards Peckham, and Collins had just filled him in on what she had learned from Sammy.

She was preoccupied. Talking to Sammy, somehow, had been like talking to Daniel himself. The kidnapper could so easily have taken either boy. And Woods was right: the little boy had given them practically nothing. But when all you have

74

is straws, she thought to herself, you have no choice but to clutch at them.

'I mean,' added Woods, 'you're looking for something suspicious but don't know what. It's bad enough looking for a needle in a haystack. You're looking for a piece of hay in a haystack.'

Collins snapped out of the thoughts she had been losing herself in. 'What's your point, Tony? That it's too difficult? Shall I drop you back at Daniel's house so you can tell the parents that, while we'd like to find out who killed their son, we're not going to because it's a bit difficult? The last time I checked, this job wasn't supposed to be a piece of piss.'

They drove in silence for a few seconds. 'Sorry, guv,' Woods said at last. 'I'm just frustrated. I want to catch a break on this thing. I feel like whoever is behind it, they're really fucking around with us, playing a game. The emails and the whole money-drop business. I just want to catch the sick bastard.'

Collins nodded. 'I guess the strain is getting to both of us.' She picked up her phone and started to punch in a few numbers.

DC Natalie Cooper was at her desk at the incident room in Peckham, working her way through computer files of registered sex offenders living close to the church where Daniel's body had been found, when her direct line started to ring.

'I need you to check some CCTV,' Collins explained breathlessly, 'for any suspicious activity around the Eliots' home and the parade of shops on Crown Street.'

'But I'm running HOLMES. And anyway

Higgins gave Drabble's team the CCTV job.'

'Then you'll have to ask nicely. We're not covering the same ground anyway. They're focusing on the church and the money-drop site. I want to go back to before the abduction.'

'What am I looking for?' asked Cooper.

'A white van.'

There was a pause. 'This is some kind of joke, right?'

'No joke. One of Daniel's friends was out with him an hour or so before he went missing. He saw a white van in an alleyway next to the parade of shops with a dog tied to it. I want to know where it went.'

Collins could hear Cooper scribbling down the information. 'It might take me a bit of time. Do you have any idea how much footage that will involve? You're probably talking thousands of hours. It could even–'

'Yeah, yeah. I've already had this conversation with Woods. Just do it. We'll be back in an hour or so and can help you out then, but in the meantime just get on with it.'

Collins ended the call and turned back to Woods. 'Did you get anything new out of Sammy's parents?'

Woods shook his head. 'Nothing we didn't already know, apart from a few more horror stories about Daniel's father. What's your gut feeling about him?'

'Not sure at the moment. A violent man, yes, but why would he mutilate his own son so horrifically? Whoever killed Daniel did it in a controlled manner, not in a drunken rage. And anyway his voice doesn't match the one on the video.'

'So are we looking for someone else?'

'Yes.'

10

It was late afternoon by the time Woods and Collins got back to the incident room. Natalie Cooper was painstakingly going through a pile of CCTV tapes that had accumulated on her desk.

'Anything?' Collins asked her without any pleasantries.

'Not on these,' Cooper replied briskly. 'DI Drabble got a bit shirty with me. I managed to get a few tapes, but she wasn't going to let go of the rest. Said she was going to call Higgins. I told her you'd sort it out when you got here.'

'Thanks.'

'That's why you're the boss, boss.'

DI Yvonne Drabble, thirty-one and stocky with dark hair and darker eyes, was the type of police woman who had made her way up the ranks by being even more of a lad than the men who surrounded her. Collins had run into her a few times at training courses and seminars over the years, but they had never actually worked together. When they had tried to engage in conversation it had all fizzled out to nothing once the two women realized that they had absolutely nothing in common, including their approach to police work.

Collins had only just reached Drabble's desk

when the woman looked up, sneered and folded her arms. 'What the hell do you think you're playing at?' she hissed. 'The whole reason Higgins put us into different teams was to make sure no one trod on anyone else's toes. My team were assigned to CCTV duty, but then I get back here and find your little DC sticking her nose into our work.'

'It's not like that,' Collins replied. 'We're following up a different set of leads, something that might have occurred just prior to the actual kidnapping.'

'And you didn't have the courtesy to ask me yourself?'

'We're on the same side, you know.'

'Don't give me that bollocks. We may be looking for the same guy, but we all want to be the one to find him first. Anyone who says different is just talking crap.' Drabble leaned back in her chair. 'I'll let you have the tapes but only because my guys are busy going through the CCTV for every one of the stops the kidnapper sent us to during the money-drop.'

It suddenly occurred to Collins that she knew little about where the money-drop had been due to take place.

'Where did it end up?'

'Didn't bother to read the briefing papers, huh? He started off at Embankment underground station and then gave our man about ten minutes to get to Holborn, then another ten minutes to King's Cross. From there it was a run down to London Bridge and then an overland train to Peckham. The whole thing ended up at a tower block on the Blenheim Estate.

'We figure he must have been near each stop, watching. We're going through the footage to see if anyone is at more than one of the locations during the same time as our man. It's the best lead we have.'

But Collins was no longer listening. She was staring into space, her mind going over something Drabble had just said.

'You okay?' asked Drabble. 'You look like you've seen a ghost.'

Collins swallowed hard before she spoke. 'Did you say the Blenheim Estate?'

'Yeah, our guy ended up there. He was told to drop the money into the lift in one of the tower blocks and press the button for the top floor. He did that and then the team moved in and cordoned off the area. No one could get in or out. When they were satisfied they had the whole place locked down, they moved in and that's when they found it.'

'Found what?'

'The money. It was still there. The kidnapper never collected it. Guess the team must have spooked him or something.'

'Do you think the kidnapper lives on the estate?'

'Not unless he's stupid, but they're doing house-to-house anyway.'

'Who else knows the estate was where they ended up for the drop?'

Drabble shook her head slightly. 'No one apart from SCD7 and those working on the case; it's one of the holdbacks.'

It was common practice in all major criminal

investigations to hold back certain pieces of information as a way of sorting out the crank callers from those with genuine information or knowledge of the crime.

Yvonne Drabble blinked hard several times and looked at Collins strangely. 'Something you want to tell me?'

'It's just that ... I used to know the place pretty well.'

'Doesn't surprise me. I hear it's a bit of a dump.'

Collins leaned over the desk and stared directly at Drabble. 'Listen to me, you piece of shit: I get results and I don't need to climb the same greasy pole as you. So carry on acting like a fucking man in a skirt, you fucking He-Bitch.' Drabble was taken aback by the onslaught and noticeably embarrassed by the fact that those close to her had overheard.

Just then the sound of a small, slightly high-pitched cough came from behind Collins. 'Excuse me,' said Khan, looking from one woman to the other and finally fixing his gaze on Yvonne Drabble. 'Excuse me, sir.'

Drabble's eyes widened ominously. 'Are you trying to be funny?'

Khan's mouth opened and closed, but no words came out. It was obvious to Collins at least that he had no idea what he was supposed to have done wrong. DI Drabble finally lost patience and stormed off.

'What did I do?' said Khan at last.

'Didn't they teach you anything when you joined?' said Collins with a smirk. 'It's "sir" for the men, "ma'am" for the women. Everyone likes "guv" too. You're Khan, aren't you?'

She held out her hand, and he took it gratefully. His handshake was surprisingly firm. 'I'm DI Collins. How are you finding it?'

Khan shrugged his shoulders. 'It's okay, I guess. Equipment's not exactly state of the art. And the stuff I do, well, you know, I could do so much more if only they let me bend the rules slightly. It's like working with one hand tied behind my back.'

'I know the feeling,' said Collins. 'I have the same problem myself. Tell you what.' She leaned forward so she could speak softly in his ear. 'Next time it becomes an issue for you, just come and see me.'

Khan's young face broke into a broad smile, and Collins could see that one of his incisors was missing. 'Cool. Thanks. That's what I came over for. I need a bit of advice about something I'm working on.'

Collins and Khan headed for the corner of the room where his computer was situated. As they walked, Collins looked around to see that many of those in the incident room were now staring at Drabble as she returned to the room. 'And how are the people, how are they treating you?'

Khan glanced over to where Drabble was settling down at her desk. He shrugged. 'It's okay. Kinda weird being surrounded by coppers all day long. I feel like I'm walking on eggshells, you know? And I have to make sure none of my friends see me coming in or out of here. I'd get lynched.'

'I didn't think people like you, computer nerds,

I mean, had friends.'

Khan knew she was only winding him up and was happy to play the game. 'Cyber friends are still friends, though I suppose most of them don't know what I actually look like.'

They reached his computer and sat down. Khan pulled the keyboard towards him and began to type quickly.

'What have you got?' Collins asked him.

Khan didn't turn to look at her; indeed he didn't stop typing, his fingers lightly flying over the keyboard with unstudied skill. 'Dead-drop,' he said cryptically.

'What you talking about?'

Khan stopped typing and swung round on his chair to look at her. 'A virtual dead-drop. It's how the 9/11 terrorists communicated with each other without being traced. You get yourself a webmail account – this geezer used Hotmail – and then save any message as a draft. What he did then was give the parents the user name and password to access the account for themselves.'

'What's the point of that?'

Khan shrugged. 'There's no electronic trail. The email doesn't actually travel anywhere once it's in the Hotmail draft server. Only thing is, he'll have had to upload the email somehow, and that means connecting to his Internet account.'

'Can you trace where he uploaded?'

'It's difficult. Hotmail don't keep a record of people accessing to leave draft emails, only actual mail that comes in or out. I'll have to work round it, but, even if I do that, chances are he used several layers of encryption.'

'What's the alternative?'

'I could put a worm on to his account. A kind of virus,' Khan said nonchalantly. 'It's what hackers use when they want to drain information from someone's computer – credit card numbers, bank details, that sort of thing. You can also use it to steal someone's ISP address. When this guy logs in, which he'll have to do even just to leave a draft email, the sleeper will wake up and attach the worm without him even knowing about it. But that only works if he logs on again.'

'Sounds good,' said Collins. 'So what's the problem, then?'

'Well, there are two problems.'

'What's the first one?'

'It's kinda illegal.'

'How illegal?'

'I've got to hack into Hotmail to place the worm. I could get into serious trouble.'

Collins nodded. 'Surely they would give us permission if they knew what we were trying to do. What's the next problem?'

'The machine they've given me simply isn't capable of creating that kind of worm.'

'Could you bring your own equipment here?'

'Yes, but I don't think the boss will want me to plug my stuff into the police network. He'd see it as giving a bank robber the key to the vault.'

Collins focused on the screen and brushed a strand of hair away from her eyes. 'What about outside the building – if you did this from, say, an Internet café?'

It was Khan's turn to nod. 'That would work. Better still, I can do it from home and log into my computer from here.'

'Then let's do that. You go home and set up this worm, and in the meantime I'll get someone to contact Hotmail and tell them what we are doing. If they object, we'll get a warrant.'

'But I'll still get into trouble for using illegal software...'

Collins leaned forward and moved her head down so that it was level with Khan's. 'Then let's just keep it between you and me. And if you get anything, bring it to me first.'

'No problem, ma'am.' Khan flashed a toothy smile.

She reached for a scrap of paper on his desk and began to scribble something down. 'Here's my mobile number, so you can get hold of me any time. How long to get this all in place?'

Khan looked sarcastically at his watch, then grinned. 'Oh, about ten minutes.'

Collins smiled back. 'Then what are you waiting for?'

Khan grabbed his bag and began to collect his things as Collins returned to her desk and began to send a text message to the last person in the world she wanted to see: WILL MEET U TONIGHT. USUAL PLACE. 7.

11

It was a warm Saturday evening, and the sun still shone brightly as Stacey's car pulled up outside the slightly rundown, three-bedroom home in Streatham where she and Sophie lived.

As soon as she put the key into the lock, she could hear the sound of excited chatter and footfalls coming from inside. The door swung open, and she saw Sophie standing at the top of the stairs with a huge smile on her face. 'Mum!' she squealed with delight, taking the steps two at a time as she ran down towards the hallway. But the girl's joy lasted only as long as it took for her to get close enough to see the look of sadness and regret on her mother's face. When Sophie spoke again, all the excitement had drained away, and her voice was flat and monotone. 'You're not staying, are you?'

Deep inside her chest Stacey could feel her heart breaking as she watched Sophie struggling to fight back the tears that were welling up inside her. 'I'm sorry, love,' Stacey began. 'I just popped back to pick up a couple of things. I've still got some work to do... I won't be long. I promise I'll...'

But Sophie had already started to make her way back up the stairs. 'It's not fair,' she sobbed. 'You never spend any time with me these days.'

The shift-work patterns of life in the Metropolitan Police had always been disruptive, but ever since Stacey had made it on to the murder squad she had broken her promises to her daughter so many times that they now seemed almost meaningless. Although Stacey's parents had a home of their own, they were constantly round her house. This was both a blessing and a curse. It meant there was always someone on hand to look after Sophie but it also meant that Stacey was prone to work late because she never had to worry about child care.

'I hate you,' Sophie hissed bitterly. 'When I go to school, all my friends talk about fun things they did at the weekend with their parents.'

'Sophie, please...'

'They say, "What did you do at the weekend, Sophie?" And I tell them I did nothing at all because my mum loves her job so much more than she loves me.'

'Now just wait one minute, young lady. My job puts food on the table. And the work I do is important because–'

Sophie spun round at the top of the stairs. This time her eyes held fire as well as tears. 'More important than me?'

Stacey hesitated a moment too long. Sophie spun back around and continued to make her way towards her room. 'And the worst part of it is that none of this would matter if we were a proper family,' Sophie muttered under her breath but still loud enough for Stacey to hear. 'None of it would matter at all if...'

Stacey knew what was coming next: the words that cut her to the quick every single time she heard them. And in recent months she seemed to have heard them more and more.

'None of it would matter,' Sophie said again, 'if I had a dad.' And with that she slammed the door of her room behind her.

Stacey fought to compose herself, closing her eyes and taking deep breaths as she closed the front door behind her. When she opened them again, her mother's face was peeking out from around the doorway to the living room. Penny Collins said nothing. She didn't have to. Her disapproval of the situation was written, all over her face in giant capital letters.

When her mother finally made to open her mouth, Stacey held up a hand to silence her. 'I don't have time for this, Mum,' she snapped. 'I've got to get back to work.'

The evening traffic as she headed across South London was heavier than she had expected, and Collins found herself watching the clock on the car's dashboard and wondering if she would make it on time.

It was almost an hour before Stacey turned into the narrow driveway that led to the vast, uneven patch of scrub and woodland that was her final destination. She was almost twenty minutes late.

She parked her car and gingerly made her way along a footpath on the common, until she came to the ruins of a medieval manor house. All that remained was a scattering of worn red bricks marking out the floorplan of the once grand residence. In the centre of it all stood Jack Stanley.

'I was beginning to think that you were

avoiding me.'

Jack was tall and physically impressive, with thick jet-black hair and sparkling, piercing green eyes that shone like diamonds. He was dressed in designer jeans and an expensive linen shirt that fitted him perfectly. Two days' worth of stubble clung to his chin, and a large unlit cigar was clenched between his fingers. He struck a match as he moved towards her and lit the end, blowing out the first puff of smoke in her direction.

'How long has it been, Stacey? A year? You haven't changed a bit. You're looking good, very good.'

Stacey said nothing but felt uncomfortable as his eyes looked her up and down. Jack began to close the gap between them, finally coming close enough for her to smell his cologne over the cigar smoke that lingered around him. 'How's your dad?' Jack continued. 'And how's that little girl of yours? Susie, isn't it?'

'Her name's Sophie,' Collins replied. 'She's good. And my dad's as well as can be expected. But I'm pretty sure you didn't call me every day this week to catch up on old times. What's all this about? I mean, even by your crazy standards you're acting pretty desperate.'

Stacey knew all about Jack Stanley's standards. She had known him for just about as long as she had known anyone in her entire life. As a young girl growing up on the Blenheim Estate, Jack had been a leading figure in the small gang of oh-so-cool older boys who hung around in the shadowy corners at night smoking cigarettes and passing around cans of cheap cider.

He and his friends had pretty much ignored her back then. It was only when puberty kicked in and Stacey made the transition from schoolgirl and gangly teenager to stunningly attractive young woman that the eyes of Jack and his mates began to follow her around whenever she came into view. Then he would whistle and call out 'All right, Princess' every time she went past, much to her embarrassment.

By the time Jack had turned twenty it was an open secret that he was making his living from petty crime – mostly burglary and car theft – though no one on the estate seemed overly concerned, because he always struck far from home. He had one or two minor run-ins with the law but was lucky enough to come away with nothing more than a couple of official warnings.

Things got more serious a few years later when the head of a gang of drug dealers was found stabbed to death on the edge of the estate. Jack was arrested and charged with murder within weeks but insisted he wasn't guilty; he was victim of a simple case of mistaken identity. Four days before the trial one of the main prosecution witnesses vanished off the face of the earth; two days later, two witnesses informed the police they would be withdrawing their statements. The case collapsed.

Everyone knew what had happened, and from then on Jack's reputation as a ruthless gang leader only grew.

Within five years Jack had moved away from the estate and into a house in the leafy South London suburb of Chislehurst. In his absence his lieutenants still ran the Blenheim Estate, which ensured that Jack retained a financial stake in every gram of smack, coke and weed, as well as every stolen video camera and cloned credit card that passed through the place.

By the time Stacey Collins joined the police force, Jack's empire had expanded to include several other estates and a wide range of other contraband. When Stacey made detective, Jack became her secret weapon in the fight against crime.

The agreement between them was mutual. Stacey was an ambitious officer looking to get results, and Jack wanted to protect his investments. Therefore he would provide her with tips about the activities of rival drug gangs, point out good places to look for clues about the identities of unknown armed robbers and let her have samples of counterfeit currency being produced by foreign syndicates. On more than one occasion he even told her where to find the bodies of victims of contract killings.

It was a covenant with the Devil. Stacey's career went from strength to strength, and she rapidly gained a reputation as a hard-nosed detective who got results, but Jack benefited too. Most of his information led to action against gangs who were trying to muscle in on his patch, which resulted in a huge boost to his profits.

There were other advantages for Jack. He was given occasional, subtle hints about potential police investigations into his growing criminal empire, detailed explanations about the latest technology and how the police could use it to build cases against him – information that he then used when deciding how to focus his resources.

For the most part, Stacey managed to avoid doing anything illegal – not that she ever wanted Jack to know that. The hints about police investigations amounted to little more than underworld gossip. The information about new technology came from sources available to the public if they looked hard enough: the Internet, technical journals, law reports and court cases.

But Stacey knew that when you made a deal with the Devil, you were putting your soul on the line, and one day he would come along to collect. She had tried time and time again to cut her ties to Jack, which was why it had been so long since she had seen him, but it had proved almost as impossible as cutting her ties to the Blenheim. You can take the girl out of the estate, but you can't take the estate out of the girl.

Jack had a similar problem. He had made so much money in his criminal career that he could easily afford to go legit, but the adrenalin rush he got from criminal activity had proved every bit as addictive as the drugs his gang sold on the estates he controlled.

The question of why Jack had wanted to meet with Stacey so urgently was still hanging in the air, so she repeated it. 'So what's all this about?'

He tried to smile, but it came out as a slight sneer. 'Well, I don't get out much these days, so I thought I might as well combine seeing you with a little bit of sightseeing.'

'Really?' Stacey looked around her. There was nothing to see but rubble. 'Maybe I'm missing something, but isn't that sort of thing usually a lot more rewarding if you go somewhere more interesting?'

'Not always the case, Stacey,' Jack replied. 'This place is supposed to be haunted. I'm pretty sure that ghosts only come out at night. And I don't think either of us would want to miss those, would we?'

They stared at each other for a few moments. Finally Stacey broke the silence. 'No more games, Jack. What do you want from me? I'm guessing it has something to do with that depot robbery.'

'What robbery was that, then?'

'Don't play the idiot. It doesn't suit you, not any more.'

Jack eyed her suspiciously. 'You on the job or something? Is that the reason you agreed to meet me, to question me about the fucking depot job? You trying to pull the wool over my eyes?' He took another draw on his cigar and let the smoke escape from his lips slowly. 'That's not the way our arrangement works, sweetheart, and you know it. We both have too much to lose for either of us to ever turn on the other.'

'Jesus, Jack, it's got your fucking MO all over it. And if that's as clear as a bell to someone like me, it's only a matter of time before the Flying Squad realize it too, if they haven't already.'

Jack smiled. 'You trying to tell me something, Princess?'

'I'm just telling you what you already know. And don't call me that, I always hated it. Even when I was a teenager.'

Stacey took a deep breath. If she was going to

get what she wanted, she was going to have to start again. 'Listen, Jack. I've had a hell of a week. I don't know why you called me, but the only reason I agreed to meet with you is that I need something. I need a favour. You've heard about this kid being kidnapped and murdered.'

Jack brightened up and smirked big and wide. 'Yeah, of course, it's all over the place.'

'Well, here's one thing you haven't heard. Something you won't hear anywhere and you need to keep a hundred per cent confidential. You understand me.'

Jack's voice was suddenly serious. 'Okay.'

'The final money-drop for the kidnap, it was on the Blenheim Estate. Block C.'

'You don't think–'

'That it was down to you? Of course not. Don't be ridiculous. But you and I both know that nothing moves in or out of the estate without your people knowing about it. If this guy had set up a drop, he must have been hanging around scoping it out. Your people must have seen something.'

Jack moved thoughtfully to his right, sat down on a low pile of bricks and ran his fingers through his thick dark hair. 'This drop-off, was it arranged for around 5.30 p.m. last night?'

'It started at 5 p.m. and was given the runaround to the Blenheim Estate, so they would have been there, say, 5.30, 5.40.'

'Some of the guys got spooked because there was a bunch of armed coppers milling around just after that. And now there's a bunch of uniforms and forensic guys around there.'

'Now you know why. You think you can help

me out?'

Jack stood up, brushing the dust from the seat of his jeans with the back of his hand. 'I don't know, Stacey. What's in it for me?'

'Be serious, Jack. This is different. We're talking about someone who goes around killing kids here. I was always led to believe that you took exception to that kind of thing, that you'd be eager to help out in any way you could.'

'I need a favour.'

Stacey felt a tiny chill run down her spine. 'What?'

Jack took another long final drag on his cigar, then dropped it to the ground and crushed it with the heel of his boot. He looked up at Stacey. 'There's an informant in the outfit. I'm certain of it.'

Stacey knew all too well never to speak to Jack about particular deals or people for fear of being drawn too closely into his organization. Their arrangement worked only if she kept her distance from him.

'Are you fucking serious?' The tone in her voice was hard. 'You bring me here to tell me you've got a fucking grass – do you know what would happen to me if anyone found out that I was with you? Tough fucking luck. What do you expect me to do about it?'

Jack stared at her, his growing anger obvious. 'You need to tell me who it is.'

12

'This really isn't the best time, Khan, I'm kinda busy.'

Jack's words were bouncing around Collins's mind as she drove home as fast as she could in the vain hope that she could get back and see Sophie before she went to bed. Khan sounded slightly hurt.

'But I'm only calling because you told me to.'

'What are you talking about?'

'You know, that thing we talked about, the thing you wanted me to do with, erm, the thing. Well, I did it. I did the thing, loaded it up and now ... well, the other thing...'

'Khan, are you at home?'

'Yeah, why?'

'I'm in my car. I don't think anyone's listening in on this call. You can feel free to make use of a few more words, give me a bit more of a chance to understand what you're trying to say.'

Khan sighed with relief. 'I put the worm on the kidnapper's account and set up a remote link to my pocket PC. The alarm's just gone off, so I logged in and got the ISP. I thought it was going to be another Internet café, but it's not. It's a house, a house in Dulwich.'

'Jesus, Khan, are you telling me you know where this guy is?'

'I know where he is right now, yeah.'

Collins couldn't believe what she was hearing. 'Then why the fuck didn't you tell anyone?' she asked urgently.

'He's only just logged on and I'm telling *you*. Right now!'

Shortly after the call a team from homicide were screaming through the streets of South London. Collins and Woods were in a car with Khan, who was there to secure any evidence they found on the computer. Two armed-response vehicles had been diverted from their usual patrols around the capital and were also on their way.

Woods was at the wheel, expertly weaving his way through the evening traffic. Khan was in the back, half excited and half terrified about the events that were unfolding around him. Collins tried her best to concentrate on the task at hand, but her thoughts drifted back to her meeting with Jack Stanley. His words kept turning over in her mind. 'There's a grass in my organization. You need to tell me who it is.' It was an impossible request. Although Jack hadn't said as much, it was obvious what would happen to the grass as soon as he had been identified: he'd be killed, which would make Collins an accessory to murder.

Collins snapped her thoughts back to the present as Woods quietly pulled up several houses away from their target – the place where, according to Khan, the kidnapper had logged on to the Hotmail account that was used to send the ransom demands. He switched off the engine, killed the lights and waited for the others to arrive.

The house itself was a run-of-the-mill semi-detached Victorian property; an iron railing marked the boundary between the pavement and the small front garden. The lights on the ground floor were off, but there were signs of life upstairs.

Collins turned to Khan. 'Listen carefully. The armed-response unit are going to gain entry to the house. Once they've secured it, DS Woods and I will go inside along with the senior officers. What I want you to do is wait right here. Don't even think about coming in until I call you. Is that clear?'

Khan nodded. 'Crystal,' he said meekly.

Out of the corner of her eye Collins noticed something moving at the other end of the street. She turned her head and saw, bathed in the orange glow of the street lights, a team of armed police officers in black combat trousers, bullet-proof vests and helmets silently approaching the house from two directions. Each member of the team was holding a standard-issue MP5 semi-automatic rifle across his chest.

Three members of the team vanished around the back of the house to cover the rear entrance. The remainder lined up on the left of the door, weapons pointed dead ahead. The first man touched his hand to the side of his head, waiting for the go signal. At that moment the radio in the car crackled to life. 'Go, go, go.'

The lead firearms officer nodded at the man beside him, then took a step back. The second officer lifted an enforcer battering-ram and swung it at the front door, reducing it to splinters. The man behind him flung himself on to one knee in the doorway and raised the sight of his gun to his eye. 'Clear,' he yelled, signalling to the other members of the team to move in ahead of him.

Khan was watching the scene open-mouthed. It was amazing to think that all this was being done because of him. As the officers vanished inside the house, and the sounds of shouting and breaking furniture started to come through the windows, Khan suddenly noticed something on the pavement. He jumped out of the car to meet Collins, his eyes scanning the footpath.

'Oh, shit,' he said, 'shit.'

'What is it?'

'Shit, shit, shit,' he said. 'He's good. He's really good.'

'What's going on, Khan?'

The young man slowly lifted a finger and pointed to the pavement outside the house. Two faint semicircles were barely visible close to the kerb next to a glowing lamp-post. To the untrained eye they looked like the kind of marks left by those responsible for painting lines or digging up pipes, but Khan knew better.

'Warchalk.'

'Khan, I need you to stop speaking fucking jargon.'

Khan's eyes switched from the road to meet Collins full on. 'It's warchalk. It's a sign people use to show there's an unsecured wireless network near by. Whoever lives in that house has installed a wireless Internet system and their coverage leaks out into the street. They call it "wardriving": you drive around and make a note of places where they don't have a firewall to their network but they do have a strong wireless signal,

98

then list them on the Internet and leave the marks. It means people with laptops can sit out here and get on the Internet for free, or, more to the point, they can get on by piggybacking on someone else's ISP.'

'Fuck's sake, what are you trying to tell me?'

Khan spoke without making eye contact. 'I don't think this is his house. In fact, I'd stake my granny's life on it.'

Suddenly a scream came from within the house, followed by a commotion at the front. Officers from the firearms team dragged out a middle-aged man and his wife, then carried out their two small daughters. Everyone in the family looked absolutely terrified: the woman was hyperventilating, and a small streak of blood ran down from the man's lower lip. Both children were crying hysterically.

Collins watched the scene before her with growing horror. 'Bollocks.' She glanced around the street. Curtains were twitching; a few people were emerging from their doorways to get a better look at what was going on. Collins could easily read what they were all thinking: what on earth had that poor family done to deserve such heavy-handed treatment?

It was a horrible scene, a nightmare of the worst possible order, and she could bear it no more. She turned to Woods. 'Get us out of here. I've had enough of this fucking shitty day.'

Sunday

13

*Five a.m. Time for breakfast. He had cooked the eggs
and bacon to perfection, then placed them in the oven
to keep them warm while he cleaned up around him.
He didn't stop until the kitchen was spotless and all
that was left behind was the faint odour of fried food.
Cleanliness was next to godliness, and breakfast was
the most important meal of the day.*

*He rarely needed to sleep more than a couple of
hours each night and had got into the habit of collecting the morning papers the night before, driving to
Central London to pick up the first editions ahead of
time.*

*He laid the papers out, just as he had always done,
neatly stacked on the right-hand side of the breakfast
table. Everything was in place. Once he'd had his
shower and washed his hair, he'd be ready.*

*As he showered, his thoughts reverted back to the
night before. He had just logged on and was about to
send the parents another email when his state-of-the-
art software flashed up an alert warning him about a
worm on the account. He couldn't risk uploading the
file and being caught before his work was done. He
immediately broke the connection and retreated to a
safe distance.*

*The police got there far faster than he had expected.
He almost enjoyed the sight of them dragging out that
poor, innocent family. He particularly liked the look of
anger on the face of the young Asian man who had*

pointed to the chalk marks on the pavement and the look of frustration on the face of the older woman with the blonde highlights beside him.

It was a minor setback. He would need to open a new Hotmail account before he could continue, but in the meantime he would send his latest message to the parents of Daniel Eliot in the old-fashioned way.

Five minutes after his shower he sat down to eat. He picked up the first paper from the pile. The headlines were all about the murder of Daniel Eliot, page after page of pictures, interviews and eyewitness accounts of the scene around the church. He ignored it all. Occasionally he picked up a pair of scissors and cut out a word or two, some large, some small, collecting them together into a pile on his left.

After breakfast he cleaned up after himself and went downstairs to the room he liked to call his study. He pulled on a pair of latex gloves from the box on the side of his desk and began to work his way through the pile of words cut from that morning's papers, carefully wiping each and every one clean.

14

Jack Stanley wound down the window of the six series BMW and flicked the remains of his cigar butt out on to the rough grassland that led down to the deserted beach just a few miles along the coast from Margate.

He was sitting in the passenger seat, facing out to sea, waiting for the first sign of the inflatable speedboat that was making its way across the Channel. Danny Thompson, his long-time friend and enforcer, was sitting beside him. 'Why do we use this cunt when he's always late?' asked Danny, glancing at his watch.

'That's why I got out of bed at fucking half three this morning. To sort it out.'

'This cunt's gonna get us into trouble.'

'I know. We'll deal with that when he arrives.'

The two men had grown up together on the Blenheim Estate, and from an early age Danny had idolized Jack. Danny had always been short-tempered and confrontational. At the age of fourteen he had been sentenced to two years at Feltham Young Offenders Institution after slashing a sixteen-year-old boy across the face with a Stanley knife in revenge for losing a football match. Since then Jack had learned to use Danny's natural propensity for violence to his advantage, trusting him to enforce Jack's authority on the estate, a position Danny took great pride in. He therefore knew exactly what their trip to Margate this morning was all about and had come prepared. Rarely now did Jack ever do his own dirty work.

Under Danny's seat was a semi-automatic Glock 17L pistol and silencer.

'What about Collins?'

'She's not turning our way at the moment.'

'You want me to sort it out?'

'Nah. Leave it to me. For now anyway. If she doesn't come round to our way of thinking, we'll have to teach her a lesson.'

'Like what?'

'We'll set her up.'

'About time. I've never liked the bitch.'

Jack turned to face Danny. 'Keep your fucking opinions to yourself.'

Before Danny could reply, their attention was drawn by the faint sound of a powerful outboard motor heading to shore.

As the first rays of the early-morning sun appeared and began to burn off the mist, they got out of the car and started to make their way across the rough dunes towards the sea. Danny tucked the gun into the back of his jeans, while Jack kept a look out for any passers-by.

The RIB pulled up on shore and out climbed Mark Dennings, a small-time dealer from the estate who worked for Jack as one of his couriers. He pulled a large duffel bag out of the boat and began to walk towards the two men.

'Where the fuck have you been?' said Jack. 'This is the third time you haven't done what we asked you to do.'

Mark's face broke into a broad grin. 'Chill out. I got the gear, ain't I? I always get the gear. You know that, Jack.' And with that Mark gave him a pat on the back.

Danny and Jack exchanged a glance that said they knew he was high again. Jack nodded his head at Danny, who without a moment's hesiation pulled out the gun from behind him and shot Mark twice in the head, his body slumping down on to the wet sand.

Danny replaced the gun in his trousers, stepped forward and picked up the bag, then looked straight out to sea.

'Fuck me, look at that sunrise, isn't it beautiful?'

Jack rolled his eyes. 'Fuck that, I'm hungry. Let's get some breakfast.'

15

Stacey needed only the fingers of one hand to count the words Sophie had spoken to her from the time she had woken up to the time she had dropped her daughter off at the weekly drama class she attended every Sunday morning during the summer.

The drive to Streatham community hall had taken place in complete silence, with Stacey periodically glancing at her daughter's face in the rear-view mirror – Sophie had refused to sit next to her mother in the front. It was only when they arrived that Sophie uttered her final word.

'Grandma is going to pick you up and cook your tea. I should be home early tonight,' said Stacey, as Sophie clambered out.

'Yeah.'

It was spoken in a monotone voice. What Sophie was really saying was that she no longer believed a single word her mother said. In that same instant Stacey Collins seemed to travel back in time, back to when she had been only a little older than Sophie and had uttered the same word in the same style to her own mother.

It happens to every child. You grow up thinking your parents are invincible, all-knowing and the masters of their universe. You spend years believing there is no question they cannot answer, no task they cannot accomplish. Most of all, you grow up believing that whatever danger you might face, from monsters in the wardrobe to trolls under bridges, they will always be there to protect you. And then one day the reality hits home and you realize that the only person you can really rely on is yourself.

For Stacey that day came when she, her mum and her dad had been walking through the Blenheim Estate on the way back from the local supermarket, all of them carrying heavy bags of shopping. The lifts were out of order, as they almost always were, so the trio had no choice but to struggle up the stairs to the fifth floor of E block where their flat was.

As they rounded the third flight of stairs, three young men emerged from a corner and blocked their way. Even now Stacey could remember their faces, the casual smirks they wore as her father asked them, please, to step out of the way.

'No one gets past here without paying,' one of them had said.

Stacey's father looked at them, put down his bags at the top of the steps and smirked in mock disbelief. He pointed at the lad in the middle of the group. 'You're Brian's lad, aren't you? Does he know this is what you've been getting up to? I don't think he'd be very impressed.'

The three teenagers glanced at each other, their earlier confidence fading away fast. This wasn't what they had expected, but Stacey's dad was not the sort of man to be easily intimated. Stacey watched her father in silent awe. Her mother reached over and took her hand, giving it a little squeeze of reassurance.

Her father stepped towards them, seizing the initiative. 'Now clear off, the lot of you, before I give you a clip round the ear.'

Stacey and her mother moved to one side of the stairs as the three boys, heads bowed slightly, began to shuffle past on their way downstairs. After that everything seemed to happen so fast.

As the last boy walked past, his hand flashed out and grabbed the straps of her mother's handbag, which was hanging from her shoulder. Her mother screamed in shock and surprise, and the boy tugged harder, jerking her body roughly away from the wall.

Stacey remembered seeing her father's mouth wide open in a fierce scream of disapproval as he tore down the few steps that separated him from the boy. His right arm stretched out and clamped around the boy's neck. The two other boys turned and began to make their way up the stairs to help their friend.

The boy tried to punch and claw and scratch away the man's hands, but Stacey's father was too strong. His two friends grabbed his shoulders and pulled him down. Stacey's father somehow lost his footing and fell towards them. The boys swerved to avoid him, and he crashed head first on to the stairs, cartwheeling over and over, until he landed at the bottom of the steps, his body twisted and broken in a way that even a child could tell was simply not natural.

The boys ran off. Stacey and her mother tried to help her dad to his feet, but, as soon as they moved him, he started coughing up blood. So they called an ambulance. The rest of that night was a blur of flashing blue lights, hospital rooms and polite but grim-faced doctors. His spine had been badly damaged. He was going to survive, they were told, but they should prepare themselves for the fact that he'd probably never walk again.

When the police turned up at the hospital bed, Stacey's father refused to identify his attackers, for fear of reprisals against his family – a family he felt he could no longer protect.

After four months in hospital John Collins was able to return home, but a shortage of available housing stock meant they had to stay on the estate and were allocated a ground-floor flat on block E – the only level that was even vaguely wheelchair accessible and just five floors away from their old home.

The youths themselves were eventually caught for a similar offence and given a two-year stretch. But they were back on the estate within a year – time off for good behaviour. It never seemed quite right to Stacey.

The day they moved into their new home. Stacey's mother tried to put a brave face on it all. 'We're going to be all right, my darling,' she said in her gentlest voice. 'You'll see, once you've got used to the changes, we'll be just as happy as we always were.'

Stacey had looked at her mother for a few

moments, searching out the truth of those statements in her eyes. Then she replied with a single word.

'Yeah.'

Collins was on her way back to the incident room when her mobile phone began to ring. Somewhere at the back of her mind she hoped it might be Sophie phoning to try to make things up. She had never been a fan of hands-free devices or Bluetooth headsets, and hated the new law that made it illegal to drive and speak on a phone at the same time – therefore she chose to ignore it.

She put the phone to her ear. 'Hello?'

'It's him, it's him, it's him.' Christina Eliot's voice was hysterical. 'It's my baby boy. Oh, God, it's my little baby boy.'

Collins could only barely make out the words, they came so thick and fast and were delivered with such pained emotion. 'What's happened, Christina? What's going on?'

But Christina only continued to scream 'It's him, it's him, it's him', before collapsing in a mass of sobs.

Collins' adrenalin was pumping so hard she could feel the beat of her heart. 'Don't do anything,' she shouted, struggling to be heard above the sound of the woman's cries. 'Can you hear me? Don't do anything. I'm on my way.'

Collins arrived at the house twenty-five minutes later and made her way past a number of journalists and the small group of well-wishers leaving tributes outside the house. The family had received literally hundreds of cards ever since

Daniel's body had been discovered. At first they had been from friends, parents of the children in Daniel's class and others in their immediate social circle. But, as the news spread around the country, people came from further afield to pay their respects. Some of the cards had a religious theme, and contained prayers and meditations. Others came from mothers who had lost children of their own. They included telephone numbers, words of encouragement and offers of the chance to talk or meet in order to help the healing process. A few contained money, never a huge amount, but enough to show that someone cared. Not all the cards were nice. Some were distressing, put together by sick pranksters. But one card and one card alone stood out above all the rest.

Collins walked into the makeshift shrine that the lounge of the Eliots' home had become. Christina was curled up on a corner of the sofa and didn't even manage to look up. Collins looked instead at the family liaison officer beside her, who nodded silently towards a square of glossy paper in a clear plastic bag on the edge of the coffee table.

She picked it up and immediately recognized the scene. It was the interior of the church of St Andrew's, where Daniel's body had been found. The altar, with its statue of the Madonna and the stained-glass window above depicting the Last Temptation of Christ, were the first things she noticed. But what made her blood run cold was something in the top-right-hand corner of the photograph. A pair of small legs and bare, swollen feet.

On the other side of the photo were words cut

from newspapers and carefully pasted into place. *The sins of the fathers are revisited upon their children.*

It took a few minutes for the words to sink in; then she signalled to the family liaison officer to meet her in the corridor.

'Where's the father?' Collins asked.

'He went out just after the card arrived.'

'And you didn't stop him?'

'I had no reason to. He's not a suspect.'

'Well, he is now.'

16

DCS Higgins was halfway through his morning briefing when he noticed Collins arriving. He eyed her disapprovingly as she found a seat next to Woods and Cooper towards the back of the room.

'Next item. As you're almost certainly aware, we had a bit of a fiasco last night. Something that seemed like a firm lead ended up not giving us anything at all. The story is obviously being picked up by the press, and there's a hell of a lot of speculation going on out there, so we've decided that the best form of defence is attack. We're holding a press conference at the Yard at two this afternoon. That will give us the chance to make a wider appeal for witnesses to the events around the church. The parents of Daniel Eliot are still too traumatized to appear before the media, so myself and DI Collins will be conducting the briefing.'

Woods turned to Collins. 'Nice one,' he whispered, knowing how much she hated them.

'Fuck off,' she muttered back. They both smiled. Collins loathed having to deal with glib reporters and questions that said one thing but meant another. Everything was black and white to them: victims were always good, criminals always bad, and when things went wrong the police knew nothing about anything. Still, they were a necessary evil. In cases such as this maintaining a high public profile was crucial. The more press coverage there was, the greater the chance that a member of the public might come forward with that one crucial piece of information that would lead to the killer.

For the members of the press the conference could not come too soon. With little solid information to go on, they had begun to speculate wildly about the motive behind the bungled kidnapping. Appeals to leave the couple alone had fallen on deaf ears. Half a dozen reporters had been permanently camped outside the house since news of Daniel's murder had broken, and two tabloids had offered the Eliots large sums of money to tell their story.

The minute Higgins finished his briefing, Collins headed towards him with copies of both sides of the photo in hand.

'Have you got a reason for being late or did you just not want to show your face after what happened last night?'

She ignored his sarcastic comment and held up

114

the paper. 'Sir, you need to see this.'

Higgins studied the sheets carefully. 'When did this arrive?'

'Mrs Eliot got it this morning. Forensics are checking the original.'

'You think it's the father?'

'Either that, or it's something the father has done.'

'You think someone's out for revenge?'

'It would explain the torture.'

'Maybe, but why would you torture a child to that extent to get back at the father?'

'Revenge for something he's done.'

'So you think someone's punishing him?'

'Or maybe he's punishing himself.'

Higgins paused. 'Where is he?'

'We don't know. He left the house this morning. I've put out an All Points Warning.'

DC Natalie Cooper had been working solidly since Saturday morning. Her principal task within the murder team was to run the Home Office Large Major Enquiry System, known within the force as HOLMES. Introduced in 2000, it had proved invaluable to the investigation of serious crimes. All the intelligence gathered by an enquiry could now be cross-referenced – provided that the operator kept up with the flow of information. So every piece of evidence, every statement, every line of enquiry followed up, had to be logged by Cooper. This included the bungled raid on the home of the innocent family, much to Collins's annoyance.

In an enquiry this size, running the case

through HOLMES was a full-time job, but Natalie had been given another task by DI Collins: to search through hours of CCTV in the hope of spotting some suspicious activity close to the home of Daniel Eliot.

The makeshift viewing suite, with its comfortable chairs, blacked-out windows and large television, was not available, as DI Drabble and her team had based themselves there. Instead, Cooper was forced to make do with an ancient TV/video combi with a fifteen-inch screen that she had found in a corner of the canteen. But, despite these limitations, it had not taken her long to find what she was looking for. With a rough idea of when Sammy and Daniel had travelled to the shops to buy sweets, she had managed to narrow the time frame and quickly found traffic-camera footage of the two boys excitedly tearing along the pavement on their bicycles.

The newsagent had provided tapes from his own cameras, showing the front and rear entrances of the shop, the stock room and the counter. Although the clock was out by several minutes and the system split each screen into four, Cooper managed to identify the grainy images of the two boys entering and leaving.

After making an allowance for the time difference, Cooper was able to examine footage from the closest council-run CCTV camera to the scene. It had given her a fleeting glimpse of a white van pulling into the alleyway beside the newsagent's moments before the boys had arrived at the shop, followed by a second glimpse of the van leaving as the boys ate their sweets.

Cooper found various bits of footage of the boys making their way home, but one scene sent a shiver down her spine. It was the view from a traffic camera that gave only partial coverage of the side street close to where the boys lived. She first saw Daniel and then Sammy playfully cycling past – then a white van slowly following behind.

17

Tony Woods made his way slowly along Downing Street in the city of Cambridge and let three years' worth of wonderful memories flow through his mind. After the morning briefing DI Collins had suggested finding a theologist to analyse the religious elements of the murder case, and he had jumped at the chance to revisit his old stamping ground.

Having driven up from London that morning, he had arranged to have coffee with his old tutor from the Department of Experimental Psychology, Dr Marcus Panton, before meeting with the head of the university's Faculty of Divinity.

In the impressive surroundings of the faculty building, they greeted each other warmly. Dr Panton had always had a soft spot for Tony Woods and had considered him to be one of his best students.

'Good to see you again, Tony. Come in and have a coffee.'

Woods followed Panton into his study with its tall ceiling and dark-wood panelling. 'So how is life treating you?'

'Oh, can't complain. I'm hoping you've come back to discuss that Ph.D. we talked about before you left.'

'I'm afraid not. My student days are long gone.'

'So what are you up to these days, then?'

'Working for the police.'

'Fantastic. I always thought you'd do well as a criminal psychologist.'

Dr Panton's assumption made Tony laugh. 'Not quite. I'm a detective sergeant.'

'Oh, what a waste of a good talent. But I always knew you liked a bit of the rough stuff.'

Woods spent another half hour catching up with his old friend before heading over to the other site for his appointment with Professor Philip Beechwood.

'You do understand that what I'm about to show you has to be kept absolutely confidential,' Woods began.

The professor nodded excitedly, clearly pleased by being given access to information not available to the general public.

'This concerns the murder of Daniel Eliot,' Woods continued.

The initial excitement in the professor's face quickly faded as Woods began to divulge details of the gruesome case and showed him copies of the cryptic notes left by the killer. Beechwood put on his glasses and studied the pages carefully. Woods left him to his own thoughts for a few moments before asking his first question. 'So can you tell me what it means?'

Beechwood sighed. 'I think you know this already, but whoever is behind the death of Daniel Eliot is a very dangerous man.'

'Why do you say that?'

'Because he appears to be twisting the Scriptures in order to justify his actions. In his mind, he is doing no wrong because he is following the word of God.' He pointed to the second note. 'This is from Exodus, Chapter 20. That's where the Ten Commandments first appear in the Bible. Depending on your faith, it's part of either the first or second commandment. From memory the full text goes something like: *For I the Lord thy God am a jealous God, punishing the children for the sins of the fathers to the third and fourth generation of those who hate Me.*'

'Sorry, Professor, I'm not really the religious type, can you put that in laymen's terms?'

'Sure. In essence it says that if you commit a sin, then three or four generations of your children will suffer as a result.'

'So, someone could be going after Daniel's father and grandfather?'

'It's possible. But then there's the other passage: *By the sin of one man, all men were made sinners.* That one is from Romans 5. Tell me, Mr Woods, do you know what Original Sin is?'

'Enlighten me.'

'The Bible teaches us that in the beginning, man was without sin and man lived for ever. But when Adam ate the forbidden apple from the Tree of Knowledge, he committed a sin and since then, man has been mortal. By eating the apple,

Adam brought death to the world.'

'I don't understand how that relates to this case.'

'The person who used this quotation is saying that those who are without sin will live for ever. By the same token, those who die, no matter what the circumstances, do so because they have sinned.'

'And that even applies to an eight-year-old boy?'

Professor Beechwood nodded grimly. 'As I said, you're dealing with a very dangerous man.'

18

DI Collins arrived at the underground car-park at New Scotland Yard just as DCI Blackwell was getting out of his own vehicle. He waited for her, knowing it was his opportunity to take her down a peg or two.

'You really fucked up last night, didn't you?' he said with a smirk as soon as she opened her door. 'I always knew you were wrong for this case. I'm surprised you didn't try to fit the family up for it anyway.'

Collins knew exactly what Blackwell was getting at. 'You should get your facts straight before you start accusing people, sir.'

'Everyone knows you tried to fit up that child molester.'

Collins laughed. 'You're so full of shit. Did you know the only reason that case collapsed was because Forensics contaminated the DNA sample?'

'But that doesn't give you the right to frame him.'

'And what gave him the right to go out and rape a twelve-year-old girl seven days after we had to let him walk, sir?'

Blackwell was lost for words. He had not known the full facts of the case and could only stand silently by Collins's car as she made her way into the main building for the press conference.

DCS Higgins was waiting outside the press room, looking smart in his Met dress uniform. He smiled when he saw Collins appear, looking equally smart in her black trouser suit and white cotton blouse.

'You all right?' asked Higgins, who could tell something was bothering Collins.

'I'm fine, sir – you know how I feel about press conferences.' Collins was trying her best to put the confrontation with Blackwell out of her mind and focus on the job in hand.

'You've heard David Eliot's back home.'

'I heard it on the way here,' Collins said. 'And we've confirmed his whereabouts at the time that Daniel was taken, so we're back to square one.'

At that moment Blackwell joined them and Collins fell silent.

'Well,' Higgins said, trying to break the awkward silence between the two officers, 'they're all waiting.'

'Then let's get it over with,' said Blackwell, his tone of voice in front of DCS Higgins nothing like the one he had used in the car-park.

Collins gave him a filthy look, and then the three of them walked into the room and up on to the standard blue police podium, where they were greeted by blinding flashes of lights. The room was packed with reporters and camera crews, all of whom fell silent as the officers took to the stage.

'Good afternoon. I am Detective Chief Superintendent Mark Higgins. To my left is Detective Chief Inspector Colin Blackwell of SCD7, the Kidnap and Extortion Unit, and to my right is Detective Inspector Stacey Collins of the homicide division.

'I'd like to start by reading a short statement. As you already know, at approximately 18.45 on Friday evening, the body of eight-year-old Daniel Eliot was found inside the church of St Andrew's in Peckham.

'I can today confirm that a ransom demand had been made for Daniel's safe return.

'Daniel disappeared near his home sometime during the afternoon on Wednesday. We are today issuing some new photographs of him and making a fresh appeal for witnesses who may have seen him between Wednesday morning and the time his body was found on Friday evening.

'This is an appalling crime, perhaps the worst I have seen in my twenty-five years on the force, and it is essential that Daniel's killer is brought to justice. My colleague, Detective Inspector Stacey Collins, is heading the investigation, and we will now take any questions.'

Suddenly there was a riot of voices and a crowd of hands as each journalist tried to have their question answered first. Higgins pointed at a reporter in the front row.

'Trisha Bennett, *Daily Telegraph*. Is it true, Inspector, that this is the first time a kidnapping handled by the Met has resulted in a fatality?'

Higgins turned to Blackwell, who was struggling to keep his composure. 'Yes, I can confirm that, sadly, this is the first time we have failed to recover the victim of a kidnap alive.'

Another hand shot up, and Higgins pointed. 'Damien Groves, the *Sun*. Is it true that Daniel was murdered because the Met refused to pay the full ransom of just £25,000?'

Blackwell knew this journalist had spoken to someone on the inside. 'I'm afraid it's our policy not to comment on operational decisions of ongoing investigations.' He'd lost count of the number of times he'd recited that in his thirty-year career.

The journalist raised his voice, and everyone knew what the next question would be before he asked it. 'So are you saying the police now put a price on the life of a child?'

Blackwell looked directly at the tabloid reporter. 'The police never have and never will put a price on saving any life.' The room was suddenly filled with the scratching of shorthand.

'Sandra Gordon, ITN. So how close are you to apprehending a suspect?' The question was directed towards Collins this time.

She didn't answer for a moment, causing the murmurs in the crowd of journalists to die away; then, just as she planned, she picked out a television camera at the back of the room from one of the main broadcasters, the red light at the front indicating that it was recording. An image flashed into her head: it was of a man, a faceless man, watching the television. Watching her. There was no doubt in her mind that whatever she said would be taken in and picked over by the person she was trying to catch, and it was important to get it right.

'So far,' she said, her voice level and her eyes not leaving the camera, 'we have very little to go on. At present there are no witnesses, no leads and almost nothing in the way of forensic evidence to further our enquiry.'

There was a murmur from the crowd, and Collins could feel Higgins giving her a hot, sidelong glance. 'The truth is we don't have very much at all.'

Sandra Gordon spoke again. 'So let me get this straight, Detective. You refused to pay the full ransom and as a result Daniel Eliot was brutally murdered. And now you have almost nothing to go on. Is that the situation?'

Collins needed only one word to reply.

'Yes.'

Outside the room, Higgins pulled Collins into a vacant office a few doors down. He slammed the door and started fuming at the DI before she could speak to him. 'What are you playing at? This isn't the fucking time for games with the press.'

'It'll be fine, sir,' she told him calmly.

'What do you mean, it'll be fine?' Higgins ranted. 'You know how that lot will twist what you've just said. We're going to end up looking unprofessional and incapable.'

'Not if we find our murderer, we won't.'

Higgins was almost incandescent now. 'And how do you propose to do that, DI Collins? You've just publicly admitted we've got nothing to go on.'

'If you're going to carry on screaming at me, sir, I'll be happy to go home and spend the day with my daughter.'

There was a pause. Higgins looked as though he was about to explode again, but thought better of it. When Collins spoke again it was in a much calmer way – not conciliatory, exactly, but not far off.

'I need the killer to think we're groping in the dark. Everything he's done in the past few days has been precisely worked out in detail: he's figured out how to keep in touch with us without being traced; he knew exactly when to enter the church without anyone knowing.'

'Get to the point.' Higgins almost managed to sound surly.

'The point is this: so far he hasn't put a foot wrong. If he thinks we're on to him, he'll redouble his efforts. But if he feels overconfident – that he's in control and that we don't know what we're doing – then maybe he'll get sloppy. Frankly, I think that's worth a bit of egg on the face, don't you?'

Higgins stepped closer to her. 'Listen to me, Collins, and listen carefully. You've worked for me for over three years, and I know you can some-times be a loose cannon. But don't forget there're

125

plenty of people out there waiting for you to take a fall – just don't give them a chance to say "I told you so."' And with that, he walked out of the office.

19

The drive back from Central London to Peckham was the first free moment she had had all day and one she intended to take full advantage of. She pulled her mobile from her handbag and punched out a number without even looking at the keys. It rang twice before it was answered with a simple 'Yes?'

'Hi, Mum, it's me.'

'Oh, hello, love,' came the chirpy reply.

'Is Sophie there? Can I have a word?'

There was a pause. 'Listen, love, Sophie's still very upset by what happened yesterday. She ... she told me that she doesn't want to speak to you right now. I think it would be best if you could just come home, spend some time with her. Do you think you'll be able to do that?'

'That's why I'm calling. I'm not working late tonight so should be home in time for tea.'

'Oh, that's wonderful, dear. I'm sure it will all be sorted out in no time at all. Do you want me to tell her?'

Stacey thought for a second. 'Tell you what, don't say anything. I want to surprise her.'

Collins and her team spent the rest of the afternoon going through CCTV footage of the van that Cooper had isolated, but none of the images showed the vehicle's registration number.

Cooper could not hide her frustration. They had got what they wanted, but it wasn't enough to move the investigation forward.

'Let me go down there, guv, and I'll see for myself if there are any more cameras around showing that street.'

'Sure. See what you can get. I'm going home to see Sophie.'

At six thirty Collins was in her car. She stopped off at the local supermarket on the way home in order to pick up Sophie's favourite pudding – crème brulée – and it was only when she got back on the road that her keen sixth sense suddenly kicked in.

It took a moment for her to appreciate fully what was wrong, but, in the way that an image slowly appears on a Polaroid photograph, things filled out and came into focus. It was the car in her rear-view mirror. The red BMW. It had been there ever since she had left the office. It was newer and bigger than hers. Collins sped up and took the next right turn without indicating. A second later she saw the red BMW had done the same. She accelerated hard and vanished out of sight around another tight bend. The BMW came hurtling round after her.

So far as she could tell, there was only one person in the car behind. She took another sharp corner, braked hard and quickly got out of her car.

The BMW slowly drew up behind and mounted

the edge of the kerb. She recognized the driver straight away. Tall, drawn, in his mid thirties with a pock-marked face and shaven head, it could only be Danny Thompson, Jack Stanley's enforcer.

'Why the fuck are you following me?'

'I have a message for you.'

Thompson looked to his left and right, a pointless attempt to make sure no one was listening in. There was no one around.

'What's the message?' said Collins again, now beginning to get impatient.

'Jack Stanley wants to see you.'

'When?'

'Seven. Tonight. He say's you'll know where.'

'I can't... I've...'

But the man had already spun around and started to walk back to his car. 'All I know is that he's going to be there and that he's got something for you. If you don't want it, that's down to you.'

It took another hour to make it to Chislehurst. By the time Stacey arrived at the ruined manor house she was fuming with rage. She had made arrangements to spend some time with her daughter, but Jack Stanley had managed to get in the way.

She took deep breaths and tried to calm herself as she approached the ruins. She needed his help and that meant she had to control her emotions. At least for now. When she was ten feet from Jack, he stood up and nodded in her direction.

'What have you got for me?' asked Stacey.

'Nothing.'

'Is that supposed to be funny? Is that your idea of being fucking clever? You bring me all the way down here just to tell me that you're not going to give me any help until I do you the one favour you know I can't actually do...'

Jack held up a hand to silence her. 'Don't jump the gun,' he said calmly. 'I didn't say anything about not wanting to give you any help. I know you're struggling with the idea at the moment – but I'm pretty sure you're going to come round to my way of thinking. And in the meantime, I'm quite happy to help you out any way I can, Princess.'

Stacey winced at the sound of the nickname she had grown to hate. 'Stop playing fucking games with me.'

Jack took his time replying. 'You know I never play games,' he said at last, 'but there's nothing to tell.

'I got a couple of the boys to ask everyone who knows anything around on the estate. And I'm telling you, a pigeon can't even take a shit on the windowsill in any of those blocks on the Blenheim without someone seeing it happen.' As he came closer to her, Stacey turned her head the other way as he whispered, 'Even my lookouts have lookouts, if you know what I mean?'

'So what did they see?'

'Nothing. Nada. Zilch. I'm telling you, Princess, if your man was ever on the estate, if he ever arranged any kind of money-drop or anything to do with the kidnap when he was there, then he must be a fucking ghost because not a single person in that whole place saw him.'

Stacey took in the news. It simply didn't make any sense. The money-drop is the single most important and challenging part of any kidnap operation. No one would suggest a location for it to take place that they didn't know well or at least have spent some time in. What on earth was this guy playing at?

Jack's voice snapped Stacey out of her thoughts. 'I've done what you asked me to. So what are you going to do about my problem?'

'I can't get hold of that information, you know I can't.'

'Don't give me that. I know for a fact that a lot of the stuff you've fed me over the years, I could have found out for myself if I'd gone and looked for it. I know how careful you've been, but I also know that if there's one person who could find a way to get that information, it's you.'

Stacey didn't bother to smile at the compliment. 'But what are you going to do with the information, Jack? I know what happens to grasses in your world. They end up dead. I can't have blood on my hands. I can't be a part of anything like that.'

Jack held up his empty palms in a gesture of innocence. 'What kind of guy do you think I am? You've got me all wrong. I just want to send the guy some flowers.' As the joke he was about to tell got the better of him, Jack could no longer hold in the snigger building up inside. 'But they probably won't be for his birthday.'

He reached into his jacket and pulled out an envelope. 'It could be one of six people. Here are their names and a few details about each of them. Just do what you can, Princess.'

Jack held out his hand, and Stacey reached out

to take the envelope. Their fingers touched briefly and their eyes met. Jack started to smile, but Stacey remained stern-faced. She tried to take the envelope, but Jack refused to relax his grip.

'Stacey ... I...'

'Don't, Jack,' she said, looking down at the ground.

She pulled at the envelope once more, and it slipped through Jack's fingers. She tucked it into her bag and, without a word, spun on her heel and started to walk away.

Somewhere in the distance, the shutter of a camera with a powerful zoom lens clicked repeatedly.

20

Although the next day was the start of the school holidays, Sophie had already gone to bed by the time her mother arrived home. Stacey was once again racked with guilt at having let her daughter down, and it made her even more angry that Jack Stanley had been responsible.

Her parents were still up, watching television in the front room. She popped her head round the door to greet them.

'Hello, love,' said her father. Her mother continued to watch the TV in silence. Stacey rolled her eyes and made her way into the kitchen.

She had just opened the fridge and was trying to decide what to have for dinner when her phone started to ring.

'Good evening, Inspector. It's Dr Matthews. Sorry to call late.'

'That's not a problem, Doc. What is it?' Stacey asked quietly.

'I got some of the test results back, and I thought you'd want to hear them right away.'

Stacey pulled a small notebook and pen from her bag and leaned against the kitchen worktop. 'Okay, go ahead.'

'First off, the toxicology. There are traces of chloroform on the subject's clothes.'

'Knockout gas?'

'Exactly. We're talking very low traces so I suspect it was used to incapacitate the subject when he was taken. That's supported by the residual amounts of cotton wool that were found around his mouth and nose.'

Stacey closed her eyes as a series of disturbing images of Daniel's kidnap ran through her head. 'What about time of death?' she asked.

'Well,' replied Matthews, her voice sounding professional and firm. 'That's the curious thing. I would place it at about four o'clock on Friday afternoon. Certainly no later than four thirty.'

Stacey fell silent as the news consolidated itself in her mind. 'Jesus,' she said after a moment. 'That means Daniel was dead at least an hour before the ransom deadline.'

A riot of emotions ran through her as the reality of what the doctor was saying quickly sank in. Had the kidnap been about the money, or just about killing Daniel? Had the police in any way provoked him into killing? If so, why the torture, why such brutality against a defenceless child?

The last contact between the kidnapper and Blackwell's team had been ten minutes before the deadline, when he had instructed them to leave the bag of money in the lift of a tower block the Blenheim Estate – perhaps over an hour after he had killed Daniel.

All at once everything began to fall into place. No wonder Jack's people hadn't found any trace of the guy on the estate. He had never been there. Despite having gone to the trouble of arranging an elaborate money-drop, the kidnapper never had any intention of releasing Daniel alive.

Her mind was racing faster and faster. It couldn't have been about the money. It could only have been about the power, the control and the fear. Her gut feelings told her that this could mean only one thing.

He was going to strike again.

Monday

21

Seven a.m. It was the quietest room in the house. Upstairs and at the back, furthest away from the road, with a large south-facing window that allowed plenty of natural light to enter.

He sat perched on a padded stool, the sound of Radio 2 playing gently in the background. He had been working steadily since breakfast, and there was now only one figure left to complete. Gazing through the tabletop magnifying glass, his hand steady, and using a tiny brush loaded with silver paint, he depicted the buckles on the man's shoes and the blade of his sword. Finally the last of the Jacobite soldiers for his re-creation of the Battle of Culloden was complete.

Around the room hundreds of miniature figures from other great battles, including Waterloo, Trafalgar and the First and Second World Wars, looked down from wooden shelves, each one hand-painted in intricate detail.

With great pride he placed the finished Jacobite on the miniature landscape of hills, trees and streams that accurately simulated the battleground down to the very last detail. It had taken him more than a year to complete this latest project, a process that had involved hours of study at his local library and several trips to the Highlands.

He sat there admiring his work for some time. Everything had gone exactly to plan, and he was proud of his attention to detail. He allowed the feelings to soak in for a few more moments before getting up and moving into the bedroom next door.

All the things he needed for that day's work had been laid out on the bed, and he slowly began to pack the items into a leather bag, ticking each one off from a mental list as he did so. Latex gloves, gaffer tape, binoculars, a single padded leather glove, cotton-wool, two short lengths of rope and a bottle of chloroform.

Once all the items were packed and double-checked, he found he had a little time to kill. He read a few random passages from the Bible and then said his prayers. Outside the sun was shining, just as it had been a few days earlier. It was, he decided, a very good omen.

He picked up the bag and left the house. It was time to go to work.

22

Michael Dawney was several days into his break and was thoroughly enjoying the warm summer weather.

He was particularly looking forward to the family holiday in two weeks' time. They would spend their first week at Disneyworld and the second in the Florida Keys. It was going to be great – Dad was always so much more relaxed on holiday, and ready to play with him whenever he wanted. At home he was always much too busy for anything like that. Leaving the house early each morning and returning late at night, Peter

Dawney rarely saw his son except at weekends. Michael's mum, Alice, was around, of course, but she was pretty hopeless at sports. Today she had her friends coming around for a coffee morning.

So the morning seemed to spread out before him, the total opposite to a school day, when everything was such a frantic rush to get out of the house in time. It was nine thirty before he was sitting at the kitchen table, slowly spooning Frosties into his mouth as he watched *Ed, Edd 'n' Eddy* on the Cartoon Network.

'Can I go outside to play now, Mum?' he asked, as he finished the last mouthful of his breakfast.

'Course you can, love – I'm going up to have a shower. Just remember to clean your teeth before you go out.' She kissed him on the forehead and went upstairs.

Their large back garden bordered on an area of woodland that could be reached through a gate in the open-slatted fence. Michael had been told never to set foot in the woodland without his parents. He didn't mind – the truth was he found the woodland creepy. In the wintertime, especially when the light started to fail in the late afternoon, it started to look like the murky pictures of haunted forests that appeared in fairy-tale books, with tree trunks so gnarled that they looked like the arms and legs of old people.

He knew exactly how he planned to spend his morning. He would build himself a ramp out of a plank of wood and a few old bricks, then jump it with his bike. He'd need to work quietly, and around the corner from the kitchen – if Mum saw him doing it, she would no doubt suggest

139

that he did something a bit safer. But, in Mikey's experience, safer meant less fun, and what was the point of having a stunt bike if you weren't allowed to do a few stunts on it?

It took at least ten minutes to gather together all the bricks he wanted from the side of the patio – nine of them in all – and place them in a neat block well out of the way of Mum's gaze. The plank of wood he'd had his eye on was upended against the back of the garage; he dragged it round to his makeshift obstacle course and lifted one end on to the bricks. He was ready to go.

Walking through the woods and up the steep hill had left him sweaty and short of breath.

He had been there many times before and knew exactly where to stop for the best view of the house. He placed his bag on the ground beside the large oak tree and removed the binoculars, quickly focusing on the image of the small boy riding his bike over the low ramp. The boy was cautious at first, probably because he was afraid of falling off. But as his confidence grew, he rode more quickly and jumped further.

He laid out the contents of the bag, making sure one last time that he had not forgotten anything. He then made his way back down the hill to where he had parked his van. He opened the back doors and smiled as a mongrel puppy began excitedly jumping up towards him. He picked the dog up gently and cradled it in his arms, allowing it to lick his face as he carried it back up into the woods.

When he reached his vantage point, he placed the dog down on the ground, stroking it firmly enough to hold it in place. His eyes lit up as he slipped the leather gauntlet on to his right hand. And then he struck. His hand moved as quick as a flash, grabbing one of the dog's rear legs hard, bracing it between his thumb and forefinger and squeezing harder and harder until ... crack ... the bone gave way, breaking clean in two.

Michael was riding faster than ever towards the ramp when he heard an almighty scream. At first it sounded like the screeching sound foxes made at night but, as the wailing continued, Michael knew it was the desperate cry of an animal in pain.

He dropped his bike and ran towards the fence, peering into the thicket. A flash of movement caught his eye – a small dog flailing around on the ground just a few feet away. He looked back towards the house and called for his mother, but there was no answer. Although he knew he shouldn't go in the woods, it would take only a few seconds to rescue the dog and bring it back to the house, where his mother could help him look after it. He gave a final look back to the house before running towards the gate.

He had already removed the top of the bottle of chloroform and soaked the cotton-wool pads when the boy emerged from the gate. He crouched down out of sight behind the trunk of the tree and peered around as the boy reached the spot where the dog lay.

He watched as the boy knelt down and began to stroke the injured animal, looking around cautiously to see if the dog's owner was anywhere to be found. The boy gently lifted the dog up into his arms, being careful not to damage the broken leg further, then turned and headed back to the gate.

The dog's screams covered up the sound of the man's approach. It took only a few steps for him to reach the boy. In one swift movement his left hand pulled the boy's head back into his lower chest while his right hand held the cotton-wool over the boy's nose and mouth.

The boy dropped the dog in fright and clawed uselessly at his hands before slowly going limp. The man released his grip, and the boy fell to the ground. He knelt beside him, running his fingers gently through the boy's hair. 'By the disobedience of one man,' he said softly, 'many were made sinners.'

Alice Dawney had showered, dressed and fixed her hair just the way she liked it. The first of her friends were due around for their coffee morning in little less than an hour, which left her just enough time to do something with Michael.

The pair had long ago decided that games of football or catch were hopeless when it was just the two of them, but perhaps they could build something out of Magnetix together – he always liked that.

She opened the back door and stepped outside. 'Mikey!' she called. 'Where are you, love? What are you doing?'

There was no reply, so she walked around the corner. That was odd. Mikey's bike was on its side, next to a not very safe-looking contraption that he had constructed out of bricks and that old plank she had been trying to get Peter to take to the tip for weeks now. But Mikey wouldn't just leave his bike like that: it was his pride and joy. He must be round the other side of the house, where they had erected the goalpost, having decided to play football instead.

Alice walked round. 'Mikey!' she called again. 'I thought we could do something together.'

Still no reply. And still no sign of him. She felt her heart start to pulse a little faster, and she quickened her step to complete the circuit of the house and bring her back to the kitchen door. 'Mikey!' Her voice was shrill now. Panicked. This wasn't like him at all. 'Joke's over now. Stop hiding.' She found herself back at the bike. It lay there, immobile. All around was still, oppressively silent.

And then she saw something that made her catch her breath. The garden gate was open. A sickness rose in her as she stepped slowly towards it and passed through it. In the woods outside, just a few feet away, she saw one of Michael's shoes. His new trainer. They had only bought them on Friday afternoon. He was so proud of them. Why would he leave it there? Why would he go into the woods at all?

She held the shoe in her hand and gazed at it; a tingling hotness enveloped her whole body, and she noticed that her hand was shaking. Instantly she turned, as though a spell had been broken, and at the same time a low moan escaped her lips. She ran back towards the kitchen door, her legs trembling beneath her. They nearly gave way as she ran through the kitchen and into the hall way, where the cordless phone was resting on its base. 'Mikey!' she yelled up the stairs, even as she found herself automatically dialing a number on the keypad. 'Mikey, are you up there?'

No answer.

The phone rang at the other end. 'Peter Dawney,' her husband answered in his 'work voice', which always sounded so different to the one he used with her.

'It's me,' she whispered breathlessly.

'Alice,' he said in surprise and concern. 'Darling, what's the matter?'

Alice found herself hyperventilating, unable to speak.

'Darling, calm down. Take a deep breath.' She did as she was told. 'What on earth's wrong?'

'It's Mikey,' she finally managed to say. 'I don't know where he is. I can't find him. He's gone.'

23

DI Collins and DS Woods had arrived at the incident room shortly before midday, having spent the morning at New Scotland Yard briefing DCS Higgins about the latest developments on the case.

As they walked towards their desks, they passed DC Cooper, who was staring intently at the small TV in front of her. The previous evening she had travelled to the area close to where Daniel Eliot had been snatched in order to look for more cameras with a view of the street where the white van had followed Daniel and Sammy. After walking for what felt like several miles, she had found two, one attached to a builder's yard, the other on the forecourt of a tyre shop.

Both timing systems were out, as was usually the case with civilian CCTV. And she had been scanning the footage all morning.

'Have you cracked the case yet?' asked Woods with a cheeky grin.

'Piss off. Why can't you do this for once?'

Collins came over to join them, having overheard the conversation. 'Because he's a DS and you're a DC,' she said. 'Anyway you need the experience,' she said, smiling.

'What did Higgins have to say, guv?'

'Not a lot. We gave him everything we've got. We really need to focus on the van. How are you doing?'

'Nothing so far on the camera from the builder's yard. I've got one more tape to go, then I'll move on to the tyre shop.'

'Okay. Woods, why don't you use your charms to see if you can get another TV from Drabble and help out?'

Cooper allowed a tiny smile to cross her lips.

'I could get two TVs, guv,' said Woods, 'then you could have one as well.'

'Nice try,' replied Collins. 'I'm off to Guy's. Matthews is ready with her full report.'

The traffic was slow as Collins headed back from Guy's, and Radio 2 was playing 'Romeo and Juliet' by Dire Straits. She let the music clear her mind. Soon, though, it ended, and the discussion returned. The topic of the day was an obvious choice considering the story dominating the headlines: the death of Daniel Eliot.

'So we're back with retired police detective Guy

145

Redgrove, and on Line 1 we have Julie from Brixton.'

Julie's voice was grating and shrill. 'If this government did what they always say they're going to do and put more police on the streets, things like this wouldn't happen.'

The smooth voice of the radio DJ interrupted. 'We're told, of course, that police numbers are increasing. Do you see any evidence of this?'

Julie snorted. 'My girl goes to school less than half a mile from where we live, and I have to take her there and pick her up to stop the drug dealers who hang around nearby from getting anywhere near her.'

The DJ adopted a note of polished incredulity. 'So, let me get this right, Julie. You're telling me that you're aware of drug dealers operating outside your daughter's school, and the police are doing nothing about it? Guy Redgrove, what do you say to that?'

'Well, clearly it's difficult for me to comment on something without having all the facts,' Redgrove began. 'But what I will say is this. The police rely heavily on intelligence, and that intelligence often comes from members of the public. If you're having a problem with drug dealers in your neighbourhood, you need to report it. Have you reported it, Julie?'

Julie gasped. 'Are you mad? I have to live there. I have to walk past those streets every day. You know what would happen to me if they thought I was a grass? What you need to do is put some more police officers outside the school to stop it–'

'But surely that won't do the situation much

good,' said the DJ, cutting in on her. 'Because the dealers would simply go round the corner and the kids would know where to find them.'

Of course they do, thought Collins to herself. And if you put police round the corner, they'd just find somewhere else to do their business.

The DJ brought the conversation to a close. 'Thank you for phoning in, Julie. We're discussing child safety and the tragic death of Daniel Eliot. Could it have been prevented? Could the police have done more? Is London still a safe place for our children? We want to hear your views. More after the one o' clock news.'

There was a musical jingle, and then a new voice took over. 'The news at one. Police are appealing for witnesses in connection with the murder of eight-year-old Daniel Eliot, who was found dead on Friday night after disappearing from near his home on Wednesday afternoon. In particular, they would like to speak to the driver of a white van seen acting suspiciously in the Selsdon area of Croydon between 3 and 4 p.m. last Wednesday. At the weekend, Detective Inspector Stacey Collins, the officer in charge of the murder investigation, conceded that the police were currently without any leads.'

Collins couldn't help thinking that those carefully chosen words might come back to haunt her.

The remaining news was the usual babble of politics and weather, after which the phone-ins continued; Collins only vaguely listened to the stream of half-formed opinions and unreliable facts that were shared and transmitted across the airwaves. The traffic, which never usually worried her, was starting to put her on edge. She wanted to get back to work. Collins was becoming convinced that the van could be the breakthrough they'd been waiting for.

'Our next caller,' the DJ announced in a voice that matched the subject matter in hand, 'is James from Camberwell. Good morning, James.'

There was an unusual silence, the sort of dead air time that brought embarrassment to announcer and listener alike.

'James from Camberwell,' the announcer repeated after a few seconds. 'Are you there, James?'

Very slowly the caller spoke, and the sound of his voice forced Collins to swerve the car to the side of the road and screech to a halt. The car behind her beeped its horn furiously, but Collins barely heard it. She was too busy listening to the radio.

Too busy listening to the voice that she knew.

Unemotional. Monotone. Dead. And all at once familiar from the videos and the recordings of the telephone calls.

'I killed Daniel Eliot,' the caller said solemnly. 'He was a good little boy. Quiet. But I had no choice. By the disobedience of one man, many were made sinners.'

The DJ clearly thought it was a prank caller. 'Okay, James, that's enough. I don't think our listeners find it very funny to make jokes about–'

'I have another boy.'

'Are you saying you've kidnapped another boy?'

'If you insist on interrupting me again,' he stated, 'I will hang up. And make no mistake – you'll want to hear what I have to say.'

The DJ started to stutter a feeble objection, but

the caller simply spoke over him. 'I killed Daniel because the police were trying to trap me. They didn't believe that I would carry out my threat.' He paused and drew a deep breath that was amplified by the telephone receiver. 'Because of this, I have obtained another child. He is eight years old, and he lives in the village of Kingswood in Surrey. If he is to be returned safely, I will require a ransom of £3 million to be paid forty-eight hours from now. Details of the delivery will be supplied to the police at a moment of my choosing. If my instructions are not followed, you may rest assured that he will meet the same fate as Daniel.'

There was a short silence interrupted by a vague hiss in the background, and suddenly the unmistakable sound of a child's voice, muffled and distant, crying for his mum. Then the phone went dead.

Collins sat rigid for a few moments, hardly believing what she had just heard. Then, as if suddenly shaken out of a dream, she grabbed the portable police siren from below her seat, thrust it out of the open window on to the roof of the car and, with the siren's screams filling her ears, pushed her way into the traffic.

It was finally starting to make sense. The real reason the kidnapper had killed Daniel Eliot, the real reason he had not even attempted to collect the ransom, the real reason why the amount being demanded was so small and the drop-off had been arranged for such an unlikely location – all of it was suddenly crystal clear.

He had been building up his bargaining power.

The kidnapper wanted to demonstrate to both

the police and the parents of his next victim that he was deadly serious.

Less than twenty-four hours earlier the world's media had captured DCI Blackwell telling them that the Metropolitan Police would never put a price on the life of a child. Now that claim was about to be put to the test. Under the circumstances, how could the police do anything other than stump up the full amount?

This was bad. This was as bad as it could possibly get. It seemed to take for ever from the end of the phone-in for Collins to get back to the incident room, and her mind was a maelstrom every inch of the way. As she battled against the traffic, she found herself shouting obscenities at cars that were in her way. It wasn't road-rage – just rage.

How the hell could she find a missing child in two days? She had already seen what his abductor was capable of. She had seen what he liked to do. She crashed her fist down on to the horn as a blue van got in her way.

Blackwell's initial perception had been wrong, oh so wrong. The untraceable emails, the use of an anonymous van, the piggybacked ISP – it all pointed to someone who had spent months, maybe even years, planning this crime. He had fooled them all. He had made them look like idiots.

Time was running out.

She had to get back to the office. And fast.

24

When Michael Dawney woke up, he thought for a terrifying moment that he had gone blind. Even though his eyes were wide open, there was nothing but pitch black – a heavy, suffocating black that was darker than anything he had ever known.

He didn't know where he was or who had brought him here. He didn't know if it was still light outside, though the hunger pangs in his stomach told him that a meal of some kind was long overdue. He was thirsty too.

The last thing Michael remembered was rushing into the woods after the dog. He found him, his leg broken, at the foot of a large tree. As he headed back home with the dog in his arms, he felt his head being held back and all around him going dark, the way it does when a cloud crosses in front of the sun.

As his eyes began to adjust to the lack of light, he was able to make out his surroundings. The walls were bare, plastered but not painted. There were only a few items of furniture: a filthy mattress, a small bucket in one corner, a single chair and a cold metal table. Everywhere smelled of damp and decay.

Michael shivered with fear. His young mind was groggy, but he was too young to understand that he had not only been kidnapped but also drugged. He tried to move, to reach out and make some sense of his surroundings, but his arms refused to function. It took a few more seconds of foggy thoughts and confusion for him to realize that he had been tied up.

His body rubbed painfully against the hard concrete floor as he tried to move and look around.

There was a metallic 'clink' in a distant corner, followed by the sound of a bolt being drawn back. Then the door opened, and the room was filled with a light from outside so bright and painful that Michael was forced to close his eyes.

The initial burst of brightness had burned itself into his retina, and when he opened his eyes again his vision was blurred and confused. Then heavy footsteps began to sound across the floor towards him.

'Please,' Michael gasped. 'Please...'

The voice that replied was gruff and uncompromising. There was no room here for negotiation. 'Shut up.'

It was a lesson he chose not to heed. 'Please,' he said again, 'please help me.'

Two large strong hands grabbed him painfully by his wrists and lifted him up to a standing position. The pain was intense, the shock of it enough to make him open his eyes again. He found himself staring into the face of his attacker.

The man was clean-shaven and what little hair he had was cut short. He was tall and wore a blue-and-white-striped kitchen apron over his pristine white shirt, which accentuated his pot belly. The shirt was open at the collar, and Michael could see a line of mottled skin snaking its way down from the back of his right ear and round to the top of his chest and beyond. The scars looked painful and raw, but what Michael could not tear his gaze away from were the man's eyes: they were dead, cold and emotionless.

One burly arm held him out, the other smacked him across the face with an open palm, knocking him back down to the floor. A trickle of blood began to seep out of his nose. 'Shut up,' the voice said again.

Michael lay on the floor, tears in his eyes, but too scared to cry. The man made to hit him again, but the boy lurched back with fear, only to find his shoulder slipping into a sticky patch on the ground. He looked over and saw at once that the patch was made up of partly congealed blood. For a moment he was confused. The blood coming out of his own nose was still fresh, and in any case there had not been enough of it to gather on the floor.

Then, with a growing sense of horror, Michael realized that the blood was not his own. He wasn't the first person to have been brought to this room.

25

Collins sat in a corner office of the incident room along with Woods, Cooper, Drabble and other members of the team, all listening intently to a digital recording of the Radio 2 show that the BBC had sent over immediately after the kidnapper's call.

'Could it be a hoax?' asked Cooper.

'Unlikely. Missing Persons have already confirmed that the parents of a boy named Michael Dawney from Kingswood filed a report just after ten,' said Collins grimly. 'Besides, he quoted from the line of Scripture that was at the scene of the crime. That was a holdback. Few people outside this room know about it.'

'There's the voice as well,' said Woods. 'To my ear it sounds like the bloke from the videos. Khan ran it through some Internet voice-recognition program. It's going up to the lab for a proper analysis, but I think it's safe to say that it's our man.'

Collins nodded and looked around the room: every face was serious and lined with concentration.

'Initial thoughts?'

'He's increased the ransom by a factor of more than a hundred,' observed Drabble. 'And we suspect that he always intended to kill Daniel. To force our hand – to make it clear that, if this second ransom isn't paid, we know what to expect.'

'My thoughts exactly,' said Collins. 'By killing the first child, he's just trying to increase his chances of having the larger ransom paid.'

Cooper shook her head slowly. 'But that's not going to happen. There's no way in the world the Commissioner is going to authorize the release of £3 million. Any kind of cooperation is against the rules.'

'Jesus,' gasped Woods. 'He's an eight-year-old kid, and we know what this monster's capable of.

Isn't it time to just forget about the rule book, pay the bastard the money he wants and make sure the poor kid lives to see another birthday?'

'For what it's worth, Woods,' Collins replied, 'I agree. But it's over our heads, and you know as well as I do that there's no way the Commissioner would agree to it. It's political now, and there's no politician in the land that would agree to giving in to this kind of stuff, even if they get a dead body at the end of it. If they paid, it would open the floodgates.'

'So what do we want to do?' asked Cooper.

'The call went through to the radio station just after 1 p.m. He gave a deadline of two days for the ransom to be paid. That takes us up to Wednesday at 1 p.m.'

The room was filled with a sense of urgency and adrenalin as the task ahead of the team became clear.

'Where do you want us to start?'

'Get on to the station, Tony. He must have given the show a telephone number – they always phone their callers back – so find out what it was and where the call was made from.'

'Knowing this guy's form,' said Drabble, 'it's going to be a pay-as-you-go mobile. Untraceable.'

'I agree,' said Collins. 'But if we can track the signal we might be able to get an idea of where he was calling from. That might narrow down the area where we want to start our enquiries.'

'Cooper–'

'Let me guess. CCTV from the Dawney household.'

'You got it. Get on to Missing Persons and find

out everything they have on the case. Let's get as much footage from the area close to the site where Michael went missing as we can. There's every chance he used the same vehicle.'

Everyone set about their tasks as Collins opened the door of the meeting room, only to find DCS Higgins standing directly in front of her.

'I was just about to call you, sir,' she said. 'I take it you know all about the phone call to the radio station?'

'Of course,' he replied. Higgins looked a little hesitant. 'Collins, I need to have a quick word with you. In private.'

The pair made their way back into the meeting room, and Higgins gestured for Collins to sit down.

'What is it, sir?'

'Listen, Collins. I know this is a tough case, but–'

'Sir, if it's about what I said at the press conference, then I apologize. I played what I thought was the best strategy at the time. I really don't think anything I did has changed the kidnapper's actions one bit...'

He held up his hand to silence her. 'We're all very emotionally involved in this case, especially now that another child has been taken by the same man. But you have to understand that what was a murder case has now become another live kidnap.'

'I don't follow you, sir.'

'SCD7 are taking over the investigation. DCI Blackwell is going to be running the show from now on.'

'For how long? Until he fucks it up again? Until Michael Dawney is dead and I have to pick up the pieces?'

'You're out of line, Collins. You know the way this works. I don't want you to make a move without Blackwell's say-so. We all need to be one team on this. I need to know that you're on board, that you can work with and not against him. Can you do that?'

There was a long pause, then Collins sighed helplessly. 'Yes, sir.'

'Good. DCI Blackwell will be here to brief your team in a couple of hours.'

Collins stood up. 'If it's all the same with you, sir, I'd like to see Blackwell now.'

'You can't. Blackwell's not here right now.'

'Where the hell is he?'

Higgins looked at Collins as if what he was about to say was screamingly obvious. 'I told you, he's running the investigation. He's on his way to see the parents.'

26

DCI Colin Blackwell sat motionless in the centre of the spacious living room while his team waited outside. The house he was in could not have been more different from the one he had sat in a few days earlier while working on the Daniel Eliot case.

The room smelled incredible. A mix of hot

coffee, fresh bread, fresh flowers and soft supple leather from a large living-room suite. It smelled like money.

He let his eyes wander over his surroundings. There was a state-of-the-art home entertainment system, complete with giant plasma TV. Heating, lighting and air conditioning were controlled from LCD panels built into the walls by each doorway.

It was all fitting for a man said to be at the cutting edge of British innovation. Blackwell had heard of Peter Dawney of course. Everyone had. In recent weeks he had become a regular face on television chat shows, talking about technology and his artificial intelligence program that could run your entire home.

Alice Dawney sat on a sofa at the other end of the room, her eyes red and puffy from crying. She had not said a word since Blackwell had arrived, and he knew from experience that she was in shock, terrified that Michael would suffer the same fate as Daniel Eliot.

Blackwell heard footsteps and turned to see Peter Dawney standing at the doorway. The man who walked towards him had an elegant demeanour: tailored grey suit, light blue shirt with no tie, and scooped-back dark hair that was parted in the middle and starting to grey at the sides. Usually he looked distinguished and handsome; today, frightened and vulnerable.

He smiled weakly and sat down next to his wife, gently putting his arm round her as she continued to sob quietly.

'Thank you for agreeing to see me, Mr and Mrs Dawney,' he began, 'on what must be an extremely difficult day for you. I won't waste your time with trivia. Has the kidnapper made direct contact with you?'

Peter sighed deeply, leaned forward in his chair and pinched the bridge of his nose between his fingers. 'No – the first we heard about it was when a friend called to tell us about the radio show. I've just got off the phone to the bank.'

'How are you getting on?'

'We're getting there. Not quickly enough for my liking, but we're getting there. My friends have been ... incredible ... agreeing to hand over thousands of pounds of their money. And we've had offers of help from all over the country. Such generosity. But still...'

Peter looked up and met Blackwell's gaze. The strain showed in his eyes, and he looked close to breaking point. 'You have to understand, everything I have is tied up in the company. I've only ever drawn a relatively modest salary and put all the profits back into the business. Of the wealth I have, a lot of it is there only on paper. When it comes to turning it into hard cash, there are difficulties, especially on such a short timescale.'

'How confident are you of raising the money?' asked Blackwell.

'I didn't say it wasn't possible. After all, we are talking about the life of my son here. I just said it was going to be difficult. People see me on TV and assume I've got millions sitting in my bank account. It's not like that. The firm, like any technology company, soaks up money, and the new software is far from ready. My house is worth two million, but that just means I have a large mortgage. I'll get the money. Christ, I have to, but it's going to ruin me. I don't care. All I want is my son back.'

Blackwell nodded. 'I understand that. And I want you to know that I have exactly the same priority. I won't lie to you. The money is important. We know this kidnapper, and we know that he won't accept anything less than the full amount. In every case of kidnap, the time when the money is handed over is the time when those responsible are most vulnerable. If we can put £3 million on the table, it gives us our best chance of drawing him out.'

'But I can just hand over the money myself, can't I?'

'It's entirely your decision as to whether you want the police involved at this stage or not. Obviously we can't force you, but what makes this case unusual is that the announcement was made not to the parents but to the public as a whole through a radio programme. It means the kidnapper knows that the whole world is going to be watching everything he does. He hasn't said anything about not getting the police involved, so my advice would be to allow us to handle this.'

Peter snorted, a sound somewhere between a laugh and a groan. 'You'll understand if I'm a little sceptical. Your track record of late doesn't give me a lot of confidence.'

Blackwell shuffled uncomfortably in his seat. That one had hit close to home. 'You're entitled to your opinion and believe me no one in the force feels the tragedy of the outcome of the Daniel Eliot case more than I do. But we firmly believe that the kidnapper always intended to kill Daniel in order to prove that he was a serious threat. He wanted to make sure there would be no question of trying to negotiate over a future ransom. But, at the same time, your son is the only leverage he has. If he wants the money, he absolutely has to keep Michael alive.'

The words seemed to breathe new life into Alice, whose face had been hidden in the nook of her husband's shoulder. She looked up, her face stained with tears. 'Then you think Michael is okay?'

'At this stage,' said Blackwell, choosing his words carefully. 'Everything we know tells us that Michael is alive.'

Alice looked at her husband, her bottom lip quivering, then collapsed into his shoulder and began to cry once more. Peter gently stroked her back, comforting her.

'If I say yes and let you come in and take over, what will happen?'

'We'll bring in a couple of family liaison officers. They'll be your direct link to the investigation and keep you updated at all times. They'll also act as a buffer between you and the press or anybody else. They'd remain here on a permanent basis until ... until Michael is recovered.'

'Okay.'

'On top of that there will be a technical team. They'll intercept any messages from the kidnapper in a bid to help us track him down. Everything we've learned so far tells us that the kidnapper is working alone. This means that when he goes to collect the money, Michael will be alone. If we can find out where Michael is, that will be our opportunity to pick him up and capture the kidnapper without risk to your son.'

Blackwell looked away briefly, as if searching the room for an extra thought, then turned back to Peter. 'I should let you know that standard Met policy in cases of this kind is not to pay the full amount of the ransom. Instead we would pay a portion and leave a note explaining to the kidnapper that the full amount is simply not available at the moment. The idea is to draw the kidnappers into a dialogue and give us more time to rescue the victim.'

'Is that what you did with that other boy?'

'Yes.'

'I see. Do you perhaps think that the kidnapper somehow knew that and that's why he killed him? Do you think that's why he came after my Mikey?'

'I'm sorry, there's really no way of knowing that.'

An uncomfortable silence settled on the room, only to be broken by a knock at the door. 'Come in,' said Peter. All heads turned to see a smartly dressed woman in her thirties push the door open slightly and poke her head around it.

'I'm sorry, Peter,' said the small round woman with an apologetic smile. 'I really need you to sign these right now to authorize the release of the funds in the escrow account if you want to be sure of having them today.'

'That's fine, Martha. Come right on in. Detective, this is my secretary, Martha Day. She's helping to coordinate getting the ransom money together.'

The woman smiled politely at the officer, then

crouched down beside Peter and spread a few sheets of paper out on the coffee table in front of him, indicating with a brightly polished fingernail where he needed to sign.

Peter waited until Martha had left the room before he spoke again. 'How close are you to actually finding Michael?'

Again Blackwell shuffled stiffly in his seat. 'We have a number of lines of enquiry that we're pursuing. That's really all I can say at the moment. Though I can assure you, Mr Dawney, that all our resources will be going into finding your son.'

Peter stared hard at the man. 'My wife and I need a few minutes to think about this. Would you mind waiting outside?'

As Blackwell left the room, Peter shut his eyes and thought back to the events of the previous four hours.

When he had first called 999 to report Mikey missing – Alice being in no state to do it herself – they had been rewarded with two local officers fifteen minutes later. But any thoughts that Mikey might simply have got lost or run away from home had been erased by the sick bastard making his ransom demand on that radio show.

Since then the house had been surrounded by police officers and squad cars. Suddenly the Dawneys were prisoners in their own home.

It was unreal – like a persistent nightmare that refused to allow him to wake up. By two o'clock they had replied to so many questions by concerned and polite police officers that Peter had begun to grow confused by his own answers. What was there to say? When he had left the house that morning everything was normal. Now their world had been turned upside down. He found he could hardly bear to be in the same room as Alice, her raw despair too sharp a contrast to his calm, almost anaesthetized lack of emotion. He felt he should be crying too, howling in frustration, sorrow and despair. But for some reason he wasn't; he was just finding the information impossible to process. It simply couldn't be true. It couldn't be real. There had to be some sort of mistake.

It was almost as if whoever was doing this knew exactly how devastating a financial blow this would be. Everything he had worked for his whole life would be gone in an instant. His company, his home, his dignity. Some might say he could do it all over again. He had started out with nothing. But that was years ago. He was younger, without a family, more willing to take risks. Now he honestly didn't have the energy.

Damn. Peter wanted to slap himself. He shouldn't be thinking like that. Not while Mikey's life was at stake. All that mattered was his son.

And then the man from the Met's kidnap squad had arrived. He hadn't asked many questions at all. Just one, really: did he want them to handle the negotiations with the kidnapper?

Peter had taken an instant dislike to the man. He couldn't bear people who seemed unable to use their authority or make proper decisions, and Blackwell seemed just that type. When he had quizzed him about what the police were doing – actually doing, now – to find his son, he found his vague replies and evasions to be infuriating.

The only good thing that had come out of the conversation was precisely how important it was for him to get hold of all the money. It was what he needed: something to divert his attention, to take his mind off the feeling of desperate helplessness that had come over him the minute he'd heard the news that Mikey was missing. Getting all the money really was the best way of getting his son back. Failure to come up with the full amount was not an option. There was no way he was going to let the police fuck it up, as they had with the other boy.

There was a picture of Mikey on the coffee table, taken on a glorious sandy beach when they were on holiday in America two years ago. He had grown up so much since then. Peter took the little silver frame in his hand, held it to his chest and bowed his head.

And, for the first time since his son's disappearance, he felt tears stream down his face, desperation crashing over him like the waves in the picture he held tightly against his chest.

As soon as he left the Dawneys' house, Blackwell was on the phone to Higgins back at the incident room. 'Good news, sir,' he said.

'What do you mean?' Higgins asked.

'The parents are allowing us to take over the case, and they think they can raise the money.'

'That's good, is it?'

Blackwell nodded enthusiastically before realizing this was useless when his boss was on the other end of a phone line. 'I think so. We need to draw this guy out into the open. If there's even a hint that anything less than the full amount is on offer, then I think we might be looking at the Daniel Eliot case all over again.'

'It goes without saying,' said Higgins, 'that we have to avoid that at any cost.'

'Absolutely. For that reason, I'd like to bring in a profiler.'

'You think that's necessary? The clock is already ticking.'

'Last time the guy ran rings around us. I think we need to be more prepared. The more we know, the better we'll be able to deal with whatever tricks he's going to pull in the next two days.'

'I agree. Go ahead. Anyone in mind?'

'I was thinking Michelle Rivers.'

'Name rings a bell.'

'She was the one West Midlands Police used on that serial rapist case. By all accounts her profile was spot on. Virtually led them right to him.'

'Okay, bring her in. In the meantime, if we're going ahead with a full money-drop, then that's where our attention should be focused: setting up an effective perimeter and working out a foolproof way of making sure our man doesn't get away.'

'I'll get right on it, sir.'

'One more thing,' said Higgins.

'Sir?'

'What about Collins and her team? She has a lot to offer, just as you had when she took over your case.'

'I'm happy to work with her if I have to, but I want her kept right out of the way.'

'She's a good detective.'

'Is she? You saw how she was at that press conference. I'm concerned that if she says the wrong thing it could push this guy over the edge. And Michael Dawney will be dead.'

27

Collins felt useless. The killer she had been hunting for the past three days had kidnapped another child and was on the verge of killing again, but because she was on the murder, rather than the kidnap, squad the only thing she could do was sit on her thumbs and wait for instructions from DCI Blackwell.

She knew the protocol only too well, for she had quoted it at Blackwell a few days before, but it still infuriated her. She needed a break, so headed off to a local pub with Woods for a liquid lunch.

She had never believed in the saying 'When it rains, it pours', but lately she felt as if one thing after another was getting on top of her. The job, her daughter and Jack Stanley were pulling her down. She thought back to the way she had felt after her father had been attacked. It had been the driving force behind her decision to join the police. But lately it seemed that everything negative in her life was a direct result of her job.

'You all right, guv? You seem miles away.'

Collins snapped herself out of her daydream. 'What the fuck are we doing sitting here? We should be doing something, anything, to help find the killer. Instead we have to wait for that obnoxious prick Blackwell.'

'What do you want us to do?'

'Anything.'

'Like what? Get a transvestite to give him a blowjob for his birthday?'

'Knowing him, he'd like it too much.'

They both laughed. Collins stood up and drained her glass of Jack Daniel's and Coke. 'I've had enough of this shit. Let's get back to the office.'

Rajid Khan sat quietly at his desk in the corner of the incident room, a pair of large noise-cancelling headphones clamped over his ears.

The top-left-hand corner of his screen showed a small window with a live feed from MTV, and it was the sound of The Editors playing their latest release that was blasting into his skull at full volume. Some people found it distracting, but, for Khan, a little background music was the perfect way to concentrate his thoughts on the task in hand.

The remainder of his screen was taken up with multicoloured boxes filled with streams of numbers, a mix of complex logarithms and mathematical formulae. Another, much larger video box showed the distant image of a white van passing down a main road in a three-second loop. Next to this was a smaller, static box that seemed to contain nothing but a pattern of random dots.

Twenty minutes earlier DC Cooper had made her way over to his desk with a serious look on her face. She had finally struck gold. The camera from the tyre shop had been fitted at an unusual angle in order to capture images of customers entering the forecourt. Because of this it had managed to capture a single fleeting picture of the white van's registration plate, though it was too blurry for Cooper to read. She immediately passed it on to Khan, who had been eager to help.

He still had his issues about working for the police and felt certain that he always would, but this case had got to him – because of the callousness of the killer, the age of the child, and the complete and utter brutality of the crime.

The revelation that Daniel had been killed even before the deadline for the ransom money had disturbed him deeply, as had DI Collins's suspicions that the killer might strike again. Sometimes the law was an ass, and there were plenty of cases where Khan found himself siding with the supposed wrongdoers. This was not one of them. He wanted to catch the killer of Daniel Eliot every bit as much as the rest of the team.

He nearly jumped out of his skin when DI Collins tapped him on the shoulder. 'Don't sneak up on people like that,' he gasped, clutching at his chest in mock agony with one hand while pulling off his headphones with the other.

'You're too young for a heart attack,' she said, grinning. 'What's that's shit coming out of your headphones?'

Khan smiled warmly. 'For your information that is the sound of the best band in Britain.' Then he shook his head slowly. 'Man, your daughter must be so embarrassed by you.'

Collins nodded towards the images on the

screen. 'How are you getting on?'

'I'm getting there. It's not easy, but I'm making progress.'

'Can't you just magnify the image?'

The way this process was portrayed on television always made Khan laugh. Invariably the scene would take place in an FBI lab. An agent would sit down with the office geek and call up a video, then ask for a tiny corner of the image to be magnified. A few strokes of the keys and up the picture would come, allowing the agent to read the suspect's name off his credit card or some such nonsense.

'If only it was that simple,' said Khan. 'Each pixel – they're the little dots the pictures are made out of – each one only holds a certain amount of information. You simply can't blow up a picture to show that kind of detail if the detail isn't there in the first place. All you get is a giant blur.'

'So what are you doing?'

'Well, one of Blackwell's people has taken a copy of the images to Scotland Yard, but I know I can do the job faster and better. At the moment the best image-clarification software in the world comes from NASA and was developed to sharpen up images of distant planets and stars using pattern-recognition algorithms. Luckily I've managed to acquire a copy of it.'

'What do you mean "acquire"?'

Khan smiled, and Collins decided not to enquire any further.

She squinted slightly as she stared at the screen. It looked as though the software was working already. In the time she had been sitting there, the still image of the van was slowly but surely becoming clearer and clearer. Each time the three-second video played through, a new layer of pixels was added to the image. Collins could begin to make out one of the letters from the number plate: an *E*.

'How long before you're done?'

'If I was at home right now using my computer, it would already be finished. Since I'm in here using Met Police gear, which is more state-of-the-ark than state-of-the-art, I'll be another twenty minutes.'

'Okay. Let me know as soon as you've got something we can read.'

She was interrupted by the ringing of her mobile. The number was withheld, and she assumed it was Higgins or Blackwell calling from Scotland Yard.

'Hello, Princess.' She paused and looked around guiltily, convinced that every pair of eyes in the room was staring at her.

'What the hell do you want!' she hissed.

'I've tried calling but you wouldn't answer. So I had to withhold my number. I'm getting the funny feeling that you don't want to talk to me any more, and that's not good for either of us.'

She made her way out of the station and headed for a quite side street near by. 'What the fuck do you want?'

'You know what I want.'

'I can't do it. You know I can't be a part of anything like that. I can't have blood on my hands.'

Jack's voice suddenly became threatening. 'If you don't, then there's going to be a war.'

'What the fuck are you talking about?'

'Because this guy is not only talking to the police, he's also talking to the Kosovans.'

Jack was talking about a rival gang that had tried on several occasions in the past two years to take over two of his estates. 'If I can't put a stop to it, there's gonna be blood on the streets.'

'Don't you dare try to put blood on my hands,' she hissed into the mouthpiece. 'You hear me? Don't you fucking dare.'

Stacey was suddenly aware of someone standing behind her. She turned to see Woods with an excited look on his face.

'What is it?' she asked.

'The kid's got the registration number of the van. I think we've got him.'

28

'Do we have a name?'

Collins walked purposefully into the incident room. As she did so, Cooper handed her a grainy black-and-white photograph. It was unmistakably the white transit van, but the number plate was now completely in focus and clear.

'Excellent,' she breathed softly.

Cooper nodded towards Khan. 'Einstein over there managed to do something with it. Don't ask me what.'

Collins moved over to where Khan was sitting. 'Are you sure about this?'

'Course.' He looked offended.

'I'll ask you again – are you absolutely sure? Last time we ended up looking like idiots and raiding the wrong house.'

For a moment Khan didn't reply. Then he glanced down at his screen. 'One hundred per cent.'

'Well done, Khan,' she murmured, before turning back to Woods. 'Who's it registered to?'

'Address in Coulsdon.' Woods pointed to a large map of London and its surrounding areas on a wall, indicating an area to the south of Croydon, just inside the M25. 'His name's Richard Morgan, a plumber by trade. Ran a PNC check. No convictions, but then we ran him through ViSOR and got a hit. He was cautioned two years ago.'

Collins could feel her pulse quicken. ViSOR, the Violent and Sex Offenders Register, was a huge database containing the names of all those convicted or cautioned with sexual offences. Although there had been no sign of sexual abuse on the body of Daniel Eliot, there had been cases in the past where paedophiles had snatched children with every intention of molesting them but killed them out of panic before any abuse could take place.

'Has DCI Blackwell been informed?' she asked.

'Not yet, he's over at the Yard.'

'Okay.' Collins played with a pen as she collected her thoughts. 'I'll call him right now. You go and arrange back-up.'

'Armed?'

'Yes. And get some people down there now to make sure he's there.'

Collins moved to a meeting room in order to be able to talk to Blackwell in private. She was trying hard to keep the excitement growing within her from raging out of control. In a few hours' time they just might have the killer of Daniel Eliot and the kidnapper of Michael Dawney behind bars. For all she knew, Michael could be being held at that very address.

She dialled his number.

'Blackwell.'

'Sir, it's DI Collins.'

'I'll be over to brief you and your team in an hour.' His tone was sullen, and it was obvious that her team was not his priority.

'But, sir, we've had a breakthrough.'

'What do you mean?'

'We've got the registration number of the white transit van that was seen following Daniel Eliot.'

Blackwell was suddenly focused on what Collins was telling him. SOCO had reported that fresh tyre tracks consistent with a transit van had been found on the edge of the woods close to where Michael Dawney had been snatched.

'Who is it?'

'His name's Richard Morgan. A plumber by trade. And we also got a hit on ViSOR.'

Blackwell felt his pulse quicken. 'Give me the address.' The tension between the two officers had faded away with the prospect of making an arrest.

'Get everyone into position and wait for me,' Blackwell continued. 'I don't want anyone to breathe until I'm there. Our top priority is

Michael's safety.'

'I understand.'

'One more thing, Collins.'

'Yes, sir?'

'Well done.'

It took less than an hour before everyone was in situ.

The house in question was situated just off the A23. For such a busy location, it was strangely quiet. By the time Blackwell and Collins had arrived, unmarked vans from SO19 had sealed off either end of the road.

The house itself, No.18, was nondescript. The neat front garden looked much like all the others in the row, perhaps a little less well maintained. On one side was a gravelled area where a white transit van, identical to the one Collins had seen on the CCTV, was parked at a slightly awkward angle.

The two detectives peered through the windscreen. The weather had changed dramatically in the last hour or so, the sweltering heat giving way to a blanket of thick black rain clouds that rolled ominously overhead. In the background there was a rumble of thunder. 'Speak to SO19,' Blackwell told Collins. 'Make sure they're ready.'

Collins spoke into the handset of the police radio: 'Is everyone in position?'

There was a crackly pause before a terse voice came over the airways. 'Roger that.'

'Have you confirmed that the target is in the house?'

'Roger. Thermal cameras show one occupant in

the back room.'

Collins and Blackwell glanced at each other as the SO19 officer continued: 'A white male was seen entering forty-five minutes ago. The back entrance is being watched, and nobody has left. He's there, all right.'

Collins passed Blackwell the handset. He took a deep breath before he spoke. 'This is DCI Blackwell,' he announced.

'Go, go, go.'

Again the standard response: 'Roger that.'

The moment Blackwell spoke the words, the backs of the unmarked vans opened and a dozen black-helmeted officers sprang out. Each carried a dull black MP5 assault rifle and moved with choreographed swiftness to the front of the house. Half stood guard to one side of the door, their rifles trained directly at the house. The remaining men moved forward and one swung a battering-ram at the door's hinges and kicked it to the ground. The second team repeated the action at the rear of the building.

The shouts of the armed response team could only barely be heard above the commotion. 'Get on the floor! Get on the floor!'

'Let's go,' Blackwell told Collins.

The scene that presented itself inside the house was one of chaos. Broken glass and pieces of furniture upturned by the entry team were scattered around. Splayed out in a kneeling position, his head and his arms pressed firmly against the brown leather of a sofa, was a well-built, balding man. His face was pointing away from Collins, but his voice spoke more of anger than fear.

'What the fuck's going on?' he shouted as Black-well and Collins entered.

One of the armed police bent down and frisked him thoroughly. He looked up at the officers.

'He's clean.'

Blackwell approached the man. 'Richard Morgan, I am arresting you on suspicion of the murder of Daniel Eliot. You do not have to say anything but anything you do say...' Blackwell continued to read him his rights as Morgan was lifted to his feet.

'You've got no evidence.' As he was led out of the house, he continued his protest. 'I'll be back home before the pub shuts.'

29

Alice Dawney sat quietly in the living room of her home. The family liaison officers were starting to get on her nerves, asking if she was okay every five minutes. Of course she wasn't okay, her son was missing. She had read in the paper about the terrible things the killer had done to Daniel Eliot. Visions of the same things being done to her son were constantly running through her mind.

Peter was in his study, desperately trying to raise the money before the deadline. He had already raised £1.5 million, secured against the home and business, both of which would have to be sold in order the repay the debt. Well-wishers had so far donated and pledged another £300,000. That left

£1.2 million still to find, and he was fast running out of time.

Alice tried to occupy her mind with anything other than the words that the kidnapper had said on Radio 2 earlier that morning.

A few cards had arrived from neighbours who had heard that Michael had gone missing and assumed that he was the kidnapped boy. Alice flicked through them out of little more than politeness. The people meant well, she knew that for sure, but at the same time there was nothing that any of them could say or do that would make any difference to their current situation. Under the circumstances, she would rather have simply put the letters to one side, but somehow that seemed disloyal to Michael. It would almost be as if she was saying that she didn't really care about him as much as she actually did. No matter how quickly, she had to go through each and every one by hand.

There was another reason too. The kidnapper of Daniel Eliot had sent the parents a card, and there was always the possibility that he might do the same in this case. The post office had been alerted, and in the meantime the family liaison officers had been given additional instructions to check all hand-delivered items. Alice had had enough of them and sent them to another room. They meant well but she needed space.

As she worked her way through the small pile, she came across a jiffy bag addressed to Peter. The handwriting was incredibly neat and regular, and it took Alice a few moments to realize that whoever had done it had used a stencil.

As she braced the package against her leg and ripped open the top, something rolled out and hit the floor with a wet, slapping sound. She looked down and saw a child's hand, severed at the wrist, surrounded by a pool of blood.

The sound of Alice's excruciating scream brought everyone rushing to the room. As Peter entered, he could see the hand on the floor in front of him. He started crying as Alice began to wail. 'Oh, God, Michael, what has he done to you?'

He moved over to his wife, cradling her in his arms and turning her head away from the horrific sight. But Peter himself could not stop looking at the hand, and, as he peered more closely, he saw that something had been written on the palm with a black marker pen: *Behold the hand of your son.*

30

'What was inside it, Woods?' asked Blackwell again, still not quite believing what he was hearing.

'A hand. A child's hand, severed at the wrist.'

Collins recalled the body on the autopsy table. 'Just like Daniel Eliot.'

'Exactly like Daniel Eliot,' said Woods grimly. 'So Michael Dawney could be dead.'

Tony Woods had pulled Collins and Blackwell aside just as they were about to conduct their first interview with Richard Morgan to inform

179

them of the latest development at the Dawney house.

'We don't know that for sure,' said Blackwell.

'The parents are convinced. And there was a message too?'

'What did it say?'

'Something along the lines of "here is the hand of your son". Written on the palm.'

Collins had to hold back her emotions, fearing that if she let them rise she would lose control when she came face to face with the prime suspect. But, no matter how hard she tried, she couldn't get the image of the small hand being cut from the wrist out of her head. Except that, in her mind's eye, the child's face was that of her daughter. She knew that if she was alone, she would break down.

'The bastard,' she muttered.

Woods nodded in agreement. 'Yup. Bad enough killing kids, but why make some kind of game out of it? What do you think, sir?'

Blackwell's tone was firm. 'Let's wait for Forensics to confirm the DNA. Get yourself down the lab and don't leave until they give you the answer.' He turned to Collins. 'How do you want to play it with our plumber now?'

'We've got to crack this sick fuck.' Her voice was low and filled with an anger neither man had witnessed in her before. 'We need to break him down layer by layer. We've got to get him to tell us where Michael is.'

Collins excused herself and went to the toilet to splash cold water on her face. She looked at herself in the mirror and knew she would get what she wanted, whatever the cost. She wished she could hold Sophie in her arms now more than ever. She desperately needed to feel close to her. She pulled out her mobile and sent Sophie a text: I LOVE YOU SO MUCH X.

As the officers entered the interview room, Richard Morgan looked up. Beads of sweat were beginning to form on his forehead, and he was fidgeting constantly.

They sat down opposite him, and Blackwell switched on the video camera and recording machine at the side of the table. After waiting for the beep that indicated that the tape was running, he went through the standard procedures, listing the persons present in the room and the time and date.

'Richard Morgan. You've been offered the chance to be represented by a solicitor and I understand you've declined this,' Blackwell began. 'I just want to give you the opportunity to change your mind.'

'What do I need one of them for?' Morgan replied, picking away at the calluses on his hands. 'I haven't done anything wrong.'

'Then why do you look so nervous?' asked Collins.

'Nervous? I'm not nervous. I just need a fucking cigarette. I haven't gone this long without a fag since I was a kid.'

'Where were you last Wednesday between the hours of twelve and five?'

Morgan laughed. 'I can't remember what I was doing yesterday, let alone last week.'

Collins stared directly at him. 'Have you heard

of a boy called Daniel Eliot?'

'Yeah, he was that kid that was killed.'

'So you can remember beyond yesterday.'

Morgan could not look at either officer.

'I was working.'

'Where?'

'All over the place. I was doing call-outs.'

'So you must have records.'

'Don't need them. I work for myself.'

Collins sat back in her chair. 'So how do people get hold of you?'

'They call me.'

'On your mobile?'

'That's right.'

'So we can check your phone records and confirm that with your customers.'

Morgan hesitated, and started to look concerned.

Both officers waited for an answer. When Blackwell realized there would not be one, he leaned forward. 'How is your memory of earlier today?'

Morgan shrugged.

'Where have you been this morning?'

'No comment.'

'Come on, Richard, you must know where you were this morning.'

'No comment.'

'Where's Michael Dawney?'

'No comment.'

'If he's bleeding to death somewhere, you'll be up for two murders.'

'I want a lawyer. I'm not saying another word until I get a lawyer.'

Blackwell turned to the microphone. 'Interview

suspended at 20.37 hours.' He switched off the machine and pressed the buzzer to call for an officer to escort Morgan back to his cell.

'You know what happens to child killers in prison, don't you?' Collins hissed. 'They'll tear your fucking bollocks off.'

It would take at least two hours for the duty solicitor to arrive. Collins had tried her best to find someone who could attend sooner, knowing that every minute wasted took Michael closer to death. But deep down she and Blackwell already feared the worst.

She needed to get out and have a break. She headed through the summer rain over to her parents' flat, where Sophie was staying overnight. She had decided to take a couple of weeks' annual leave over the summer and wanted to talk to Sophie about taking a trip abroad. It would be a much needed rest and a chance for the two of them to get close again.

It was gone nine when Stacey arrived at her parents' flat on the Blenheim Estate. There were the usual kids and trouble-makers hanging about, trying to get a rise from whoever walked past. But they could sense Stacey was in no mood for their stupid antics and let her pass by in silence.

When she entered the flat, her father was in the living room reading a book on the First World War, a present that Stacey had bought for him last Christmas. She found her mum and Sophie in the kitchen, clearing up after a late dinner.

'Hi, love,' she said, trying to be cheerful. Sophie ignored her mother once again.

'I've booked some time off in a couple of weeks. I thought we could go abroad, just you and me.'

Sophie wouldn't even look at her. Instead she brushed past her while putting the plates away in the cupboard behind her.

'Sophie, I'm talking to you.'

Sophie continued to clear away.

Stacey was trying her best to make amends, but her daughter's rejection, on top of everything else that had happened that evening, was too much to take. 'Are you ever going to talk to me?'

Stacey's mother interrupted: 'She's okay, aren't you, darling?'

'I'm fine, Gran.'

'Stay out of this, Mum – better still, maybe sometimes you could give me a little support.'

'Leave her alone,' hissed Sophie.

'Finally you talk to me.'

'Just leave me alone.'

'Leave you alone? I rush home from work to spend time with you and that's all you can say!'

'Well, go back there – it's always more important than me.'

Stacey had had enough; she didn't deserve this. She took Sophie by the arm and swung her round. 'You listen, you ungrateful child.' She snatched up the newspaper from the kitchen worktop. 'You see this.'

Sophie looked away.

'Look at it!'

With the increasing anger in her mother's voice, Sophie began to look frightened. She glanced at the paper, and there on the front cover was a picture of Daniel Eliot in his school uniform, smiling innocently.

'This boy was murdered on Friday night, and the man who did it has taken another child. I have to find him before the same thing happens. Do you hear me, young lady?' She lifted Sophie's head so their eyes met. 'I have to find that boy before he dies.'

'That's enough, Stacey.' Her mother put her arm around Sophie, who was obviously shocked by her mother's onslaught.

'For fuck's sake, Mother, why not for once just back me up? Every time I come home lately you're giving me a filthy look or lecturing me on what little time I spend with her.'

'Sophie's too young. She doesn't need to know about things like this.'

'Well, maybe if she did, then she'd understand why I can't always be home when she wants.'

'But if it's not this case, it's some other case. You always seem to put your work before your family.'

'What I do is important.' Stacey knew as soon as the words left her lips what her mother's response would be.

'More important than your family?'

'You know that nothing is more important than my family. Ever since what happened to Dad, I've been there for you. But lately it seems as though every time I come home you two are waiting to have a go at me.'

Her mother and her daughter stood there in silence.

'Is that it, then?'

Sophie had tears in her eyes.

'Forget it,' said Stacey. 'This is bollocks.' And with that she stormed out of the flat.

The clouds had broken, and the sun was setting as Stacey headed back to the station.

The argument had left her feeling guilty. She knew she didn't spend enough time at home, and Sophie was growing up so fast. She was missing the best years of her little girl's life.

They used to be so close, but since she had transferred to the murder squad she had precious little time for anything else. She felt as if she were being pulled apart. She could not stop the tears from falling as she made her way through the evening traffic.

31

'Interview resumed at...' Collins glanced up at the clock at the back of the room. '23.18 hours. Present in the room are DI Stacey Collins and DCI Colin Blackwell. Also present is Mr Richard Morgan and duty solicitor Muhammad Sharma.' The lawyer nodded as his name was read out.

Richard Morgan was looking more confident with a solicitor by his side.

'Richard, if we can go back to your whereabouts earlier today – can you now remember where you were?' asked Blackwell.

'I've told you before, I don't recall.'

'Look, Richard, we don't have time to play

games. We need to know where you were.'

'I don't have to tell you. I haven't done anything.'

'By telling us where you were, we can eliminate you from our enquiries. If you have nothing to hide, you have no reason not to tell us.'

Sharma coughed by way of interrupting the conversation. 'I think my client has made it clear that at present he is unable to recall his exact whereabouts. I think it serves no one to keep going over the same ground.'

Blackwell turned to Collins, who picked up a sheath of papers from the table in front of her. 'For the benefit of the recording,' she began, 'I am now showing Mr Morgan copies of telephone records relating to his mobile phone.'

Collins leaned across the table. 'Richard. You told us earlier that you were out on call last Wednesday afternoon, but that you couldn't remember the customers who had requested your services.'

'That's right.'

'In that case perhaps you could explain to us why it is that your phone shows no activity between eleven on Wednesday morning and four that same afternoon.'

Morgan looked pale. 'No comment.'

'According to the phone company,' Collins continued, 'your phone was actually turned off during that time.'

Morgan said nothing.

'That's not very good business practice for someone whose livelihood depends on people being able to contact them.'

'No comment.'

Blackwell took over. 'You don't get it, do you? You're being questioned over the murder of one little boy and the kidnap of another. You're talking about offences that carry the highest possible penalty. Do you really want to reply with no comment to all of this?'

Morgan swallowed hard. 'No comment,' he said weakly.

'Did you kill Daniel Eliot?'

'No.'

'Where is Michael Dawney?'

'I don't know.'

Collins shuffled more papers from the pile in front of her. It was time to play her trump card. 'I am now showing the suspect a still photograph from CCTV footage taken close to the area where Daniel Eliot was last seen.' She flipped the photograph and thrust it in front of Morgan. 'The van in this picture was seen following Daniel Eliot and his friend as they made their way home on Wednesday afternoon. The van has been identified as belonging to you.'

Morgan studied the picture closely, then looked up, meeting Collins's eyes for the first time. The look on his face was one she had seen many times before. It was the look of a man who knew he was beaten. The look of a man who was about to give it all up.

Morgan turned to his solicitor and whispered something in his ear.

Sharma nodded and scribbled something on the notepad in front of him.

'My client wishes to have a private consultation with me,' he said. 'I would ask that you switch off the tape and leave the room.'

'You think he's stalling for time?' asked Blackwell, as he and Collins stood outside the interview room.

'I don't know. He's not the person I envisaged.'

'What do you mean?'

'I didn't question it until I showed him the picture of the van. His whole body language changed. He stopped being the cold, calculating killer that I'd expected. It was almost as if he panicked. Up until then he'd always shown such control.'

'Well, he needs the money. He's got debts of more than £50,000.'

'His voice never sounded right to me either. When we first arrested him and I heard him speak, I presumed he just put on a deeper, more menacing tone with the parents. But I've not heard it once.'

'He could always change his voice electronically. A lot of kidnappers do. The devices are so advanced that the human ear can't tell.'

'But we didn't find anything like that at his house.'

'No, but it could be where he's keeping Michael.'

'Or he could be an accomplice. Maybe someone else was driving the van that day.'

A knock on the inside of the door of the interview room told them that Morgan was ready, and the two officers entered.

When Collins and Blackwell returned to the room, Morgan did not look up at them. He kept his eyes fixed on the floor in front of the table.

Everyone in the room remained silent as the recording equipment was switched back on. Muhammad Sharma was the first to speak. 'My client now wishes to cooperate fully with your investigation.'

'Thank you, Richard,' said Blackwell. 'In that case can you tell me where Michael Dawney is?'

'I don't know.'

'Where were you this morning?'

'I was with a girl called Patricia.'

'What's her surname?' Collins said.

'I don't know.'

'Richard, you said you were going to cooperate.'

'I am.'

'Then tell us everything you know.'

'I don't know her surname. I've known her for two years. I see her three or four times a week.'

Collins suddenly understood. 'Is Patricia a prostitute?'

'She's not a prostitute. She doesn't walk the streets.'

'Okay. Do you pay her for sex?'

He moved awkwardly in his chair. 'Yes.'

'What's her number?'

Morgan knew it off by heart. Collins smoothed out the sheets of paper containing the phone records and looked through them. The number appeared on many occasions.

'Why didn't you tell us this when you were first questioned?' asked Blackwell.

'I'm about to get married. I don't want her to know.'

'I take it that's why you're more than £50,000

in debt.'

Morgan nodded. 'For the benefit of the recording,' said Blackwell, 'Richard Morgan is nodding his head.'

Collins flicked through the papers until she found the picture of the van once more. 'It still doesn't explain where you were on Wednesday afternoon.'

'I was with her then as well.' Morgan saw the disappointment in the officers' eyes. 'Look, guys. Why would I take a child and kill him? I'm not into children.'

'Then why are you on the register?' countered Blackwell.

'Why do you think?'

Collins couldn't resist the temptation. 'Because you're a danger to children?'

'You trying to be funny?' said Morgan, his tone changing. He was now struggling to keep his temper.

He cleared his throat. 'Two years ago I was on a night out with the lads. We ended up getting a bit merry and hit a club. I meet this girl, we get chatting and end up back at her place and do the business. I'm not proud of it, but I'm no angel and these things happen.' He lifted his eyes to look sheepishly at the detectives, hoping for a nod of acknowledgement. They remained stony-faced. 'When I wake up in the morning, in bursts this bloke. At first I think it's her fella, but it turns out to be even worse – it's her dad. She's only fifteen. How the hell was I supposed to know that? She looked at least twenty. Then her dad calls in you lot and I get nicked. My brief gets it

191

knocked down to a caution, but I have no choice but to go on the register. So rumours spread that I'm a nonce and I get people trying to burn my house down.'

A knock at the door led Blackwell to pause the interview. DS Woods had received a report from Forensics and needed to speak to Collins and Blackwell urgently outside the room.

'Two bits of news for you. First, the hand doesn't belong to Michael Dawney.'

'Who does it belong to?'

'Daniel Eliot.'

The relief was visible on the faces of both officers.

'So Michael could still be alive,' said Blackwell.

Collins looked at her watch. 'For the next thirty-seven hours at least. Morgan's come up with an alibi. I need you to check out a local prostitute.'

'No problem,' said Woods. 'I'll do it now. But you should know that the lab say the tyres on his van don't match the tracks from the scene where Dawney was taken.'

All three stood in silence for a moment.

'We must be looking at a different van with copied number plates,' said Collins.

'If we are, then this isn't our man,' said Blackwell. 'And whoever has Michael Dawney is still out there.'

Tuesday

32

The middle-aged woman with long dark hair, gold wire-framed glasses and thin pale lips walked in through the open door of the incident room and looked around disapprovingly as if she had detected a bad smell.

Tony Woods, sitting a few desks away, caught a whiff of an unfamiliar fragrance in the room and whipped around to see who it belonged to. The striking woman he found himself staring at was just his type. Her smooth hair was scraped back tightly over her scalp, and her glasses seemed to accentuate her brown eyes. Her clothes were businesslike: a grey trouser suit and an off-white blouse, with sensible black shoes. She carried a slim brown leather briefcase. Woods was at her side in an instant.

'Hi, I'm Tony. And you are...'

When she lifted her hand to meet his own, Woods clasped it eagerly, then clamped his other hand on top, startling the woman enough to make her pause and draw breath.

'My name is Dr Rivers. I'm here to see DCI Blackwell.'

Woods's lips curled into a charismatic smile, one he had used many times before, usually to devastating effect. 'Ah, you're the profiler? I'm sure you're going to be incredibly busy, but it would be great if we could find some time to chat.

It's an area I've always had an interest in. I actually have a degree in Experimental Psychology from Cambridge. In fact, I considered going into profiling before I decided to get involved in nuts-and-bolts police work.'

Dr Rivers gently shook her hand out of Woods's grasp. 'You do know that there's no such job, don't you?'

'What do you mean? The FBI's full of profilers.'

The woman shook her head. 'I assure you there is no one in the FBI whose job title is profiler. What they do have, down at the National Center for the Analysis of Violent Crime in Quantico, Virginia, is the best unit in the world for analysing the most deviant criminal minds in the world.' Her tone put Woods back in his place.

Woods cocked his head to one side and tried to twist his features into his most charming smile. 'So what does that make you?'

'I'm a senior lecturer at the University of Durham. I have a Ph.D. in Forensic Psychology and an MA in Behavioural Science. I'm an expert in the motivations that drive the criminal mind. My job is to work out what leads people to make certain decisions and take certain actions.' Her voice was condescending and put Woods back in the place she wanted him to be: as far away from her as possible.

Woods nodded, realizing that his chances of getting this gorgeous woman to go out for a drink with him were virtually zero. He looked up, his eyes searching the room for his colleague.

'Dixon,' he called out to a passing detective sergeant, 'the profiler's here, go tell your guv.'

The woman's face revealed her anger at once again being called a profiler. Woods, with a smug grin, turned and went back to his desk.

The radio played quietly but just loud enough for him to hear. All the talk was of Michael Dawney and Daniel Eliot, he noted with satisfaction. Pundits and experts were giving their half-formed views and hastily cobbled-together, paid-for opinions. Not many were near the mark. Most seemed to think his handiwork was that of a madman. What did they know? One man's madness was another man's sanity, of that he was sure. One man's death, another's redemption. That's what the Bible said.

He had spent the morning fighting the Battle of Culloden. He took such pride in each of the miniature figures and armaments he had painted. They looked so exact. But something had gone wrong. One figure was missing – how could he have forgotten? When it happened, he felt his muscles tense up and a surge of stress well through his veins. He took a spare figure from the cupboard and began to paint.

Almost at once he lost control of the brush. The white oil paint that he had been applying to the face flicked over the red uniform. His hands stopped still, and he held the soldier for some time – maybe thirty seconds – before slowly moving the brush away and removing the offending item from under the magnifying glass. He stood up, walked out of his bedroom and down the stairs into the kitchen. He opened the back door and threw the soldier into the garden.

He couldn't return to painting now – it was all ruined – so he washed the brush meticulously and left it on the draining board to dry. He was so angry with himself that he slapped himself hard on the forehead, leaving a vicious hand mark on his face.

But that wasn't enough, so he made his way down to the basement. He pulled the chain that held the key to the cell from around his neck and opened the door. Michael Dawney sat on the corner of the bed, shivering with fear. His body was covered in dry blood and bruises. The man locked the door behind him. He turned and, as he approached, Michael began to scream.

Dr Michelle Rivers emerged from the office where she had been reading through all the files on the case that had been given to her an hour before. Her eyes searched the room until she found DCI Blackwell, who was talking to DS Dixon. She strode over towards him, her confident demeanour apparent in every step.

'DCI Blackwell, I'm ready when you are. Do you want to talk in private or shall I address the whole team?'

'We'll talk in private first. Let's go into the meeting room.'

Collins had watched the two talk, and, as they passed her desk, she pulled Blackwell to one side. 'Do you mind if I sit in on this?'

She could see the tension in the muscles around his jaw. Their relationship had reverted to what it had been before the raid on the plumber.

'Fine,' said Blackwell tersely. 'But try to keep your opinions to yourself.'

The two officers sat on one side of the large oval table in the centre of the room, while Dr Rivers sat opposite.

'Are you up to speed?' Blackwell asked.

'Only in the most general sense. Under normal circumstances I'd require several more hours with the files to form even the most superficial profile. In addition I'd need to visit the place where Daniel Eliot's body was found and retrace his last-known movements as well as those of Michael Dawney. But I'm all too aware that the clock is ticking. Forty-eight hours is–'

'Twenty-eight,' Collins corrected her.

'Twenty-eight hours isn't very much time at all,' she agreed. 'First, I'll need to see the video-clips that were emailed to the parents as soon as possible.'

'I'll have Dixon get those ready for you,' said Blackwell. 'In the meantime are you ready to answer some basic questions?'

'Sure.'

'What I want to know,' said Blackwell, 'is exactly what kind of person we're dealing with. I've been assuming it's someone of higher-than-average intelligence.'

Rivers sighed deeply. 'Hollywood has to shoulder a lot of the blame. Everyone goes around thinking that serial killers are always super-clever, just like Hannibal Lecter, but the truth is that most of these people are of only average intelligence. If you dig into the history of it, you find most multiple killers are working in pretty mundane jobs, doing only semi-skilled work. They're certainly not doctors or psychologists.'

'What about Harold Shipman?' asked Collins.

'I guess he's the exception that proves the rule, but even then he was hardly brilliant. A pretty mediocre doctor by all accounts. Certainly not a high-flyer in the Hannibal Lecter mould.' Rivers smiled in a slightly condescending way. 'If anyone like that really got involved in murder, you people wouldn't stand a chance.

'People think they must be smart because it always takes the police a long time to figure out who they are, but that's far more to do with the nature of the crime than anything else. If you live in a big city and you kill someone who is a complete stranger and no one sees you do it, the police don't have an awful lot to go on. Of course it's going to take them a while to work out who's responsible.'

'I need to know about this man's motivation,' said Blackwell. 'Why he's doing what he's doing.'

Rivers nodded. 'What you want to know is whether you're dealing with a genuine serial killer or a genuine kidnapper. If it's the latter, then paying the ransom is your best chance of getting Michael Dawney safely home. If it's the former, then there's every chance that Michael is already dead.'

'So which is it?' asked Blackwell eagerly.

Michelle pulled her briefcase up on to her lap and took out some academic studies. 'Here's the situation. There isn't a great deal of research about any of this in the UK. Most of what we have comes from the US. That said, apart from a few obvious cultural differences, the data we have from there is actually pretty useful when it comes to working out exactly what is likely to happen over here.

'You have to understand at the outset that this is a singular crime. Unique, I would say. The data we have for profiling in these situations is scant, to say the least. Most kidnappings are gang-related and don't come to police attention very often. When they do, there are obvious sociological indicators that obviously don't apply in this situation.

'Those kidnappings that aren't gang-related are almost exclusively money-motivated: generally the children of extremely wealthy parents who pay the ransom without question. Clearly only the second crime could fit into this category.'

'We believe he may have killed Daniel Eliot in order to prove that he was serious, in order to ensure the second ransom was paid,' said Blackwell soberly.

'That's very much my opinion too. I don't know a great deal about the standard procedure within the Kidnap and Extortion Unit, but I understand that standard policy is not to pay the full amount of the ransom.'

'That's correct.'

'So, regardless of whether this kidnapper had asked for one hundred pounds, one million pounds or ten million pounds in the first instance, you would have paid only a small proportion of the amount, even if the parents had wanted to pay it all.'

'That's right, but we would get the parents to leave a note asking for more time.'

'But my understanding is that you're now going to hand over the full amount.'

Blackwell looked at Collins. 'That's right. The parents are trying to raise it as we speak.'

This was the first Collins had heard of all the money being handed over, and it gave her an uncomfortable feeling.

'What this tells me is that the kidnapper's main motivation has been to get hold of a large sum of money. He's prepared to kill, maim and torture for it.'

'I'm still finding it hard to believe that anyone could live with themselves after killing a completely innocent child in that way, just as a stepping stone to a bigger pay day.'

'Of course you are. This is Britain, not Colombia. In almost all of the kidnappings you deal with, the victim isn't in any genuine danger. It's the threat of violence that makes people pay up, not the actual use of it. This is different. Here we have someone to whom life means so little that killing a child means nothing.'

'How can that be?'

Rivers flicked through files until she found the photograph of the page torn from the Bible that had been found in the church. 'Because of this. An interesting piece of Scripture. In the wrong hands, this can be used as the justification for any act of violence or brutality. If you read the entire passage, what you're effectively saying is that all men are sinners and therefore that all men deserve to die.'

'And that applies to children?'

'Absolutely. It applies to everyone.'

Collins shook her head.

'DI Collins, is there something else you'd like to say?' asked Rivers pointedly.

'No. As I said we already know all of this. DS Woods got most of it from the theologist. And in any case you're contradicting yourself. You're saying his motivation is to get hold of the money, but at the same time he wants to derive pleasure from the suffering of a child and his family. It doesn't make sense.'

'Such cases rarely make sense. You're talking about someone who wants to obtain a large sum of money and believes the best way to do that is through kidnapping and murdering children. It's hardly rational, is it? But, at the end of the day, I can only tell you what the profiling suggests, DI Collins. I can't tell you whether to listen to me.'

'You still haven't told us what kind of man he is. How old, married or single, children of his own – that sort of thing,' said Blackwell.

'The fact that he's planned everything so meticulously suggests that he's very much in control of his actions. That sort of control comes with maturity, so I would expect him to be at least in his forties. And he's a single white male living alone.'

'What makes you say that?' asked Blackwell.

'Because most child killers come from the same ethnic group as their victims and because he needs privacy for his work.'

'Work,' Collins interrupted. 'You mean murder.'

'He would definitely consider it as work: work is how you make your money, and this is how he intends to make his. It gives him another layer of justification.'

'Is he working alone? It would have taken a man of some strength to get the body into the church and then string it up all by himself.'

'Almost certainly,' Rivers replied. 'My preliminary profile suggests that he's a loner, so I believe he would definitely be working by himself. He's a man of great strength, maybe even working in manual labour.'

'But that doesn't fit in with his knowledge of computers and telephone networks. He had software that alerted him to the fact we were trying to trace his location when he logged on to Hotmail.'

Rivers gave Collins a sideward glance. Her voice showed she was getting weary of what she considered petty interruptions. 'Detective, it's not hard to find the information you're talking about on the Internet.'

'Okay,' Blackwell said finally. 'Do you think he'll release Michael if we hand over the money?'

Rivers paused, considering her words carefully. 'My preliminary conclusions are that he knew your protocols in cases of kidnap and therefore killed the first child to show that he wouldn't hesitate to do it again unless he got the £3 million on his own terms.'

'Do you think he's a former police officer?' Collins asked.

'Could be. He knows enough of your procedures. But then again he could have looked back on previous cases that got to court or, once again, searched the Internet.'

'Does he take pleasure in brutalizing the child?' Blackwell asked.

'That's an interesting question,' Rivers conceded. 'Not sexual pleasure, certainly – we know there were no signs of sexual abuse. But the fact that he recorded himself beating Daniel Eliot and sent the video to his parents suggests to me that he derives great pleasure not only from the fear and desperation of the child and the love he has for his parents; but also from knowing that the parents' suffering is as acute as it can possibly be.'

'Will he have done something like this before?'

'It's highly unlikely that he's ever killed before. Hundreds of children go missing each year, and it's likely that a fair proportion of them have been murdered, their bodies hidden away somewhere where they'll never be found. But this man wants public recognition for what he's doing. That was the reason he left the body of Daniel Eliot hanging in a church where he knew it would be found just a few hours later.

'This man clearly has the intelligence and the wherewithal to find some remote farmland and dig a grave to dispose of the body, but he deliberately chose not to do so. The notes are another indication, a desire to ensure that the parents know of his existence in a specific, rather than a generalized, way. I think the likelihood is that if he had done anything like this before, he would have exhibited the same desire for recognition, so you would already have heard of him.'

'This desire for recognition – is there any way we can use it to our advantage?'

Rivers pressed the tips of her fingers together in thought. 'I think it might be an idea to get the parents to make a public appeal if you can. That didn't happen last time round, but I think it's important to get them to appear. You want the kidnapper to feel that he has all the power, that the parents are begging him to spare the life of their child.'

205

'Doesn't that just flatter his ego?' said Collins. 'I don't see how it helps us at all.'

'It doesn't really,' agreed Rivers. 'But it will make him believe that the parents are going to follow his rules and that everything is going according to plan. It makes him less likely to do anything unexpected or to kill the child before the ransom is paid.'

'Okay,' said Blackwell. 'You say he hasn't killed before. What might he have done?'

'All serial killers – which is what he is becoming – graduate from minor offences. He's hurt before. Look for someone who's hurt children. There's also a strong possibility that he might have been involved in zoo-sadism.'

'What's that?'

'The torture and killing of animals. It's very common among those who grow up to become serial killers. They become fascinated with death, and killing animals is the easiest way for them to experience it close up and first hand. It's easier to kill an animal than a human.'

Collins suddenly thought about the dog that Sammy had mentioned. 'The boy that last saw Daniel Eliot mentioned seeing an injured dog in an alleyway next to the white van.'

Rivers smiled at Collins for the first time. 'That would be consistent with a progression towards serial killing.'

Blackwell said, with some frustration, 'So is he a serial killer or is he after the money?'

'I think what makes this case unique is that you are possibly dealing with both. His prime motivation is definitely the money; otherwise he would just kill the children. I know I've been talking to you as if you're dealing with a serial killer. That's because it's clear he enjoys his work. He enjoys inflicting pain on children and shows signs of progressing to the next level. The only reason I'm saying this is because I believe that if he gets hold of the money and gets away with it, there will be nothing to stop him from doing this again.'

33

Penny Collins arrived back at her flat on the Blenheim Estate, having done the weekly shopping. John was in the lounge reading his book. The windows were open, but with no breeze it was still stiflingly hot inside.

She kissed her husband on the forehead. 'I'm glad I got that out of the way,' she told him. 'It's going to be such a hot day today. Is she up yet?'

'No. I thought I'd let her sleep in. I think she's still upset after last night.'

'Okay, I'll make a cup of tea and take it to her. Do you want one?'

'Thanks, love.'

The curtains were drawn inside the spare bedroom, and, as Penny walked inside, she could see Sophie tucked up under the covers. She placed the mug on the bedside table and went over to the window. 'Morning, darling, time to get up,' she called out cheerfully. 'Let's not waste all day in bed.'

There was no reply and no movement from under the covers.

'Come on, sleepyhead, up you get.' Penny went over to the bed and reached for Sophie's shoulder. Her hand sank easily down to the mattress. She pulled the cover back to find two pillows in place of her granddaughter.

Penny ran into the kitchen, picked up the phone and dialled Stacey's number.

After her argument with her mother on Monday night, Sophie had lain in bed going over her mother's rant in her mind.

She hated the way her mother was treating her at the moment – like a little kid. Every time she let her down, she would try to buy her way back into her affections with sweets and extra pocket money, when all Sophie wanted was for her mum not to let her down in the first place.

Her friends weren't treated like that, she was sure of it. Well, some of them, maybe, but not the older ones, not the ones she had been spending more time with lately. Mum didn't know about them, but that was nothing new. She didn't know much about anything Sophie got up to lately.

Soon after her mother had stormed out, she had reassured her grandparents that she was okay, kissed them goodnight and gone to bed. They were so gullible, so eager to make up for their daughter's shortcomings. It meant she could do anything, really. It was gone midnight when the blare of the television in the lounge came to a stop, by which time Sophie had been fighting sleep for at least two hours; the sound of them getting ready for bed, though, suddenly pinned her eyes open.

Once everything fell quiet, she waited for half an hour before silently slipping out of bed and changing from pyjamas into jeans and her red T-shirt with the strap that kept falling from her left shoulder. Carefully, and with a skill that belied her age, she applied scarlet lipstick and eyeliner; she noted with approval that the make-up instantly made her look older. Quietly she opened her cupboard and rummaged around at the bottom, until she found an old shoe; she dug her fingers inside and pulled out a crumpled packet containing six Marlboro Lights. They had been stolen by her friend Katie, who was a full two years older than her; she had given them to Sophie in a gesture of big-sister solidarity. Truth be told, she didn't much like the taste of the cigarettes, but she wasn't going to tell anyone that.

She stuffed two pillows underneath the duvet, trying to make the shape of her sleeping body, turned off her light and peered out of the scrupulously clean but old-fashioned curtains. The room looked out on to a small grass verge that was always littered with debris and that faced on to an area where the residents of this part of the estate parked their cars. Sophie had lost count of the number of times she had been lulled to sleep by the whining sound of vehicle alarms. She looked left and right to check that nobody was watching, then opened the window and climbed out, closing it as best she could behind her and scurrying off.

She knew exactly where she was heading. Katie lived two blocks away with her mum, though her mum was very rarely there, at least not at night-time. It didn't seem to worry Katie much; she had become adept at cooking simple meals and skipping school. Once Sophie was well away from her grandparents' flat, she pulled out one of her cigarettes, lit it with a small lighter and took a series of tiny puffs, trying not to inhale too much; she didn't want to end up wheezing or collapsed in a racking cough.

As she had predicted, Katie's mother was out and Katie herself was still up. She opened the door to Sophie with a glazed look in her eyes. Sophie smiled at her, her mouth flickering slightly nervously, then took another drag on her cigarette. Katie turned without saying anything and walked back into the flat, leaving the door open so that Sophie could follow her.

The flat was musty and untidy. Sophie knew without looking that the kitchen would be piled high with unwashed plates and rotting, half-eaten bits of food; there was the smell of tobacco, and something else: a thick, almost spicy aroma that Sophie could never quite identify. The television was on, and Katie slumped down in front of it; she continued to watch the late-night goings on of the latest reality show as though Sophie wasn't even there.

'So how's it going?' Sophie stood awkwardly by the door to the front room.

Katie shrugged. 'All right.'

'Where's your mum?'

'Dunno.'

There was a silence before Sophie spoke again. 'I've brought some fags...' she started to say, the adult words falling uncomfortably from her lips, but she was soon put in her place when Katie produced a fat hand-rolled joint from a tobacco tin.

'Is that what I think it is?' she said excitedly. Katie didn't answer. Instead she lit the tip of the joint and waited until the flame died before taking a deep drag and then holding it out to Sophie.

She held it up to her lips and inhaled cautiously, this being the first time she had ever tried cannabis. As soon as it hit her lungs, she began to cough violently and her throat felt raw. A few seconds later the coughing died down, and she took another drag, this one a little longer. She felt light-headed and sat beside Katie. As she passed the joint back, both girls began to laugh hysterically.

The girls' laughter was interrupted by the ringing of Katie's mobile phone. Katie's hands shot out to the phone. 'Yeah,' she answered, her voice betraying none of the eagerness with which she had answered. Her eyes flickered over to Sophie as she listened to what her caller had to say. 'I've got a friend with me,' she said finally. 'Can she come?' Another pause. 'Okay, we'll be there in twenty minutes.' She flicked her phone closed and turned to Sophie, smiling.

'Who was that?' Sophie asked.

Katie grinned and jumped up to turn off the television. 'Party.' She reached down the side of the sofa and pulled out a small money bag. Inside it was half of an off-white pill.

'What's that?' asked Sophie, still giggling.

Katie broke the tablet in half, slipping one part under her tongue and handing the other to Sophie.

'The start of the best night of your life.'

34

Stacey's car screamed through the streets of South London. She drove almost on autopilot, doing her best to keep her mind blank, trying not to concentrate on the horrible possibilities of what had happened to Sophie. She'd gone to play with a friend, she kept telling herself, slipped out without telling her grandparents. She'd be home by the time Stacey got there, asking for her lunch.

Stacey was doing her best to convince herself but without much success. She felt overcome by the nausea of dread.

She parked up on a yellow line outside her parents' ground-floor flat, clicking the car shut with her key fob as she ran to the front door. It was open. She'd told them more times than she could count to keep the door locked during the day, but they never listened to her – they'd grown up able to keep their houses unlocked, and they didn't like the idea of changing that, despite everything. Her mum was waiting for her in the hallway, an expression of the deepest concern, worry even, on, her face. 'Oh, thank God you're here,' she started to say as Stacey strode straight past her and into the bedroom Sophie used.

212

The curtains were open, but the bed was unmade; Sophie's pyjamas lay in a crumpled heap on the floor. Stacey heard her mother speak again. 'Your dad's out looking for her. I told him not to go, but he wouldn't hear of it.'

'When did you last see her?' Stacey demanded, almost as though she were interviewing a key witness. The older woman stood in the doorway, her elderly hands clutched together. 'Last night, love. She went to bed before we did.'

Stacey looked at her watch. Three minutes past eleven. 'So how come you didn't know she was missing until now?'

'Oh, I don't know.' Her eyes started to fill with tears. 'We thought we'd let her sleep. She looks so tired sometimes. And especially after the argument last night...'

But Stacey appeared to be only half listening. She pulled the net curtains to one side and gently pushed the window: it opened with no resistance. 'Shit,' she muttered softly to herself, before turning back to her mother. 'Sophie let herself out,' she told her.

'Should we call the police?'

Stacey gave her mother a withering look. 'I am the police, Mum. I'll make some calls. If she comes back home, phone me immediately, okay?'

'All right, love, but are you sure we shouldn't–'

'Just leave it to me.'

Halfway to the front door, she stopped and turned back. Her mum was still in the bedroom doorway, watching her, her lips thin with fear. A pitiful sight. 'Who does she see?' Stacey asked, seemingly out of the blue.

Penny looked back at her, not appearing to understand the question.

'When she stays with you,' Stacey repeated impatiently, 'who does she see? Who's her best friend?'

'I don't really know,' Penny stuttered slightly as she spoke. 'There's a lad called Stephen, lives in the next block. She sometimes goes and watches the telly with him.'

'Where does he live?'

'Flat 83, I think.' Her body started to tremble. 'Oh, Stacey. She is going to be all right, isn't she?'

Stacey closed her eyes momentarily, then walked back to her mother and put her arms around her in a rare embrace. She felt her mother's body shake with a silent sob. Stacey clenched her jaw, forcing herself to keep from doing the same. If she started now, she'd never stop.

They remained in that quiet embrace for a few moments before the older woman spoke. 'Sophie needs her mother, Stacey,' she whispered. 'I can't do it all for you. I'm getting too old.'

Stacey didn't reply. She knew her mum was right, but what was there to say? She squeezed her tightly just once, then let her arms fall to her side. 'I'm going to find her,' was all that came out, delivered in a hoarse, cracked voice that almost sounded like that of a different person. Then she turned and walked purposefully out of the front door.

Stacey sprinted to Flat 83, and, less than a minute after leaving her mother, she was hammering vigorously on the front door. It was opened quickly by a matronly woman with a kind face, though it showed signs of concern at the way in which the person at her door was demanding attention. Stacey, towering above her, spoke before the woman had a chance to open her mouth. 'Where's Stephen?'

'He's inside,' the woman replied. 'Who are you?'

'Police,' Stacey said starkly.

'Oh.' The woman put one hand to her mouth. 'He's not in any trouble is he?' She stepped involuntarily away from the door as she spoke.

'I need to speak to him.' Stacey pushed past her and strode into the flat, the little woman tottering worriedly behind her.

Stacey followed the sound of the television and found herself in an immaculately presented living room. The furniture seemed old but well cared for, and the room was dominated by an enormous wide-screen TV, in front of which sat a boy whose age Stacey found it difficult to determine – though he was certainly older than Sophie, she observed with a pang.

'Stephen?' she asked, without the soft tone of voice she would usually use when interviewing a child.

The boy didn't respond; he just kept looking at the telly.

'Answer the lady, Stephen,' Stacey heard his mother say from the doorway. Then she moved in front of him, bent down and turned off the television. The boy immediately looked sulkily outraged.

Stacey knelt on one knee in front of him and gazed unsmilingly into his face. At this distance

215

she could see not very recently shaved hair sprouting unevenly from his chin, and she found it somehow repugnant. 'I'm Stacey Collins,' she said in a low, even voice. 'Sophie's mum. And if you know what's good for you, you're going to tell me when you last saw my daughter.'

Stephen's eyes flickered over to his mum before resting uncomfortably back on Stacey.

'Don't mess me around,' she whispered dangerously.

Stephen's face twitched. 'Saw her about a week ago,' he mumbled. 'She's weird,' he added spitefully.

Stacey stared straight into his eyes. 'You know I'm a police officer?'

Stephen nodded.

'If I find out you're lying to me, I'll have you in for questioning before you know it. Your mum and dad too. Got it?'

Stephen nodded, his face giving nothing away.

Stacey stood up, pulled a telephone directory from one of the shelves and scrawled her mobile number on the cover. 'You hear from her, you call me,' she told the boy, before throwing the directory on to the sofa next to him. She left the flat as quickly as she had entered it, slamming the door behind her.

As soon as she was outside, her demeanour changed. She almost fell back against the wall, leaning heavily against the stained concrete as she breathed deeply. The bright sun felt warm against her skin, but it did nothing to dispel the chill she was feeling. It was momentarily all she could do to remain standing as Penny's words

216

rang in her ears: 'Sophie needs a mother, Stacey.' She was right. Of course she was. And the guilt weighed more heavily on Stacey with each passing day, no matter how much she told herself that Sophie was just growing up, becoming a teenager, doing what every young girl had done before her.

The voices of children from a nearby playground broke into her consciousness, and, looking around her, she could see people going about their business. Sometimes the Blenheim Estate looked just like any ordinary community: mothers pushing their kids around in pushchairs, a red post office van sitting by the kerb with its hazard lights blinking. No matter how much Stacey wanted to deny it, her daughter – just like the people she saw around her – felt at home here. Why shouldn't she? This was where she spent a lot of her time. She was no different to Stacey at that age; like Stacey, she had not yet been forced to grow up. Perhaps that wasn't such a bad thing. Images of her old friend Cat, gaunt and bedraggled as she sat in the prison visiting room, flashed through her head; and the picture of her dad, bloodied and unconscious on the concrete floor; and Daniel Eliot and Michael Dawney, one of them dead, the other as good as if Stacey didn't come through for him.

Growing up could be so brutal. Surely she wasn't doing Sophie a disservice, trying to delay it for a little longer? And yet, in the moments when she was most brutally honest with herself, Stacey knew that her daughter needed more from her. More time.

She knew things had to change, but it just wasn't that simple.

How long Stacey stood there, the whirlwind of emotions spinning through her, she couldn't tell. But suddenly she was brought back to reality by one simple thought: Sophie was missing. She had left the flat of her own free will, and she was here somewhere. Of that Stacey, with her mother's instinct, was sure.

She pulled out her phone and started to dial a number. As the phone rang, she heard a little beep indicating that someone was leaving her a message. Higgins, probably. She knew she should hang up and listen to it, but she didn't. Finally her call was answered.

'James,' she said curtly. 'It's Stacey Collins. I need you to do something.'

James McNultie headed up the local station that had the Blenheim Estate under its juris-diction – had done for years. Stacey had known him since he was a lowly sergeant going up through the ranks. Although McNultie was initially sceptical of the confident, brash young policewoman from the roughest estate in London, they soon struck up a wary friendship. Stacey quickly made it clear that she was very well informed about the goings-on in that place. Her information was never wrong, and McNultie never questioned her closely about how she came by it. As a result, he was one of the few people in the Met outside her own team that had any time for her. 'Jesus, Stacey, I didn't expect to hear from you. Aren't you supposed to be dealing with this sick fucker from the radio?'

'Listen, James,' Stacey said, ignoring his question. 'You know my daughter, Sophie?'

'Yes.'

'She was staying with my parents last night and let herself out of her bedroom window, and she's still not back. I need you to find her for me.'

McNultie fell momentarily quiet. 'Christ, Stacey...' he started to say.

'She's on the estate somewhere, James.'

'There're a thousand people living there. Isn't she answering her phone?'

'It's switched off. I've left a dozen messages,' Stacey snapped.

'Have you called her friends? You'll probably find she's with one of them, playing games.'

How could Stacey admit to this man that she didn't even know who Sophie's friends were? 'Come off it, James. Kids don't sneak out in the middle of the night to play games. Can you find her or can't you?'

McNultie hesitated. 'All right,' he said finally. 'I'll do what I can.'

'Thank you.' Her voice sounded more relieved than she felt. 'Call me when you hear anything, okay?' She hung up and walked to her car.

Normally Stacey couldn't wait to leave the estate. This time, all she wanted to do was stay – stay and scour the place, to find Sophie and gather her up in her arms and say sorry. She looked fiercely through the windscreen as she negotiated her way around the grey concrete tower blocks and out on to the main road, leaving behind someone she loved when they needed her the most, and not for the first time.

On the way to Peckham, her phone rang, and she answered it expecting news of Sophie.

'Hello,' she said anxiously.

'Hello, Princess.'

'Not now, Jack.'

There was a pause. And then: 'What's wrong? You sound worried.'

Without even thinking, Stacey blurted out, 'It's Sophie – she's been missing all night and no one knows where she is.'

'Where was she last?'

'She was staying with my parents on the estate.'

The sickening realization dawned on her that Jack Stanley and his associates knew the estate better than anyone.

'Jack, you've got to help me find her.'

There was another pause at the other end of the line before Jack spoke again. 'I'll help you, of course I will, but you know exactly what you have to do for me in return.'

35

It was early evening, and Christina Eliot had not moved from the lounge all day. David was still upstairs in bed, sleeping off yet another drinking session. As she sat curled up on the sofa, she was unable to get the image of Daniel lying in the morgue out of her mind. The scars on his face had made him look like a grotesque caricature. He didn't look at peace, and it was obvious that he had suffered right up until the very end.

Ever since then she had been numb. Unable to work, unable to eat, unable to do anything at all apart from cry, she had become little more than a zombie. The news about the second child being kidnapped had come as a terrible shock. More than anyone in the world she knew what his parents would be going through. Though a part of her wanted to reach out to them, she couldn't. She was still grieving for her own son.

Her attention was suddenly drawn to the background noise of the television, which had been tuned to Sky News ever since Daniel's body had been found.

'We now go live to Scotland Yard,' said the reporter, 'where police are to release the identity of the child kidnapped yesterday. This will be followed by an appeal by the parents.'

Christina turned her head to the screen just as the familiar face of DCI Colin Blackwell appeared; he was walking into a press room with a middle-aged couple following behind.

She sat bolt upright, staring with disbelief at the face of the man who sat down beside Blackwell. 'It can't be,' she whispered to herself. 'Jesus, no, it can't be.'

She grabbed the remote control and turned up the volume as her stomach began to churn and her palms became slippery with sweat. She then reached for the phone.

They had waited longer than he had expected before going public with the name.

He could only barely contain his excitement as he

sat in front of the television watching the start of the press conference. It was plain for all to see just how much the parents were suffering. That was good. It was just as it should be. He allowed a smile to cross his lips as the camera focused on the father, who began his statement with tears in his eyes, choking on every word.

'Whoever you are, I want you to know that Michael is a good boy. A very good boy. He has a family that loves him, a family that will do anything you want in order to see him returned safely. Please don't hurt our little Michael. We'll give you the money, we'll do whatever you want. There will be no tricks, no games. We just want our little boy back home safe.' His voice cracked as he tried to repeat the line: 'We just want our little Michael back safe…'

The man collapsed in a flood of tears, his words no longer audible. The police officer beside him took over, talking about the need for the public to remain alert and report anything unusual or suspicious.

It was obvious that the police didn't have a clue who he was and that they had made no progress at all in their investigation.

Everything was going according to plan. He was going to get the money. All £3 million of it. He had the rest of the evening to review his plans for the drop-off. Upstairs in the back room he had built a scale model of the place where the money was to be left. Every detail had been faithfully re-created, including the location of CCTV cameras, strategic viewpoints, transport links and potential sniper positions.

The model was filled with dozens of figures representing the police and members of the public. He had gone through the scenario many times and *allowed for every possible eventuality. Although he would be greatly outnumbered, he had no doubt in his mind that he would be able to pull it off.*

'Stacey, it's Christina. Daniel's mother.' There was a note of panic in her voice.

'Hello, Christina,' said Collins. She tried to sound as sympathetic as possible.

Christina sounded upset, devastated. The news of the second kidnap seemed to have brought the worst of her own trauma back to her. Collins found herself emphasizing just how hard it must be to know that, whatever was happening to this new victim, her own son had already been through it.

'What can I do for you?'

Collins sensed she needed a shoulder to cry on, but this was a bad time. She was in the midst of the enquiry with no leads and less than twenty-four hours to find Michael Dawney. On top of that, her daughter had gone missing. She had told Christina that she could call her whenever she needed to, but this was the worst possible time for a comfort chat.

'I've just been watching the press conference,' Christina said softly. She was keeping her voice low, as if she didn't want anyone around her to hear.

'It must be upsetting for you,' said Collins, who needed to get her to speak with the family liaison officer. 'Have you tried talking to–'

'Something has come up; I need to tell you something.' Christina interrupted.

Her tone instantly told Collins that this was

related to the enquiry. And that it was important.

'What is it, Christina?'

'I was watching the press conference and ... I couldn't believe it. The father. When he was talking...' She was crying now. 'It's the father.'

'What about the father? What about him?'

'I couldn't believe it,' she said again. 'I know him.'

'What do you mean you know him?'

'I mean I know Peter Dawney.'

'How?'

Christina let out something midway between a sob and a wail as the pain of the memory rose to the top of her consciousness. 'I used to work for him.' Her voice went into a whisper. 'But there's something else. It was almost ten years ago.' Christina hesitated. 'It was a stupid mistake.'

'What was?'

'We had an affair just before Alice became pregnant.'

Christina didn't say anything for a long time. Collins let the silence grow, waiting for her to speak again.

'You see, Stacey, I ended it when I found out I was pregnant as well. With Daniel. David doesn't know. Peter never knew. I never told anyone.'

'What are you saying?'

'I'm saying that Peter Dawney is Daniel's father.'

36

The kitchen was bursting with a range of wonderful aromas. He was standing over the stove placing fresh scallops wrapped in pancetta on the hot griddle pan. They would take only a few minutes to cook. He liked to have a break between each course to better savour the flavours of the dishes he had prepared. A buzzer sounded to tell him that now was the right time to place the Beef Wellington that he had prepared earlier into the oven.

He was a good chef when he wanted to be, time and practice having honed his skills. He didn't always go to so much trouble, but this was a special occasion. He would be using the special china and the sterling silver cutlery. On the table a decanted bottle of Château Pétrus 1981, Pomerol, and a single crystal glass. Tonight was a celebration.

Once everything was prepared and the Beef Wellington was simmering in the oven, he went through his usual ritual of cleaning the kitchen from top to bottom and changing his clothes before congratulating himself and taking his first mouthful.

It took more than two hours before the lavish meal was completed, nicely rounded off by a rich crème brûlée and freshly ground coffee. He glanced up at the kitchen clock. Nine thirty. The clock wasn't moving fast enough for his liking. There was still so much time to go before his final plan went into action. His head was heavy from the wine, but he knew he wouldn't *sleep tonight.*

He had felt exactly the same way when he was a little boy, the night before Christmas or his birthday. There was so much excitement in the air you could almost feel it. It was like that again now, he could feel it all around him. It made his pulse race.

It had taken so long for this day to finally arrive. All that was left of his work for this evening was to make the final preparations for tomorrow.

He went down to the basement and checked the replacement number plates, copied from an identical vehicle a few weeks earlier. He took his leather bag from the shelf and packed them away, along with everything else he needed: cotton wool, surgical knife, a cloth for a blindfold, gaffer tape and a bottle of chloroform. There were two items remaining, one of them too big for the bag. He took a long rope curled round a hook on the wall and placed it on the floor. The other item was in a chest of drawers opposite the rope. He opened the second drawer down and removed a small parcel wrapped in thick brown paper.

As soon as everything was prepared, he felt much better. Perhaps tonight be would sleep after all. That would be a good thing.

Tomorrow there was much to do.

37

Alice Dawney had taken a sleeping pill and gone to bed. Peter, sitting alone in the living room of his comfortable home, was starting to realize just how little everything in his life would mean if he did not have his son. Horrific thoughts were running wild through his mind about what the kidnapper might be doing at that very moment.

The human hand that had arrived through the post. At first it had seemed to provide absolute proof that Michael had been mutilated, but that had turned out to be a sick ploy on behalf of whoever had taken his boy. For a brief moment all hope had been lost, but now it had been restored.

The final £1.2 million had been donated by a very wealthy businessman following the press conference. That meant Peter could give the kidnapper exactly what he had asked for. More than anything he wanted the kidnapper to call. He wanted to tell him that he had the money ready and that he need not do anything to his son.

The doorbell rang, but Peter did not move, knowing that one of the family liaison officers would answer it. He heard footsteps coming towards him and turned as the living-room door was opened. He found himself face to face with an elegant woman in her mid thirties in a smart but casual outfit of blue jeans, black linen blouse and black trainers.

'Good evening, Mr Dawney, sorry to disturb you so late. My name is Detective Inspector Stacey Collins. I need to have a word with you in private.' The family liaison officer heard her request and quietly shut the door, leaving the two of them alone.

Collins sat down beside Peter on the sofa, keeping her eyes focused on his the whole time.

'I need to ask you a question. It's very sensitive and personal. I understand what you're going through and how hard this question will be to answer right now, but it's imperative that you answer truthfully.'

Peter frowned slightly, unsure of where the detective would be going with her questions. 'Okay,' he said hesitantly.

'Who knew about your affair with Christina Eliot?'

'I don't know a Christina Eliot.'

'She's the mother of Daniel Eliot, the boy killed by the same man who has your son.'

Peter stood up and began to pace around the room. Collins followed him with her eyes as she remained on the sofa. 'Her maiden name was Christina Rogers.'

Peter's voice suddenly became hostile: 'What the fuck does my personal life have to do with you?'

'For God's sake, we don't have time to mess about here. Michael's life is at stake. Listen. I wish there was a more sensitive way for me to tell you this, but the reason why Christina ended your affair was because she fell pregnant. She never told you. She knew you would never leave your wife and child. That's why she left the company.'

Peter collapsed into a nearby armchair with the realization of what he was being told. His mouth fell open in shock as he tried to absorb the news.

'You mean...'

'Yes, Daniel Eliot was your son.'

'Are you sure?'

'I had Forensics run a DNA test from the hand that you were sent, and it confirms that the two boys share a single bloodline.'

Peter shut his eyes and recalled the image of the child's hand lying on the floor and the words that had been written on the palm. 'Behold the hand of your son,' Collins heard him whisper. He turned to her. 'Once we found out the hand didn't belong to Michael, I thought he'd just been trying to scare us. Oh, my God.'

Collins got up and moved to the other side of the room, crouching down beside Peter and placing her hand on his knee as a small gesture of comfort. 'I know this is a lot to take in, but you need to think. Who knew about your affair?'

'No one. No one knew about it. We worked hard to keep it quiet. My wife still doesn't know about it.' He was suddenly struck with the thought of the effect this revelation would have on his wife.

'You're not going to tell her, are you? After what's happened to Michael, it would destroy her.'

'I'm not here to make judgements about your personal life. I'm trying to find a killer. Someone must have known about the affair.'

'What about Christina's husband?'

'He was our first thought as well, but we've

229

already eliminated him from our enquiries. He never knew about the affair and still believes Daniel was his son.'

Peter buried his head in his hands. 'Jesus Christ, who would do this to me?'

'Please. You need to focus. Who could possibly have known about your having a child that you didn't know about yourself?'

'No one. I'm sure of it. No one.'

'Someone you've sacked? Someone you've hurt? Have you ever been threatened?'

'No,' he gasped. 'Never.'

Collins desperately tried to think through the various possibilities. She had to try to block the fact that Sophie had gone missing from her mind. If she let herself dwell on it, even for a moment, she simply wouldn't be able to do her job.

'Then who holds a grudge against you, against your children?' she continued.

'No one. There's nothing like that.'

'The lines of Scripture that he quoted: they refer to the sins of the father. Could it be something your father did, something that happened when you were a child?'

'My father died six years ago. He worked for the railways all his life. I don't think he had an enemy in the world.'

'There's nothing you can recall that happened when you were younger, perhaps something he told you about? Anything. Anything at all. Please, I know it's hard after what I've told you, but there must be something.'

'There isn't. Nothing.'

Peter suddenly paused as a distant memory

formed itself in his mind. 'Unless...'

Collins leaned forward, willing him to go on. 'What? What were you going to say?'

Peter sat back in his chair and shook his head. 'It can't be. This is crazy. This is totally crazy.'

'What, what?'

He leaned forward to within a few inches of her face. 'When I was at primary school, there was a kid in my class.' He slapped his palm gently against his forehead. 'Can't remember his name. His mother taught Sunday School somewhere, I remember that much. We're talking back when I was seven or eight, something like that. There was an accident. I can't even remember what happened, but there was some kind of accident and this kid ended up getting hurt. I remember his hand being burned. Acid or something. But that was thirty years ago. Surely you don't think...'

His voice faded away as he ran through the images in his mind. Suddenly he got up out of his chair. 'Wait here,' he told Collins, and rushed out the door.

Peter returned with a dusty cardboard box and began to remove envelopes full of old school reports and photographs. He pulled out a long cardboard folder from his days at primary school and opened it, searching through until he found what he was looking for.

'Here,' he said. Collins leaned forward and saw that Peter was holding a large black-and-white photograph. It showed three neat lines of young boys and girls wearing white shirts and ties over grey shorts or skirts, sitting on tiered benches and smiling at the camera. At the far left of the group a woman in her early forties stood in a below-the-knee skirt and cardigan that beamed brightly.

Peter's fingers traced along the photograph. 'That was the teacher. Miss ... Miss Riding. That was it. I don't know the rest.' His finger moved along the bottom row of children and stopped underneath a boy who bore a strong resemblance to Michael Dawney. 'That's me.' His finger moved a fraction to the right. 'And that's him, next to me. We were best friends. This must be before the accident, because he stopped coming to school soon afterwards.'

'But you don't remember his name?'

Peter shut his eyes, and Collins could see lines of concentration forming on his face. 'No. But Miss Riding probably does. If you can find her.'

'What was the name of the school?'

Peter shut the folder and handed it to Collins, who read out the name beneath the crest on the front. 'Dulwich Park School.'

38

The minute Collins left Peter Dawney's home, she pulled her mobile from her bag in order to call her mother. As the screen lit up, she saw that there were three missed calls, all from Penny Collins, and she immediately speed-dialled her mother.

'It's me, Mum. What's happening? Have you

found her?'

'Yes, dear. Sophie's home safe and sound. She's all right.'

'Where the hell was she?'

'I don't know. I think she was out with some friends or something. But that's not important right now. Let's just be thankful that she's home and she's safe.'

'Okay. I'm on my way.'

It took Stacey forty-five minutes to reach her parents' flat. She paused only briefly in the hallway to greet them before rushing through to the spare room and gently opening the door.

Sophie was lying on her front, her head turned to one side, asleep. Even though the lights in the room were off, Stacey could tell that her daughter's skin was unusually pale and she immediately became suspicious about her condition.

Her eyes scanned the room. There were three empty glasses on the side of the bed and five chocolate wrappers on the floor. Stacey gently peeled back the lid of one of her daughter's eyes. Her pupils were the size of saucers.

The excessive thirst, the snacking on sweets and the dilated pupils could mean only one thing: Sophie had been experimenting with Ecstasy. Her own trained eyes had picked up clues that her parents had easily mistaken.

'Oh, Sophie,' Stacey whispered. 'You stupid, stupid girl.'

Stacey wanted to shake her awake and demand answers, but she knew that much of the blame for what had happened would inevitably come to rest on her own shoulders. She worked too hard, she spent far too little time with her. Christ, she didn't even know the names of any of her friends. Tears began to well up in the corners of her eyes as the guilty feelings started to overwhelm her.

She collected herself before leaving Sophie to sleep off the remainder of the drug and went to see her parents, who were chatting in the kitchen.

'Thank God she's home.' Her mother couldn't contain her relief and gave Stacey a warm embrace. Stacey held her mother tightly.

'I'm sorry for last night, Mum.'

'We all are. Even Sophie.'

They stepped back from their embrace.

'What has she told you?'

'She hasn't said anything,' said her father, 'but she was brought home by an old friend of yours.'

Stacey turned to face him. 'Who?'

'Jack Stanley.'

Wednesday

39

DCI Chris Blackwell had been cynical, to say the least.

Although it was clearly relevant to the investigation that the two victims shared the same father, the notion that the killer of Daniel Eliot and the kidnapper of Michael Dawney was some old schoolfriend of Peter Dawney who had been hurt in an accident simply didn't add up.

'Why would he wait so long to take his revenge?' asked Blackwell, when Collins explained what she had found. 'How on earth would he have known about the affair? And why would he go after Dawney's children instead of just Dawney himself?'

'I think he killed Daniel Eliot to prove to Dawney that he was serious, that he would go through with his threat to kill his other son if the full ransom wasn't paid.'

'But Dawney didn't even know that Eliot was his child.'

'The note from the kidnapper that was sent on the severed hand said it belonged to Dawney's son. We thought it was a sick joke, but now it seems the kidnapper was trying to tell him that he had another son.'

'What do you want to do Collins?'

'With your permission, Woods and I would like to go to see Dawney's old schoolteacher this morning. I'm hoping she'll be able to throw some light on the subject.'

Blackwell sighed. He had been led up the garden path before by Collins, and, with only six hours to go until the money-drop, he didn't want any distractions, especially from her. The idea of keeping her out of the way with a wild-goose chase was extremely appealing.

Although he wanted Michael to be found safe and sound, he also needed the drop-off to take place. The whisper campaign blaming his incompetence for the death of Daniel Eliot was still circulating through the Met and beyond. This time there would be no mistake. The full amount of the ransom would be delivered as per the kidnapper's instructions. If Michael Dawney was subsequently killed, it would be a tragedy for sure, but no one would be able to blame Blackwell himself. It would be the act of a ruthless killer and nothing to do with his failings as a detective.

'Go ahead and see what she says. Just don't do anything that jeopardizes the money-drop.'

'Thank you, sir. I'll let you know what we come up with.'

Lesley Riding had long since retired from the world of teaching and moved into a small pretty cottage in Limpsfield, a village on the southern Surrey and Kent border. She now enjoyed her retirement working as a part-time fundraiser for the NSPCC. She had never married, and now believed she'd left it too late and so shared her home with three cats and a lifetime of memories.

238

Collins and Woods arrived outside her house just before eight. She rang the bell and after a few moments the yellow door was opened by a large woman with a tidy mop of bright-white hair and a warm smile.

'Lesley Riding?' asked Collins.

The woman nodded, confusion crossing her face as she looked first to Collins, then to Woods, and back again to Collins. 'That's right. How can I help you?'

Collins stood forward slightly and lifted her warrant card up to the woman's face. 'My name is Detective Inspector Stacey Collins. This is my colleague Detective Sergeant Tony Woods. We're investigating the murder and kidnap of a child, and we have reason to believe that you might be able to help us with some background information about a possible suspect.'

The old woman's jaw fell open with shock and surprise. 'Please come in,' she said, after taking a moment to compose herself. She led the two officers into her small living room, with Woods having to duck down in order to avoid hitting the low wooden beams above. Lesley gestured for the two officers to sit down. 'The kidnap and murder of a child! You must mean Peter Dawney's son, Michael, and the other boy, Daniel Eliot. I've been following the case. I used to teach Peter, you know. It's so awful.'

Collins nodded. 'Yes. I saw Peter last night, and he mentioned that there was an accident in your class involving another pupil. Do you remember it?'

It was as if Lesley Riding's body had been full

239

of hot air and had suddenly developed a leak. She seemed to collapse under her own weight at the memory. Her knees began to wobble, her hand went up to her face, and she fell on to the floor, hitting the ground before Collins or Woods had a chance to move forward and catch her.

When Lesley came round, she found she had been placed in a large armchair, and Collins offered her a glass of water that she had fetched from the kitchen.

'Are you okay?' Collins asked gently.

'I think so. I'm sorry. It's just that I haven't really thought about the accident for years, and yet at the same time I've always feared that one day it would come back to haunt me. You see, I've never forgiven myself for what happened to Duncan. I couldn't go back to teaching after that. I couldn't face it.'

Collins placed the glass of water on the coffee table behind her. 'I know this is going to be difficult, Lesley,' said Collins. 'But this is what we have come to ask you about. We're totally in the dark. We need to know what happened to Duncan. We need to know absolutely everything.'

Lesley nodded. 'I understand. I think perhaps you'd both better sit back down. This could take a while.'

40

White paint.

That was what it had looked like, and that was what Lesley Riding had assumed it was when she had put away the unmarked bottle in the cupboard that morning before the children arrived. Many of the bottles they used were unmarked. It meant the only way of knowing the paint's colour was by the lid. But this time the plastic bottle contained a thick caustic-soda solution that one of the cleaners had been using to clear a small blockage in the class sink.

She had been teaching ever since she had graduated from university some twenty years before. She had dreamed of teaching primary-school children ever since she herself had been a child, and discovered that, with the right guidance and support, those early years at school can be a wonderful and magical time. She wanted to find a way to show children that books were better than cartoons, that competitive sports were better than games that had no clear winner or loser, that studying hard was something to be proud of.

She had spent fifteen years working at a private prep school in London and was looking forward to the challenge of teaching Year 4 children at a state school in Dulwich. The first moment she had stepped into the classroom of the South

London school and seen twenty-five eager faces staring up at her in anticipation, she knew she had made the right choice.

She loved them all, of course, but it didn't take long for the individual personalities of the children to emerge and for her to have her secret favourites.

Susan Flemming was delightful in every way. At seven she was one of the youngest in the class and had only just lost her two front baby teeth. With a head full of bright blonde curls and sparkling blue eyes, Susan was already the kind of girl who lit up a room when she walked into it. Whenever she was in the class, the mood of all the other children seemed to lift. As bright as she was beautiful, Susan was a delight to teach and just the sort of girl that Lesley hoped to have when she eventually got around to having children of her own.

Mary Harris was equally chirpy, though she had a tendency to be as loud as some of the boys. And the boys were a handful in themselves. Max Carter's father was a manual labourer from a rough working-class background and had already instilled in his son an unwillingness to take orders from women.

Every class has its clown, and this one was no exception. Little Duncan Jenkins didn't just make her laugh, he made everybody laugh. His infectious smile and playful manner made him popular wherever he went. He was one of those children who had developed the knack of saying the sweetest possible thing at just the right time to make everyone fall in love with him.

In truth, Duncan was of way-above-average intelligence. He loved to learn. At the age of eight his reading skills were already on a par with those of a twelve-year-old, and his mathematical abilities were not far behind.

Miss Riding could have done with more pupils like Duncan and fewer like Peter Dawney. Right away she could tell he was the boy who would be most likely to end up behind bars in later life. When he acted up, as he often did, he claimed that it was because he was bored and needed to find a way to liven things up. Whenever the fire alarms were tripped, Peter Dawney was the first person the head teacher looked to. Whenever the toilets backed up because they had been stuffed with unflushable objects, Peter Dawney's name rang out through the corridors. Whenever money went missing from the cloakroom, Peter Dawney was the one who got the blame, even though he insisted he was innocent. If ever a boy seemed destined to have a criminal record by the time he was sixteen, Peter Dawney was that boy.

Duncan Jenkins and Peter Dawney were like chalk and cheese. They were living proof of the old saying that opposites attract. They were the very best of friends.

That morning had been set aside for arts and crafts. Lesley encouraged the children to get the paints out for themselves. Knowing how to put things away and how to get ready for each class was a valuable lesson. They often forgot to tidy up after themselves, but that was all part of the learning journey.

Two days earlier, during the last art class,

Duncan had accidentally knocked over a paint pot that was sitting on Peter's desk. Red paint had spilled all over the picture of a house Peter had spent ages working on. Peter and Duncan soon began to flick paint at each other.

Halfway through that morning's art class, Peter saw that Duncan was working on a picture using a red piece of paper. Peter decided it would be funny to 'accidentally' spill a pot of white paint on top of it. With a half-smirk on his face, he glanced round to make sure Miss Riding wasn't watching. He took the white paint from the cupboard, flicked open the lid and began to make his way back to his own desk on the other side of the classroom. As he passed his best friend's desk, he turned and squeezed the contents in the direction of the picture.

Duncan had been concentrating hard on drawing swirls of smoke coming from the funnel of a steam train. Instinct took over. Eager to stop his picture being ruined, he reached across with his hand and brushed the liquid away. It was warm to the touch and slippery, like soap. It began to spill over the edge of his desk and on to his lap. As he stood up, his clothes began to dissolve and the sensation of warmth was quickly replaced by one of intense burning.

The sound of his agonized squeals made Lesley instantly look over: what she saw would haunt her for the rest of her life. Duncan had turned to face her, his young features distorted by pain and fear. His left hand was held high in the air, a mass of charred black flesh dripping down on to his neck and the floor. Everything from the top of his bellybutton down to his ankles had been replaced by a bubbling, steaming mixture of what looked like melted candle wax, slowly dripping down.

Within a split second everyone in the class was screaming, backing away from the vision of horror that was now staggering towards the teacher. Finally the pain became too much for Duncan to bear, and he collapsed, twitching slowly on the classroom floor.

Duncan Jenkins spent the next eight months in hospital. He had received third-degree burns to more than thirty per cent of his body, and the doctors told his agonized parents that he would never fully recover.

There were nineteen operations in all, using grafts of skin from the unaffected parts of his body to cover up the gaping holes that had been left by the caustic soda. Soon Duncan's lower body began to resemble a patchwork quilt of ragged scar tissue. There was nothing cosmetic about the work – it was merely an attempt to prevent the wounds from constantly getting infected.

But there was a limit to what the grafts could do. Three fingers of his left hand had been permanently fused together. It would, the doctors decided, be better not to attempt to separate them. His genitals had been damaged beyond recognition. Yet his face remained untouched.

His parents were at his bedside night and day. They had been devout Catholics all their lives and prayed constantly for their son to make a full recovery. Lesley Riding came to visit him regularly, but she was so overcome by grief and guilt that she was unable to look the little boy or his parents in the eye. She left teaching shortly afterwards, abandoning her dream for fear that her incompetence might one day ruin the life of another child.

During the first few months in hospital Duncan was on such high doses of painkillers that he was unaware of what was going on around him, but the doctors gradually began to wean him off the drugs, concerned that be would be addicted for life.

'But surely he's still in great pain,' said his mother, Grace.

'Yes, but the risk of addiction is too great,' came the reply. 'I'm afraid that he's just going to have to learn to live with the pain.'

'But he's only a little boy,' said his father. 'Why should he have to bear such a burden?'

'I'm sorry, Mr Jenkins, but the fact of the matter is that Duncan is going to be in pain, day in, day out, for the next few years of his life.'

While Duncan was in hospital he suffered another terrible blow. He had always been incredibly close to his father. They spent a lot of time together, just the two of them, playing in the garden, going fishing and watching the local football team on Saturday mornings. Best of all they spent hours together wargaming: re-creating famous battles using miniature soldiers that they lovingly painted. But ever since the accident Duncan could sense that his father was suffering too. It saddened him greatly to see his little boy in such pain.

Five months after the accident Matthew Jenkins died of a massive heart attack. His mother believed her husband had never recovered from the shock of their son's suffering. Duncan cried non-stop the day he was buried, as he was unable to leave the hospital to attend the funeral.

Having lost her husband and seen her son horribly mutilated, Grace increasingly relied on the Church for comfort. She spent most afternoons with her son in hospital, and one Sunday after church she produced a Bible from her bag and began to read from it. 'For whatsoever man he be that hath a blemish ... or he that hath anything maimed ... shall not come nigh to offer the offerings of the Lord.

'Sin came into the world through one man, and death through sin, and so death spread to all men because all sinned.'

'What does that mean, Mum?' asked Duncan.

'It means anyone who sins will be punished.'

'I don't understand.'

She placed the Bible on Duncan's bed and rose to leave. 'It means our family has been punished for something you've done.'

Duncan looked at his mother in disbelief. 'But I haven't done anything wrong.'

She leaned over and kissed him gently on the forehead. 'You must have, son,' she said, as she turned and left.

The January after he was finally discharged from hospital Duncan returned to school, the same school where the accident had taken place, for the start of the spring term. It was a miserable experience. Before the accident he had been one of the most popular boys at the school. Afterwards everyone shunned him. His most visible disability was his left hand, which he kept permanently covered in a long leather gauntlet, and a roll-neck top hid the scars down his neck, but rumours about the full extent of his injuries persisted throughout the playground. He was now considered a freak.

No one except his mother knew the truth for sure – Duncan had been excused PE because of the pain it would cause. But it was clear to everyone that something was very, very wrong.

As the doctors had previously warned, he was in constant pain. After a while he managed to all but ignore it as a dull ache in his lower body, but every now and then there would be a sharp, stabbing sensation in one of his legs or stomach, and it took every ounce of willpower and strength not to cry out loud.

The boy who had once sat at the front of the class and put his hand up to answer every question now languished at the back. During break time he usually sat on a bench by himself, lost in his own thoughts and being sniggered at by those who were once his friends.

By this time his mother's life revolved around the church of St Andrew in Peckham. She attended Mass several times each week, sang in the choir and taught Sunday School. It gave her much comfort, and she also believed it helped to repay the sins that had been committed by her son.

By contrast the accident turned out to be the best thing that could have ever happened to Peter Dawney. He was expelled from the school where the accident had taken place, and his parents struggled to find anywhere willing to take him. In the end the last remaining option was the local prep school. Knowing of the boy's reputation, the headmaster dismissively told the parents that if Peter passed the entrance exam, he would be able to attend.

To everyone's astonishment, Peter not only passed the entrance exam but achieved the highest pass rate in the school's history. Once installed at the new school,

Peter's behaviour changed to the extent that be became virtually unrecognizable. His past complaints of 'boredom' turned out to be just that. Highly intelligent, he had been acting up because none of the schoolwork he bad been assigned was challenging enough for him. In this new, high-pressure environment he thrived.

'If your son doesn't make head boy, I'll eat my hat,' the headmaster told Peter's bemused parents.

The winter was the hardest time. The icy winds made Duncan's scars and grafts burn like fire. Most of the time he would remain inside during playtime, but every now and then the teachers would insist that he get some fresh air, wrap him up warm and send him out to sit on a bench at the edge of the playing fields.

The years that followed for Duncan were hard. There was no let-up at school, and his weekends consisted of following his mother to church twice a day. He missed his father greatly and began to spend time alone in his room painting toy soldiers.

At the age of fifteen Duncan made his first real friend since the accident. Having transferred to his school in the middle of the year, Karen Sterling was something of an outsider. With no preconceived ideas about Duncan's past, she was happy to enjoy his company.

Their relationship grew from strength to strength. Duncan confessed his fears, his dreams and told Karen of his pain. She told him of her own plans for an idyllic life in the country with a family of her own.

They began to eat lunch together, talking during break time and even walking to and from school together. Before too long Duncan confessed everything about the accident that had maimed him, and Karen

249

was wonderfully sympathetic.

As time went by, he began to trust her more and more, and came to believe that their friendship would be the kind that would last for ever. Of course, Duncan wanted far more than friendship. Although his young mind could not fully understand the feelings rushing through it, he knew that he wanted Karen to be a big part of his life in the future. When he heard people jokingly talk about getting married and having children, he knew that he wanted Karen to be that woman for him.

She often asked about the scars and about the skin grafts, but in the months they had known each other she had never once seen any part of his disfigured body. Then, one night after school, as they were walking home through the local park, Karen asked Duncan what his hand was like under the gauntlet.

'You don't want to know. It's horrible,' he said.

'It can't be that bad. I've seen pictures of people with burns before.'

'Not like this, you haven't.'

'Oh, go on, Duncan. I feel like you're keeping a big secret. Sometimes I think there's nothing wrong with your hand at all, and you just wear it because you think it makes you look cool.'

After a moment's pause they both laughed at this. Then Duncan sighed and slowly started to undo the straps from the gauntlet. He looked into Karen's eyes as he slipped it from his arm and held up his hand in the fading afternoon light.

Karen knew Duncan well. She cared about him. She felt she was prepared for anything, but what she saw when he removed his gauntlet made her run away from him in fright.

And at that moment, the moment she left him alone in the cold night air, Duncan knew that he would always be alone.

After that he became a virtual recluse, splitting his time between his mother, the church and his miniature battlefields. It was also at this point that he stopped believing that his life and that of his family had been ruined because of his sin. It had been ruined because of one person and one person alone: Peter Dawney.

At first he had simply wanted to kill Peter Dawney slowly and painfully; he wanted him to suffer just as he had suffered. He got his first taste of death when a stray cat entered his garden one afternoon. He broke every bone in the animal's body before holding its neck down and watching the cat's eyes until the life slipped out of them. It was satisfying but over far too quickly.

As the years went by and his thoughts matured, Duncan realized that when you kill a man, he suffers, perhaps for a few seconds, maybe even for a few hours, but eventually he dies and his pain ends. He is at peace. Duncan himself had prayed for death for years, knowing it was the only release there would be from the constant pain he was forced to live with.

Instead of killing Peter Dawney, he wanted him to feel pain. Not just any pain but a deep-seated, long-lasting pain that, would stay with him for the rest of his life. The insurance money and his inheritance meant that he could live quite comfortably without having to work, and this gave him plenty of time to plot a far more sinister revenge, which he went about with military precision. He began to study Peter, watching him, following him. He wanted to learn everything that there was to learn about his enemy, to find every weakness.

He was there in the shadows when Peter Dawney met his wife for the first time, took out the lease on a new office building and launched his first product. He was even there in the background when Peter got married.

And of course Duncan was watching from a distance when Peter started his affair with Christina Rogers. The pair would regularly meet up at remote locations and hotels across the south-east.

And then, when Alice Dawney became pregnant, everything changed. Soon afterwards he saw with great satisfaction the look of hurt on Peter's face as the affair came to an end. But the greatest prize came a few weeks later when he was going for his six-monthly check-up at the local hospital and saw Christina Rogers enter the ante-natal unit. His mind was buzzing. The Lord did indeed work in mysterious ways. But he had to be sure. If they were both his children, they would both pay for the sins of their father.

He had learned patience from his father and knew he would not do anything while his mother was still alive; Duncan would remain the dutiful son. But six weeks after she died, he put his murderous plan into action.

41

Lesley Riding burst into tears many times as she told Collins and Woods everything she knew about Duncan Jenkins. At the end of the story, she cried once more.

'For months after it happened, I would wake up in a cold sweat. I had nightmares in which I would hear that terrible scream, see the burning skin. Sometimes I was the one who was burning. Sometimes I would see other children burst into flames. In the end I had to be prescribed sleeping tablets and antidepressants, but to be honest they made me feel worse. I know Duncan was scarred for life by what happened, but I've been scarred too – on the inside.'

Collins listened patiently to the woman's story. She had to let her speak at her own pace, but at the same time she was anxious to get on with the investigation. Duncan Jenkins was by far the strongest lead they had come across so far. He had the right kind of motive for the crime and, from what Lesley had said, was more than capable of planning something so intricate.

'Lesley,' said Collins as softly as she could manage, 'I do appreciate that this is a very difficult time for you, and that the guilt you've been carrying around for years must be spiralling out of control now that you know he's a prime suspect in this particularly heinous crime, but I need you to focus. I need you to help us. What we really need to know right now is where Duncan Jenkins is. Where does he live? Do you know anyone who might be able to tell us?'

Lesley had not been in touch with anyone from the school for many years and had no idea where Duncan could be found. Collins and Woods sat while she made a series of phone calls to long-lost friends and former teachers at Duncan's school, slowly piecing together information about what happened to the pupil after she left.

'From what I can gather,' she said, 'he stayed in the area. He returned to the school for a couple of years but didn't fit in. His mother passed away recently. They say they lived in the same house until she died.'

'Where is it?'

'I don't know the exact address. But it's in Dulwich near the park.'

42

Duncan opened the door to the makeshift cell. He could see Michael sitting in the corner, where he had been for the past two days. He smiled as he walked over to him, enjoying the sight of his suffering.

He lifted the boy up and threw him on to the bed. 'Please, no. Not again. Please no. I want to see my mummy.' The boy's face was a picture of terror. He liked that. He revelled in the control he had over him.

'Relax, Michael,' Duncan said softly. 'I just want to

talk to you. It's nearly over.'

Michael shrank away from his captor and, while still shivering with fear, curled his knees up into his belly, trying to avoid eye contact.

'Do you love your parents?'

Michael nodded.

'Do you see much of your father?' Duncan already knew the answer.

Michael shook his head.

'I always used to see my father. We used to play together all the time. Do you ever play with your father?'

Another shake of the head.

'I bet you wish you had a brother. Then you'd have someone to play with all the time.'

Michael shrugged.

'Did you know you had a brother?'

Michael whispered, 'No, I've not got a brother.'

'You have, Michael. But I killed him. Five days ago. He was in this very room.'

Michael's eyes widened with fear.

'Don't worry, I'm not going to kill you. I'm going to take you somewhere and then your father is going to come and collect you. Would you like that?'

Michael nodded as tears ran down his cheeks.

'I'm going to take you out of this room now, but I need to make sure you stay quiet.'

And with that Duncan took out a roll of gaffer tape and used it first to bind his hands and feet and then to gag him, while Michael remained motionless with fear.

When Duncan had finished, he sat Michael upright and stood in front of him. 'You've grown into a handsome boy. I've watched you from the day you were born. I saw your first birthday party, a barbecue on the lawn, and I was there for your last birthday, when you went go-karting at Streatham.'

Duncan began to unbutton his shirt and loosen his belt. 'I knew your father. We used to go to school together. He's not a nice man. Do you want to see what he did to me?'

Michael remained still.

Duncan continued to undress. 'I'm going to show you what he did to me.' And with that, he opened his shirt and allowed his trousers to fall to the ground, closing his eyes to better savour the sound of the boy's muffled screams.

43

'Cooper, it's Collins. I need a name check.'

'Sure, guv.'

'I'm looking for a Duncan Jenkins; the address is somewhere near the park in Dulwich. I need you to run a vehicle check and see if there's anything registered.'

'Okay. Give me a minute.'

Collins was in the passenger seat of Woods's Mondeo, speeding through the streets of South London as they made their way towards Dulwich, her mobile phone pressed tightly against her ear.

Cooper came back on the line. 'I've got three hits in SE21. No Duncan, though.'

'What are the first names?'

'Frank, Stephanie and Jacqueline.'

'Are any of them near the park?'

Cooper activated a second computer terminal beside her and quickly called up a road map of Dulwich. 'No, the nearest one is closer to Peckham Rye Park.'

Collins had to think fast. There had to be another way to find them. And then it clicked.

'Look up the Deaths' Register. Look for a female with the surname Jenkins from the Dulwich area who died in the last two years.'

Collins heard the sound of frantic typing on the other end of the line. 'I've got a Grace Jenkins. Died six weeks ago.'

'Okay, cross-reference that on the archives.'

'Here it is. Grace Jenkins, 42 Druce Road.' Cooper paused while she looked at the map again. 'It's just off Court Lane, right next to the park.'

'Thanks, Natalie. Stay by your desk. I might need you again.'

Her next call was to DCI Blackwell. If Jenkins was the kidnapper, then there was every possibility that Michael was being held at Druce Road. She dialled his number, but it kept ringing out, going to the answering machine. She left one message and tried again. After five attempts she gave up and called DCS Higgins.

'Sir, it's Collins.'

'Yes, Collins.'

'I've been trying to get hold of Blackwell, but he's not answering his phone – I think we've found our main suspect for the Eliot and Dawney cases.'

'Who?'

'Duncan Jenkins. I need permission to go to the address.'

'You think the boy might be there?'

She explained in brief the story of Jenkins and his reason for hating Dawney. Higgins heard what Collins was saying and knew that she definitely had a lead.

'Okay, it seems a long shot, but go and check it out – carefully, though. If it's him, the last thing we want to do is make him panic and kill Michael. Report back to me as soon as you can – we've got just over three hours before the drop-off.'

Duncan Jenkins had grown up in a classic red-brick Victorian semi-detached house with large sash windows that looked out on to a quiet residential street in South London. As Collins and Woods slowly drove past, she noticed immediately that the driveway was broad enough to allow someone to back a transit van up to the front door and take in whatever they wanted without being noticed.

'We need to have a closer look,' said Collins. 'We can't see anything from here.'

'We'd better be dead careful, though, guv,' said Woods. 'If he's in there with the kid and we go knocking on the door, he'll kill him.'

Collins glanced out of the window as Woods parked two streets away and saw a young postman pushing a trolley loaded with letters and parcels, stopping at each house as he made his deliveries.

'I've got an idea,' said Collins.

Five minutes later Tony Woods, uncomfortably

dressed in an ill-fitting Royal Mail jacket, made his way along the front path of No. 42, his eyes scanning each window for movement.

He reached the door and rang the bell. There was no response. He held open the letterbox, crouched down and peered inside. 'Postman,' he shouted. 'Got a delivery.'

Again, no response.

He turned back and went to meet Collins, who was waiting at the top of the road with the bemused postman, who took back his jacket and continued his rounds.

'No one home,' said Woods, as they headed back to the house. 'You want to go and get a warrant?'

'No time – follow me,' said Collins, cautiously keeping to the right-hand side of the property, where a narrow path led to the back garden. The high wooden gate was firmly locked. Collins immediately wished she had been wearing jeans and trainers instead of her usual black trouser suit, open-necked white blouse and low-heeled court shoes.

Woods cupped his hands together. 'You want me to give you a bunk up?'

'Piss off.'

'Worth a try, guv.'

Collins reached up, gripped the top of the fence with both hands and pulled herself up to the top, giving Woods a sly look as she dropped down on the other side.

She found herself on a small patio looking out over a garden with neat flowerbeds and grass that was perfectly manicured. As Woods dropped down beside her, the pair turned and looked in through the half-glass door at the immaculate white-laminate L-shaped kitchen.

Collins stood back and scanned the rear of the building for any open windows. There were none. She returned her attention to the door, crouching down and pushing open the cat flap.

'What's that noise?'

'What noise?'

Collins smiled mischievously as she straightened up. 'I distinctly thought I heard a baby crying. Sounds very distressed. I think that gives us probable cause.'

Before Woods could even begin to object, Collins had smashed a small pane of glass by the side of the door, reached in and unlocked it. She waited a few moments to see if the sound of breaking glass prompted any kind of reaction, then stepped inside.

'Jesus, it's like stepping back in time,' said Woods, as he looked around him, taking in the dated surroundings. The walls were covered in faded magnolia woodchip paper; the worktop was a speckled black-and-white formica. 'My grandmother had a kitchen like this, but nowhere near as clean.'

Collins led the way past the breakfast table, into the hallway and towards the front door, but she stopped short when she spotted a panelled wooden door under the staircase. She held up one hand, silently signalling to Woods that he should stand still. She turned to him and put one finger to her lips, then crept towards the door and placed her ear against it.

Woods raised a questioning eyebrow. Collins shook her head, indicating that there was no sound from the other side of the door. She stepped forward and placed her mouth close to Woods's ear. 'If he's down there, he may not have heard anything,' she whispered softly. 'Or he might have gone out and left Michael down there alone.'

Woods nodded, gripped the handle and gently pulled the door open a fraction, allowing a soft light and musty smell to rise up from the basement below.

'Shit,' she whispered again, a rush of adrenalin pulsing through her veins. 'I think he's down there.'

Collins slipped off her shoes and, with Woods following close behind, began to creep down the stairs. Her hands and forehead were covered in a thin film of sweat, her senses acutely alert and ready to face whatever horrors she might encounter. She kept her eyes fixed on the last few steps, which curved around to the left into the basement, keeping it just out of view.

She was almost at the bottom when she froze at the sound of footsteps coming up the path to the front door. She turned and stared wide-eyed at Woods, who swiftly but silently made his way back up to the top of the stairs and pulled the door to, leaving only a tiny gap for him to look through.

His heart raced as he saw a shadow approaching through the glass of the front door. He looked down at Collins and mouthed the word 'shit'. The shadow grew larger and larger, until the figure was directly outside the entrance. Woods closed his eyes and pulled the door all the way shut. At that moment he and Collins heard the distinctive sound of a pile of letters hitting the tiled floor.

'Fucking postman,' said Collins under her breath, continuing her way down the final steps to the basement. She paused at the point where the steps twisted, her back rigid against the wall as she peered round the corner.

'Shit.'

Woods came running down behind her. 'What is it?' he gasped. But as he turned the corner he immediately knew what she had meant.

In front of them was a small square room, no more than four feet wide. A pile of old paint pots sat in one corner and a collection of rusted DIY tools sat in another. The bare brick walls were stained with damp, and it was obvious that the room had been used for nothing more than storage for many years.

'Not quite what I expected, guv.'

'No. You couldn't swing a cat in here. I thought these places had huge basements. This is more like an old coal bunker. Better search the rest of the house.'

They started in the lounge. The room was dominated by a light-brown corduroy sofa and armchair, both slightly worn. The walls were bare apart from a picture of the crucifixion of Christ that sat above the dark-green tiled fire surround. The only modern thing in the room was the large flat-screen TV with a Sky box and DVD player/recorder in the corner on a glass stand.

Collins walked over to the ash-veneer side-board and drinks cabinet, and glanced at the collection of framed photographs of a young child with his parents, smiling cheekily and playing up for the camera. She reached out and picked up the picture in the centre of a young boy posing in his school uniform. At the bottom of the print, embossed in gold, were the words *Dulwich Park School.* It was the first time she had seen Duncan Jenkins up close, even though the picture was nearly thirty years old. She studied his features. He was a slightly chubby boy with mousy-coloured hair, brown eyes and an innocent angelic face. She placed the photo back and noticed that there were no photos of him after that age. It was as if time had stood still after the accident.

'Tidy fellow,' said Woods, nodding towards the armchair on which the three remote controls had been neatly arranged. Woods pulled open some drawers. They were full of yellowing newspapers and dog-eared books.

'We're wasting our time. There's nothing here.'

'Let's check the other rooms anyway.'

They made their way upstairs and started with the room at the front of the house. The pastel colours, delicately patterned floral wallpaper and lace-edged bedclothes showed this had been his mother's bedroom. Pictures of her were every-where. Collins noticed a worn leather-bound Bible on the bedside table and a wooden crucifix on the wall above the bed.

'It's like a shrine,' breathed Collins. 'What do you think?'

'I'll bet you any money that this room hasn't changed one iota since the day his mother died. This guy's got some serious personality disorders. OCD for one and an unnatural obsession with his mother.'

'OCD?'

'Obsessive compulsive disorder,' explained Woods. 'Turns you into a perfectionist. Everything has its place and function, and nothing can deviate from that. It can develop as a way of dealing with severe trauma.'

They continued their search across the hall. Compared to the master bedroom, the olive bathroom suite seemed plain and functional. Collins opened the mirrored cabinet above the sink. It contained mouthwash, toothbrush, toothpaste and a range of over-the-counter cough and cold medications.

'Don't suppose there's a bottle of chloroform in there?' asked Woods.

'Chance would be a fine thing.'

The second bedroom was more modern than the first, with a pine chest of drawers, wardrobe and double bed. Woods opened a couple of drawers. Underwear, socks and T-shirts were neatly packed away and colour coded. 'Classic OCD,' he said softly.

'He's a big guy,' said Collins. Woods turned and saw that his boss was holding up a pair of trousers she'd taken out of the wardrobe and scrutinizing the label. 'Judging by the clothes, he's over six foot and well built.'

Next door was an unremarkable box room. The real surprise came when they entered a room at the back of the house.

Expecting another bedroom, they instead found themselves staring at a richly detailed model landscape of hills and fields covered in hundreds of tiny model soldiers. More figurines stared down at them from shelves on all sides of the room, and a desk in the corner held a selection of magnifiers, paints and crafting tools.

'Look at the detail on these things,' gasped Woods, picking up one of the figures and examining it closely. 'He's done all this by hand. It's amazing.'

'It's a bit creepy,' replied Collins. 'We're wasting our time here. Let's go.'

'You think Jenkins is our man?' asked Woods, as they made their way back down the stairs.

'Maybe. Let's get one of the pictures from the lounge. Maybe Forensics can age it to give us an idea of what he looks like now.'

'Good idea, but a bit of a stretch, even with the latest software.'

'I know, but it's better than nothing. I'll take one of his dad too. That might help.'

As they returned to the lounge, Collins found herself staring at the picture of the crucifixion of Christ on the wall. She shuddered slightly.

'You okay, boss?'

'I didn't tell you this at the time, but Sophie went missing last night. I was in pieces... I kept thinking about Daniel hanging in the church...'

'Jesus, why didn't you tell me? Where is she now?'

'There was nothing you could have done – thankfully, she's back with my parents.'

'Have you been having problems? I thought you two were close.'

'It's been hard lately. The job's been getting in the way, and I keep letting her down. I'm scared that if I'm not there, she'll go off the rails.'

'I'm sure it's just a phase.'

'Maybe.'

She walked over to the sideboard and reached for the school photograph. But before her fingers could touch the frame, another of the images caught her eye. It was a picture of Duncan and his mother sitting on a wooden bench alongside a handsome, dark-haired man. The first time she had seen it, Collins had assumed he was Duncan's father, but, looking more closely now, she saw that this man was quite different.

And, more than that, she recognized him. His hair was now white and his face deeply lined with age, but there was no mistaking the younger image of him. 'Tony. Come here, you've got to see this,' she said.

As Woods appeared beside her, she held up a finger and pointed at the man in the photograph.

'Do you know who that is?'

'No. Should I?'

'It's Father Connelly. The priest from the church where Daniel's body was found.'

266

44

Duncan Jenkins eased the Volvo estate into the line of slow-moving traffic and settled back in his seat. Michael Dawney was securely bound and gagged in the boot, and the police knew only too well what would happen to the boy if they tried to give him anything less than all the money he had asked for.

Everything was going according to plan. He had always known that it would. He had spent many hours of his free time in the public gallery of courts around the country, soaking up the details of police procedure and researching forensic techniques involving both physical evidence and new technology like mobile phones.

He had read voraciously about the history of crime and criminals, examining the intimate details of previous outrages and working out exactly where those responsible had made their mistakes.

He knew he would have only one opportunity to seek revenge against Peter Dawney, and he didn't want to risk being caught or compromised before his entire plan had been set into motion. If there was one thing he had above all else, it was a detailed plan.

His disfigurement had been bad enough to live with, but worse was still to come. It was only when Duncan reached puberty that the true legacy of what had happened to him as a child emerged. He was unable to have children.

As the years went past, his bitterness grew. He

watched as those around him, those who had hurt him so cruelly, got older, married and had children of their own. He had lost everything. His childhood, and any chance of a normal life.

Not one day passed without his thinking about what Peter Dawney had done to him. It felt good to be finally taking his revenge after waiting for so many years. As he drove, he thought back to the moment when he had started to put his long-awaited plan into action. It had been exactly six weeks earlier. The day his mother had died.

It was a day he would never forget. He had spent the afternoon walking a dog he had picked up from a shelter through the woods at the back of Peter Dawney's house, watching through binoculars as Michael played in the garden before heading back to his own home.

When be reached the far end of his road, he sensed that somehow everything was different. The usual sounds of life and frivolity were missing. Instead there was an uneasy silence.

He had seen the ambulance rushing past him, its siren blaring away, but had not realized his mother was inside until be got closer to the house and saw a group of people standing awkwardly outside. They fell silent when they saw him and watched him closely as he made his way up the path to where his mother's best friend and regular church companion Maureen was standing.

'I didn't know where you were, Duncan,' she said softly. 'I tried to get hold of you. I wanted to go with her, but I knew I had to wait until you got here. I think you need to prepare yourself. Your mother is a strong woman, but I don't know if she's going to be able to recover from this.'

He remembered the tears welling up in Maureen's eyes as he asked her what had happened. 'She collapsed in the garden. They think it's a massive stroke. I'm so sorry.'

Duncan ordered a taxi to take him to the hospital. He raced through the waiting area as fast as his legs would carry him and pulled open the heavy rubber-edged double doors that led to the emergency ward. 'Grace Jenkins? Where is Grace Jenkins?' The desperation in his voice was there for all to hear.

'You are?' asked the nurse.

'Duncan. My name is Duncan Jenkins. I'm her son.'

She took him gently by the arm, led him to a private room and sat him down, then went off to fetch the doctor, who arrived a few moments later with the nurse. He stood up as they entered the room.

'Hello, Duncan, I'm Dr Montgomery.'

He reached out and put his hand on Duncan's shoulder. Duncan moved away.

'I'm sorry, we did everything we could, but we were unable to save your mother.'

'Can I see her?'

'Of course. I'll take you.'

The doctor led Duncan through the emergency ward and stopped at a cubicle that had been screened off The doctor reached across and pulled the curtain aside.

Duncan's mother was lying peacefully on the bed, her eyes closed. His first thought was one of instant relief. Somehow the doctors had got it wrong somehow they had made a mistake. She was just sleeping.

But then it sank in. The skin on her face was the wrong colour: instead of pale pink, it was yellow and waxy.

269

'We pronounced her dead ten minutes ago,' said the doctor.

Duncan moved slowly to her bedside and reached out with his fingers to touch her cheek. It felt warm, warm enough for her to still be alive. But there was no doubt about it. All the life had been drained away from her. She looked like a dummy in a shop window. Tears began to roll down his cheeks.

He leaned over and kissed her on the forehead. 'Goodbye, Mother,' he said softly. 'I love you.' Then he turned and walked out of the hospital without looking back.

The sins of the fathers will be revisited upon their sons. Peter Dawney had denied him the chance to have children, so he had started out by destroying the son that Dawney didn't even know he had. And now the final part of his plan was under way.

He knew that paying the £3 million ransom would bankrupt Dawney, but that wasn't enough. His wife now knew that he had been unfaithful to her and would almost certainly leave him. Dawney would be left with nothing. No money, no family, no home. It brought a smile to his face.

In less than two hours' time it would all be over.

45

Father Patrick Connelly looked pale and drawn when he answered the door to his home in the grounds of St Andrew's. It was obvious to Collins and Woods that the man was still in shock. He had hardly slept since finding the body of Daniel Eliot hanging from the rafters and was struggling to get the horrific image out of his mind. He had yet to return to his duties, and the church itself was still cordoned off with a police officer standing guard outside.

'Father Connelly, my name is DI Collins. Do you remember me? I spoke to you at your church on Friday evening.' He nodded weakly. 'I'm sorry to disturb you again, but I need a minute of your time. Please, may we come in?'

The two detectives followed the priest into the front room, and Collins removed a photograph from her jacket pocket.

'Is this you?'

The priest peered at the picture. 'I need to get my glasses.' He moved over to his reading chair, slipped on a pair of half-moon glasses and studied the photograph. 'Yes, that's me,' he said after a while.

'And the two people beside you on the bench?' asked Woods.

'Grace Jenkins and her son, Duncan. Grace taught Sunday School at the church for many years. She helped out in all sorts of ways. She has been greatly missed since she passed away. I haven't seen Duncan since the funeral.'

Collins suddenly recalled the fact that there had been no forced entry to the church. Perhaps Father Connelly had not left it open after all. 'Did Grace Jenkins have a key to St Andrew's?' she asked.

'Yes. Of course. She often helped before and after the services.' Father Connelly seemed puzzled by the questions. 'Why do you ask?'

Collins looked at Woods, who took her silent cue. 'Father,' he said, 'we believe that Duncan Jenkins may have been responsible for the murder of Daniel Eliot and the kidnapping of Michael Dawney.'

Father Connelly shook his head in disbelief as he sank back into his reading chair. 'But why? He was such a quiet, gentle man. Why would he do such a terrible thing?'

'We think it was revenge on the man who scarred him,' said Woods. 'Daniel and Michael share the same father – Peter Dawney – and he was the one who caused the accident.'

'Holy Mother of God,' whispered Father Connelly under his breath. 'We'd spoken about the accident a few times. Whenever it came up, he was always filled with such hatred. But I never imagined it would lead to anything like this.'

'Did he ever mention the name Peter Dawney to you?'

'Never. His mother told me the name of the boy soon after the accident happened, but that was years ago.'

'Do you have a more recent picture of Duncan?' asked Collins.

He got up and moved across to the sideboard, where he opened a drawer. 'Duncan never liked having his picture taken. Avoided cameras like the plague. I remember we caught him only once.' He began to search through a pile of photos, and soon came across the one he wanted. 'Here it is,' he said. 'I'm afraid it's not very clear.' He passed the print to Collins.

The picture showed a group of homeless men sitting at a long table and tucking into a hearty meal. At the front, serving the men, were Father Connelly and Grace Jenkins. Father Connelly reached over and pointed to the far corner of the picture, where a heavy-set man sat in the shadows. 'That's him, that's Duncan. It was taken two years ago at our Christmas soup kitchen. They always volunteered on Christmas Day. Duncan had been doing it ever since he was a little boy.' He shook his head mournfully as he gazed down at the image. 'I still can't believe he's capable of doing what you say.'

'Three million pounds can make people behave in all sorts of crazy ways, Father,' said Woods.

'I guess so, but Duncan never struck me as the kind of person who was particularly interested in money.'

46

The lift doors opened, and Collins and Woods stepped out on to the fifth floor of New Scotland Yard.

'You'd better wait here,' said Collins. 'It's going to be hard enough for me to get in there on my own let alone if I'm with you.' Woods nodded and looked down the corridor to where a uniformed officer stood guard outside unmarked double doors.

Collins headed towards the officer who was

keeping guard outside the control centre of the Kidnapping and Extortion Unit, which was known as Room 3000. Although many in the Met knew of its existence, a shroud of secrecy surrounded what actually went on inside. Only a handful of officers had permission to enter Room 3000, regardless of rank, and DCI Blackwell was one of those few.

'Can I help you?' asked the PC as Collins approached.

'I'm DI Collins. You need to let me in. I have to see DCI Blackwell right away.'

'I'm sorry, ma'am, I can't do that. No one is allowed in without an authorized escort. Have you tried calling him?'

'Several times. He's not taking any calls.'

'I know they have a big operation going on. Perhaps if you came back later–'

'Listen,' she said, her voice becoming increasingly anxious, 'a boy's life is at stake. I need to see Blackwell right now.'

The PC showed no sign of backing down. 'I'm sorry, ma'am, but I can't let you in without an authorized escort. There are no exceptions.'

'Well, in that case I need him out here.'

The growing frustration in the DI was clear for the officer to see. 'Ma'am, I'm sorry, but all I can do is phone through and ask.'

He picked up a telephone receiver that hung on the wall next to the entry keypad and didn't need to wait long before it was answered. 'Sir, I have a DI Collins out here asking for DCI Blackwell.' He paused and kept his back to Collins as he listened intently. 'Yes, sir. I'll tell her that.'

He replaced the receiver and turned to face Collins. 'I'm sorry, ma'am. DCI Blackwell is tied up and cannot be disturbed.'

'You listen to me. You tell Blackwell that I've got a picture of the man he's after. He's going to need it if he's going to catch him.'

The PC reached for the phone again. The conversation was short, and before he even had time to replace the handset Blackwell had come out.

'You'd better not be wasting my time, Collins,' he said, giving her a disdainful look. 'I'm expecting the kidnapper to make contact at any minute.'

'Then why aren't you at the Dawneys' house?' asked Collins.

'I don't need to be. We can monitor all calls to the property from here. What the hell do you want?'

Collins took a deep breath, pulled out the photograph and handed it to Blackwell. 'We found this at Duncan Jenkins's house. It's him as a young boy with his mother and Father Connelly. His mother used to teach Sunday School at St Andrew's and had keys. That's how he got Daniel Eliot into the church. I don't think there's any doubt that this is the man we're looking for.'

Blackwell studied the print as Collins pulled out a second one. 'Woods and I went to see Father Connelly, who gave us this.'

He held the picture close and squinted. 'It's not very clear.'

'I know, but it's the only picture we have of Jenkins since his accident. There's nothing else.

Not even a driver's licence or passport.'

'This isn't going to help us much,' said Blackwell. 'There's only an hour to go before the drop, which doesn't give us enough time to get the picture enhanced...' Blackwell shifted his gaze back to the first photograph, and his brow curled as a thought struck him. 'Collins, you say you got this from Jenkins's house. I wasn't aware a warrant had been authorized.'

Collins looked away. 'There was no time to wait around for–'

'For fuck's sake, Collins, what the hell were you thinking? If Jenkins is our man, then there could be crucial evidence at his house. If you've gone in without a warrant and without probable cause, then nothing we find there can be used against him.'

'There was nothing there, sir.'

'That's not the point and you know it. I can't deal with this shit right now, but this is far from over. I'm going to make sure that you answer for what you've done. You can piss all over your own cases as much as you like, but don't think for a minute that you can walk in here and fuck up one of mine.'

'I'm not fucking up anything, you needed a picture–'

Blackwell snorted in disbelief. 'Jesus, Collins, you actually think this is going to be down to you, don't you, you arrogant bitch. Listen, I've got nine teams out there raring to go. The second we get a location for the money-drop, they're going to be all over it like flies on shit. I'll be patched in to every CCTV camera within a two-mile radius.

It's going to be impossible for him to get away. Once he picks up the money, then we've got him.'

They were both distracted by the sound of the heavy double doors to Room 3000 being opened. The face of DS James Dixon appeared, flushed with excitement. He looked at Blackwell, then at Collins, then back at his boss.

'Sir, he's on the phone.'

'The kidnapper's made contact with Dawney?' asked Blackwell.

'No, sir. He's called us direct. And he's asking to speak to you.'

Blackwell rushed back into Room 3000 and snatched the phone from his desk, his breath coming in harsh bursts as he spoke.

'Yes? This is DCI Blackwell.'

He instantly recognized the voice. It was, as always, calm, cold and devoid of all emotion.

'Do you have all the money?'

'Yes.' Blackwell felt his heart pounding.

The voice continued, 'Good. Michael Dawney is alive. Whether he stays that way is entirely down to you. Your actions from this moment on will determine whether this boy survives. If you understand, say yes.'

'Yes,' said Blackwell.

'Send an officer to the small park just south of Temple underground station at 1 p.m. The officer must have a mobile phone. Do you have a mobile phone?'

Blackwell was taken aback at the question. 'Yes, I do.'

'What's the number?'

Blackwell told him.

'Okay. That's the only number I'll be calling.'

'But I need–'

'If you try to interrupt me again, I'll hang up.'

Blackwell fell silent.

The kidnapper continued: 'I'll be watching. If there's any attempt to follow your officer, any attempt to apprehend me once I've collected the suitcase, Michael Dawney will die. Once I've counted the money and ensured that no tracking device has been planted, you'll receive a further telephone call telling you where Michael can be found.'

Blackwell was wary of speaking out of turn, but he knew there was one thing he had to say before the kidnapper hung up.

'We need proof of life,' he said softly. 'We need proof of life or we don't hand over a penny,' he said again, this time more firmly.

There was a pause on the other end of the line, followed by what sounded like a half-chuckle. 'Of course you do.'

Although Blackwell could not see what happened next, he could imagine it vividly from the sounds coming through the phone. He heard the kidnapper moving, his hand clamped over the receiver. Then came the muffled sound of a child whimpering, followed by the noise of tape being ripped from skin and the sudden scream of a child in pain.

'Come here, you little bastard,' said the voice.

'Leave me alone. Please leave me alone.' The boy's voice was getting more and more distressed. Blackwell closed his eyes as he listened.

'Tell them your name,' growled the voice.

Blackwell felt his stomach lurch up towards his mouth and pictured the terrified little boy staring hard at the phone and hoping it might offer hope of salvation. 'Help me, please help me,' he squealed.

He heard the sound of a slap, followed by sobs. 'I said tell them your name.'

'Michael Dawney.'

'You have your proof. You have your instructions. Do you understand them all?'

'Yes,' said Blackwell.

'Remember, Blackwell, what happened last time when you didn't follow my orders.'

Blackwell said nothing.

'I trust your silence means you're not stupid enough to make the same mistake twice.'

'Please be assured that all the money is ready.'

'Good. There is one final stipulation.'

'What?'

'I want the money to be carried by DI Stacey Collins.'

Blackwell opened his mouth to speak, but the line had already gone dead.

47

Collins walked down the corridor towards Woods with Blackwell's words ringing in her ears: 'It's going to be impossible for him to get away.'

She knew that up to this point, everything

Jenkins had done had been planned down to the very last detail. He wouldn't have overlooked the most important part: the collection of the money. Something didn't add up.

And all at once Collins realized that there was a truth in those words that even Blackwell himself had failed to see. It *was* going to be impossible for Jenkins to get away, and it always had been. In the Daniel Eliot case there had been a massive team assigned to watch and track the money. If Jenkins had gone within half a mile of the drop zone, he would have been spotted immediately.

This time it was going to be even more difficult. Jenkins knew only too well that there was no way he could get near the money without being caught. And that was the point that they had all missed.

She looked at Woods, who shrugged in response to the look of confusion on her face. Collins quickly turned and began to run back towards Room 3000, reaching the door just as Blackwell stepped out.

'You're being set up again,' said Collins. 'He's not in it for the money. I'd be surprised if he even calls.'

'What are you talking about?'

'He's going to kill Michael Dawney, if he hasn't already.'

'How can you possibly say that? Of course it's about the money. It's obviously about the money. That's why the first ransom was so small, that's why Daniel Eliot was killed. He wanted to make sure that we took him seriously. He wanted to make sure the parents didn't hesitate when it came to handing over the cash.'

'But, *sir*,' she said, emphasizing the formal title, 'it's like you said, it's impossible for him to collect it without being caught.'

'But that's because he's underestimated our response times, our ability to follow the cash once it's been handed over–'

'He hasn't underestimated anything else so far. In fact he's always been one step ahead. What makes you so certain that he's going to fall behind now?'

Blackwell paused for a few moments, considering the point before dismissing it out of hand. 'You're wrong. He's just called. And he wants you to do the drop-off.'

'What?' She looked confused. 'Why me? That doesn't make any sense.' Blackwell's news had completely thrown her.

'What you're suggesting, Collins, doesn't make sense. Why ask for a ransom if he has no intention of collecting it?'

'He's playing a sick game with Peter Dawney. He's trying to break him in every way – emotionally and financially. In a nutshell, and excuse my language, but Jenkins is fucking with Dawney's head. He wants him to think that there's still a chance that Michael is going to be found alive. But there isn't. Please, sir,' she said, pausing to compose herself. 'I know we've had our differences in the past, but we have to get beyond them.'

'Okay. Let's say you're right about this. What are you saying I should do?'

'Call his bluff. Don't play the game. Just grab him the minute we see him and get him to tell us

281

where Michael is.'

Blackwell shook his head. 'When he collects the money, he'll call with the whereabouts of Michael Dawney. This isn't like the last time. We're talking about £3 million. No one is going to be able to resist that kind of cash. I believe your man is going to turn up for it. I've been dealing with kidnaps for over seven years. I know what I'm doing. We're going to catch him at all costs.'

'Even if that cost is the life of Michael Dawney?'

'That's not going to happen, Collins. Apart from Daniel Eliot, we've never lost a victim.'

'You're more concerned with saving your own reputation than with saving that boy's life,' Collins hissed. 'You're saving your arse. By handing over the full ransom, you know that if he then kills the boy, no one can blame you for the death of either Michael or Daniel.'

Blackwell said nothing. He didn't need to. The guilt was written all over his face.

'No price on a child's life, eh? It's just not true, is it?' continued Collins. 'Your career is worth much more to you.'

Anger rose up from within Blackwell. 'You're bang out of order, Collins. I've served in the force for nearly thirty years. I'm gonna make sure that you're reprimanded for your conduct towards me and your fellow officers, and for your blatant disregard for procedure on this case.'

Collins just glared at the DCI. He took a deep breath and sighed as he turned and keyed the entry code on the pad beside the door. 'Right now the only thing I'm concerned about is the money-drop. So you'd better come in.'

It was like a miniature version of NASA's mission control.

A screen the size of a small cinema covered the far-end wall. Collins saw that it was filled with a mixture of CCTV images and GPS map coordinates from Temple underground station and the surrounding area.

The room was a hive of activity. Between her and the screen were three tiered platforms, each containing four interlocking desks filled with a bank of computers. Each desk had an operator.

To her right a group of officers was scanning banknotes in order to record the serial numbers before stacking them into a large black wheeled duffel bag.

Blackwell led Collins to a spacious single booth on her left. 'This is the command post where I'll be based throughout the operation.'

Collins nodded a greeting at the supervisor sitting in the booth, who politely nodded back.

'You'll be using my phone, and we'll be able to listen in to everything that's said. It's being modi-fied at the moment, so it'll work even if it's switched off.'

Collins raised an eyebrow.

'We can do some pretty clever things here.' He glanced at the supervisor and smiled. 'Most of which I'm not even allowed to talk to you about. All you need to know is that we can listen in on any phone call in the UK.'

'Don't you need a warrant for that?'

'Technically yes, which is why the room is closed off. Nothing we hear can be used as evidence, but in a kidnapping case it can give us a real edge. We'll be able to hear everything, and we'll know exactly where you are from the phone's signal. Also, we're plugged into the CCTV centre at Piccadilly, and there'll be undercover teams on the ground following close behind.'

'If he sees them, he's going to kill Michael.'

'He won't. Not even you're going to see them.'

As Blackwell continued to explain how the operation was going to be run, Collins could not help but think that it was all a massive waste of time. If she was right, then Michael was in more danger than any of them realized, because if they produced every last penny of the ransom, Duncan Jenkins was not going to be anywhere near the drop-off. He wouldn't be going to get the money; he'd be too busy killing an innocent child.

48

Everyone in the Dawney house had spent the morning waiting for the kidnapper to call, only to learn that he had telephoned Scotland Yard direct and provided them with the details of the drop-off.

Peter had gone to his study, but Alice chose to remain in the living room. The revelation that her husband had fathered an illegitimate child, and that that child had been Daniel Eliot, was an extra burden she found impossible to cope with. She kept her distance from him, knowing that as soon as Michael was safely home, it would be just the two of them.

When Peter heard a knock at his door, he hoped that it was Alice, coming to check on him. Instead he found himself face to face with a police officer.

'Sir, there's a young lady at the door and she needs to speak to you urgently.'

'You've got to be kidding. At a time like this? I don't want to see anyone. Are they from the press?'

'No, sir, not from the press. She said her name was Martha. Martha Day.'

It took a moment for a flicker of recognition to cross Peter's face. 'My secretary?'

'That's what she said, sir.'

'You'd better let her in.'

Peter walked into the hallway as Martha entered; he embraced her warmly. Martha's dark hair was neatly tied back, and she wore a plain grey skirt and white blouse. She looked round nervously at the bustling members of the police team, then back at Peter, barely managing to force a smile.

'Martha,' said Peter in a low voice, 'I appreciate the sentiment, but this really isn't the best–'

'Peter, they wouldn't let me in, couldn't get past the cordon. The police are holding back so many journalists. But it's important, Peter. I'd never have come around at a time like this if it wasn't. But it's also' – she whispered the next word into his ear – 'private.'

'But the money-drop is supposed to take place in less than half an hour.'

'Please, Peter,' said Martha, her eyes becoming moist with emotion. 'It's really important.'

Peter stared hard at Martha, trying to work out what on earth could take precedence over the current situation, then pointed the way to his study. 'Come on in.'

Once they were alone, Martha shut the door, pulled a small silver phone out of her pocket and handed it to him. 'I had a phone call a few minutes ago. On my mobile. The man said he would call back in ten minutes and speak only to you. I think it's something to do with ... Michael,' she said hesitantly, looking terrified. 'He said not to tell the police, not to talk to anyone except you, otherwise he'd kill him. He said he was an old friend.'

It was clever. Very clever. Every one of Peter's phones and all of those belonging to members of his immediate family had been bugged and linked up to the call-tracing system back at Scotland Yard. But no one had thought to tap the phone of his secretary. It was as close to a secure line as the kidnapper could get.

And at that very moment the phone in Peter's hand began to vibrate softly and flash. The name on the screen said simply WITHHELD.

'Martha,' he said quietly, 'make sure nobody comes in.'

The secretary moved to the door as Peter hit the answer button and put it to his ear in one swift movement. 'Hello? Hello!'

The voice on the other end was calm, thoughtful. Steady. 'Hello, Peter. It's been a long, long time.'

'Duncan. Where's my son, you animal? Where's my son, you sick fucking bastard?'

The only response was silence, and Peter soon realized his mistake. Duncan was the one with all the power. He had his son and had already proved his willingness to kill in the most brutal manner possible. The last thing Peter wanted to do was piss him off even more.

Peter took a deep breath before speaking again. 'Look, I'm sorry. The police have got your money. Every last penny of it. You can take it. It's yours.'

The sound of a snigger. 'That's better, Peter. That's much better. I think you should be nice to me. Much nicer than you were when we were young. You wouldn't want me to ruin your life the way you ruined mine.'

'It was an accident. You know it was an accident. How can you hold a grudge after so many years? How can you do such horrible things to innocent children?'

'How can I? How could you? I was an innocent child once. But you robbed me of that innocence. You ensured I would live a life of misery and loneliness. You took absolutely everything from me and kept it all for yourself.'

'I'm sorry, I was just a kid.'

Peter heard Duncan breathing slowly. 'Tell me, was it hard to get the money?'

The question threw him for a moment. 'Of course! My God, nobody has that kind of cash available at such short notice. I've had to beg, borrow and steal, call in every favour and pull every string you can possibly imagine. I don't know how I'm ever going to sort out the mess it's put me in. But none of that matters. The only thing that matters is getting my little boy back safely. Please, Duncan, I'm begging you, please don't hurt my little boy. Please don't hurt my little boy.'

Another snigger. 'Begging now, are we? That's good, Peter. That's very good. Now you listen to me and listen well. I'm going to do something for you. I'm going to give you the chance to save your son. I'm going to tell you exactly where he is. But there are conditions. You have to find a way to leave the house without the police knowing.'

'But they need me here. How on earth can I slip out at a time like this? They'll notice I've gone right away...'

'You'll find a way. You'll have to; otherwise Michael dies.'

'Okay, okay, I'll think of something. Just don't hurt my son, please don't hurt him.'

'Stop repeating yourself. It's getting boring. Shut up and listen.'

Peter took a deep breath and fought to control his emotions. 'What do you want me to do?'

Five minutes later Peter Dawney told the police officers that he needed some fresh air and headed out into the back garden alone. When he was sure no one was watching, he ran through the gate and into the woods, then down the steep hill to where Martha was waiting for him in her car, the boot already open so he could climb in. Once he was inside, she slammed it shut, got behind the wheel and immediately sped off.

49

DI Collins sat down on the wooden bench in the corner of the small park and glanced at her watch. Just five minutes to go before the drop-off was due to take place.

It was another scorching day, and the park was busy with city workers sunning themselves during their lunch breaks. With one hand she tightly held the large black duffel bag at her side; with the other, she gripped Blackwell's mobile. All she could do now was wait for Jenkins to call.

She scanned the area around her to see if she could spot anyone from the back-up team, but if they were there, they had blended into the crowd perfectly. That made her feel comfortable. If she could not spot them, then neither could Jenkins.

She made sure she didn't move her head as she spoke into the microphone attached to her lapel. 'I'm in position,' she whispered, while constantly looking all around her. 'Do you have a visual?'

'Yes,' came the reply through her earpiece.

She had butterflies in her stomach. She didn't want to be right about Duncan Jenkins. She wanted to hand over the money and get Michael Dawney back home safely. She began to doubt herself. Perhaps Blackwell was right after all. Why would Jenkins be going to all this trouble over the ransom if he didn't intend to collect it?

Her thoughts drifted to her daughter, and how

distraught she had been when Sophie had gone missing overnight. She knew now more than ever that she must find a way to restore the bond between mother and daughter.

Her mind was still drifting when the phone in her hand began to vibrate. She pressed it against her ear. 'Hello?' she said cautiously.

'You're Detective Inspector Stacey Collins, aren't you?' said the voice.

'And that's Duncan Jenkins, isn't it?'

There was a pause. 'Very clever. I knew you would find out who I was once I'd taken Michael.'

'You're not doing this for the money, are you?'

He didn't answer.

'I know what all this is really about. I know what you're playing at.'

'Actually, Stacey, I don't think you know very much of anything at all.'

'Well...'

'How's that little girl of yours? Sophie, isn't it? What's it like to have her back home? You must have been out of your mind when she went missing. There are a lot of bad people out there.'

Collins was speechless. She had expected to be the one with the upper hand, having found out his identity. Instead she was dumbstruck and immediately on the defensive. 'How the hell do you know about my daughter?'

'Forget about that. Do as I say and don't interrupt me; otherwise I'll hang up and Michael will die.'

There was a pause; then: 'I want you to empty your pockets, your handbag and everything else. I want to see you take out your purse, your warrant card, your keys and any other items, including your earpiece and radio. There's a rubbish bin opposite the station entrance. Throw everything in there. Keep nothing but the duffel bag and the mobile phone.'

Silently, Collins got up and walked across the park to the bin – her eyes flitting about nervously, wondering just how close Jenkins was – and did what she was told.

'Good,' said the voice when she had finished. 'Now I want you to turn right and start walking up the street to your left towards the Strand. From there I want you to turn left and head towards Trafalgar Square. You're being watched every step of the way. I'll call you back to provide further instructions.'

Collins paused, waiting for Jenkins to speak again. But the line was dead.

Back at the control room, the image of DI Collins walking towards the Strand filled half of the large screen.

'Are all the cameras along the route to Trafalgar Square ready?' asked Blackwell.

'We're just lining up the last couple now,' Dixon replied. 'Should only be a few more seconds. Do you want me to get someone to collect her items out of the bin?'

'Get someone to keep an eye on it, but don't move in yet.'

Both men watched the screen as images of Collins from many different angles divided the other half of the screen. Some of the operators were busy scanning other cameras for signs of suspicious activity. All had a copy of the photograph of Duncan Jenkins on their desks. Other operators wore headphones and listened in on phone traffic, trying to pinpoint Jenkins's location.

Five members of the SO10 undercover team were also following Collins. One was dressed in the tattered and torn clothes of a homeless man, the others in more conventional attire.

'Sir, don't you wonder about the psychology of it, what's driving him to do this?' asked Dixon, his eyes focused on the screen in front of him. 'I mean, why does he inflict so much pain on these children?'

Blackwell shrugged. 'I don't know, but you're beginning to sound like DI Collins. She had some hare-brained theory about this not having anything to do with the money.'

'Could she be right?'

Blackwell gave the junior officer a hard stare. 'Listen, his motives don't change a thing about the way we're going to catch the bastard. All that psychobabble is just a bunch of crap. This man hurts kids because he wants money. Lots of money. And that's his one big weakness. If he wants to get his hands on it, he's going to have to come out to get it, and that's going to put him right in the middle of my trap.'

Blackwell held out the flat palm of his right hand, then snapped his fingers together into a fist. 'And just like that, we'll have him.'

50

Collins was walking along the Strand, passing the entrance to the Savoy Hotel, when the phone in her hand rang again.

'Yes?'

'Two hundred yards up on your right there's a jewellery shop. There's a watch that has been reserved for you in the name of Collins. Go in and pay for it.'

'But I don't have any money,' said Collins. 'You told me to leave my purse and empty all my pockets.'

'You're carrying a bag with more than three million inside, aren't you?'

All at once Collins understood. It would have been all too easy for the police to booby trap the bag so that it sprayed dye over the kidnapper and the money once it was opened, or to have filled it with counterfeit cash rather than the real thing. By forcing Collins to open it and buy something with the cash, the kidnapper would be assured that the bag was safe and the money genuine.

Collins crossed the road and made her way to the jewellery shop. The middle-aged Asian owner buzzed her in and smiled warmly as she approached the counter, struggling to pull the duffel bag behind her.

'How can I help you, madam?'

'I understand you have a watch reserved in the

name of Collins?'

'Ah, yes, madam,' said the man, reaching under the counter. 'Your husband called a little while ago. We've been expecting you.' Collins cringed as the man pulled a small case from under the counter and placed it in front of her. 'A lovely model. A Breitling chronograph. The amount payable is £2,700.'

The man's eyes followed Collins as she bent down and unzipped the edge of the duffel bag. She reached in and pulled out a wad of notes, then stood up and counted out the full amount.

'Thank you,' said the man, closing the case and putting the watch into a gift bag. 'Your husband also arranged for a courier to deliver this. He said you'd collect it along with the watch.' The man pushed forward a jiffy bag, which she immediately ripped opened. Her heart sank when she realized what was inside: a mobile phone.

A new phone meant that it would be far harder for Blackwell's team to track down the call – tens of thousands of calls were being made in that area at any one time. It all went to show just how wrong they had been when, during the first case, they had assumed they were working with an amateur.

The phone was already switched on, and Collins immediately noticed that the battery held only a single bar of charge. There was a note inside the envelope: *Take Blackwell's phone and place it in this envelope. Leave it in the shop.*

The new phone began to ring almost as soon as Collins emerged on to the street. She didn't know exactly where Duncan Jenkins was, but she knew that he was extremely close.

The undercover officer dressed like a tramp, who happened to be closest, couldn't hear what was being said but still had a visual on Collins and the money.

'Stop,' barked the voice in Collins's ear.

She was directly outside a bookshop that was under a set of narrow arches, with Nelson's Column off to her right.

'You see the No. 13 bus at the stop?'

Collins looked across and saw the red double-decker.

'Yeah.'

'Get on it. Right now.'

At that instant the last few passengers were boarding and Collins had to run, dragging the heavy bag behind her as best she could. The doors began to close just as she reached them, and she hammered furiously on the glass to attract the driver's attention. He looked at her and pressed the button to open the doors once more. She struggled to drag the heavy bag on board as the other passengers, annoyed by the delay, gave her disapproving glances.

Fifty yards along the Strand, one of the undercover officers started to bark into his radio, 'She's on the bus, she's on the fucking bus.'

Collins didn't remain there for long. Jenkins told her to get off and walk to Piccadilly Circus, then get on the underground and head for Oxford Circus. She struggled up the stairs, a passing Italian tourist helping her to carry the bag, and emerged into the bright sunshine. By now she was sweating with the exertion of it all.

Crowds were everywhere, enjoying the weather and filling both sides of the road in an endless moving sea of people. Collins had no idea whether any of the undercover team had managed to keep track of her. She knew they would no longer be able to monitor her communications. She could only assume she was all on her own.

In the control centre DCI Blackwell was tearing his hair out with frustration. Dixon had been unable to call up an image from one of the cameras on the bus's route, and there hadn't been enough undercover officers in situ to verify whether Collins had got off. Although he could now see the bus on the screen in front of him, there was no way of knowing if Collins was still on board.

The room supervisor was frantically clicking the controls of the panel in front of him, switching from camera to camera to check as much of the route as he could. One strong possibility was that the kidnapper was already on board the bus and had taken the money from her. This could only be confirmed if she came off without the bag.

'Why can't you get the picture?' barked Blackwell.

Dixon shuffled uncomfortably in his seat before speaking. 'I ... I can't.'

'Why the hell not? What's gone wrong?'

'It's a blindspot. The camera's out. There are fifteen cameras down on the system at the moment, and that's one of them.'

'What the hell are you talking about?'

Dixon sighed heavily. 'Some of them have been

out for a week. But the one on the bus route went down five minutes ago. The chips have burned out. Looks like someone's used a laser point on it. It's going to be out of commission for at least half an hour.'

'Shit,' said Blackwell, lowering his head forward over the desk until it rested on his bunched fists. 'Shit.' Laser pointers were widely available on the Internet and were occasionally used by criminals to disable CCTV cameras. The small device produced a powerful beam of light that over-loaded a camera's circuits until it burned out.

The one thing Blackwell had promised himself would not happen now seemed to be an absolute certainty: the kidnapper was going to beat him.

51

Collins had walked only a little way along Oxford Street in the direction of Centrepoint when the phone rang again. 'To the right of you is a narrow doorway leading to some flats. There you'll find a roll of bin liners. Take as many as you need and place all the cash inside them. Tie off the tops as if you were throwing away bags of rubbish. Then carry them with you until I tell you where to drop them off.'

Collins did as she was told. Leaving the empty duffel bag in the doorway, she made her way along Oxford Street. She had gone only a few more feet when the phone rang again.

'Leave the bags by the lamp-post in front of you and walk away. Thank you, DI Collins, your work is done. I want you to keep walking towards Tottenham Court Road. Don't look back.'

Collins felt sick as she put down the bags. Jenkins could be anywhere. He could have been standing right behind her. She simply had no way of knowing. If she wanted Michael to be found alive, she had to call Blackwell and let him know where she was.

She had to take the chance. She looked down at the phone in her hand and began to dial. Almost immediately the phone squealed with disapproval and a warning message flashed briefly on the screen: INCOMING CALLS ONLY. She could always just dial 999, but it would take time to convince the operator to put her through to the right department. Collins needed a phone on which she could call someone on the team direct.

She walked more than a hundred yards before slipping into a small women's clothing shop. 'I need to borrow your phone,' she said to the slim young woman behind the counter.

'What do you think this is? Go find a phone box.'

'I'm a police officer. This is urgent police business. I need to borrow your phone.'

'Got any ID?' The girl was cocky as hell, and Collins took an instant dislike to her. She instinctively reached to the back pocket of her trousers where she always kept her warrant card, only to find an empty space in its place. What she wanted to do was push the girl aside, but she knew that would only lead to the alarm being sounded and uniformed officers rushing to the scene. She didn't have time to explain what was going on.

'Shit,' she muttered, then turned and stormed out.

'Up yours, nutter,' the girl called after her.

Collins stood on the pavement, crowds surging past on both sides of her. 'Where the hell is a policeman when you need one?' she said under her breath. She looked up and down, but there were none to be seen. Although dozens of uniformed officers and community support officers regularly patrolled the street, the weight of the crowd made it impossible for her to spot one.

Time was running out. And so was her patience. Across the road she spotted a small café in a side street with a bank of tables outside. A man in a pale linen shirt was chatting nosily on his phone. Collins marched over and snatched it out of his hand.

'What the fuck.' The man looked stunned.

'I'm a police officer. I need to use your phone urgently.'

With one eye on the man, Collins began to dial one of the few numbers she knew by heart.

'Tony? It's Collins. The money is in a couple of bin bags close to Oxford and Wardour streets. Tell Blackwell and get them to swing the cameras around. I'm going to head back that way to see if I can spot anything.'

Collins clicked off the phone and handed it back to the man. 'Thanks. I didn't mean to scare you. It was an emergency. Please, call the police if you need proof. My name is Detective Inspector Stacey Collins.'

She headed back towards the place where she had left the money, hoping beyond all hope that it was not already too late.

Dixon spun his seat around so quickly that he almost fell over.

'Guv, we've got her. Collins has been in touch. She made the drop. She called Tony Woods. The money is in a couple of bin bags just outside Marks & Spencer.'

'Put it on the screen.' Blackwell looked up, but all he could see was a bright red blur. It quickly dawned on him. 'Shit. He's taken it out, hasn't he? It's another one of the blindspots, isn't it?'

Dixon bit a few buttons on his keyboard. 'The closest we've got right now is fifty yards away.'

'Then get some bodies down there. We need to get eyes on the cash, otherwise we're fucked.'

'Already done, sir. They're on their way right now. I've got the closest camera up.'

Blackwell scanned the large screen. Even with the zoom on maximum, it was still too far away to make out individual faces. All he could see was a steady stream of shoppers stepping around two plastic bags.

A middle-aged man deposited a newspaper. A bearded teenager threw a half-eaten hamburger on top of the pile. Then a man in a threadbare coat and no shoes drew up and began rummaging around.

'Who the hell's that?' said Blackwell, staring open-mouthed at the screen. 'Is that one of our men? Get him the hell away from there.'

It was quickly apparent that he wasn't an undercover officer, as the same man casually picked up the two bags and tucked one under each arm, then began walking back towards Oxford Circus. He was moving towards the camera, his image becoming clearer with each step.

'That's him,' said Blackwell. 'That's our man.'

Two streets down and hidden from view by a market stall on the pavement, Collins was also watching the man. He wasn't what she had expected at all. The photograph she had seen made him look bigger, more frightening.

There was no way of knowing exactly how close the other units were or whether they had managed to get the CCTV cameras to track the man. If Collins was going to be sure that they kept sight of the money and apprehended the kidnapper, she would have to follow him herself.

Keeping a discreet distance and using the crowds of people all around her as a cover, she kept moving in on the man, her heart racing as she got closer and closer. Suddenly she felt a burly hand on her shoulder. She looked around to see Woods. He nodded to his left and right, indicating the plain-clothes members of the SO19 firearms team who were advancing up along the street, their guns concealed so as to avoid alarming members of the public.

The man with the bags moved through the crowd, then stopped on the corner of Oxford Circus and placed them in a litter bin on the side of the street. As he began to walk away, the armed officers moved in.

'Jenkins,' an officer called out above the noise

of the crowd and the traffic.

No reaction.

'Jenkins!' This time his voice was louder, more of a bellow than a shout. The man must have heard it, unless he was deaf, but there was still no reaction. Collins felt a tingle in her spine. This wasn't Duncan Jenkins.

'Armed police. Stop right now.'

At last the man stopped and glanced back over his shoulder. The armed officers took out their police-issue baseball caps and placed them on their heads, the distinctive black-and-white check pattern clearly visible around the rim. At the same time they pulled the Velcro pads off their slim-fitting bulletproof jackets to reveal the word POLICE emblazoned above their chests.

It took only a split second for the man to realize that they were indeed talking to him rather than to anyone else. He turned around, and, as the guns were pointed towards him, he raised his hands to the sky.

Collins held back. This was a job for the armed team, and she didn't want to risk getting between them and their target. There were more than enough distractions around as it was.

The officer to the right of her began to bark instructions. 'Get down on your knees.'

The man's face was contorted with terror. He was so scared he had lost the ability to move and stood completely frozen.

'Turn around and get down on to your knees,' the officer said again.

By now, shoppers had realized what was going on. Some had stopped to stare, while others had hurried along, eager to give the whole thing a wide berth. Collins looked up and saw a double-decker bus moving slowly past, faces pressed up against the window as passengers and tourists enjoyed the free show.

The man's mouth opened and closed like a goldfish's but no sound came out.

Collins turned her head and cupped her hand against her ear in an effort to hear. She caught only a few words: '...gave me money ... told me to take bags ... promised me money...'

Collins spun around on the spot. Jenkins was there somewhere. He was probably watching them right now. He might even have Michael with him. Could she have been wrong? Was he genuinely after the money after all? He had used the man as a decoy.

And that's when it happened.

One moment the man was standing fifty feet in front of her; the next he wasn't.

The blast wave of the explosion hit her. It was as if someone had punched her hard in the stomach, knocking all the wind out of her and sending her flat on her back.

The others felt it too. In a perfect circle all around the man people were falling and scream-ing and twisting in the air as the shock wave passed through them. Then it hit the windows of the shops. They shattered, sending razor-sharp shards of glass flying in all directions. For a few seconds there was deathly silence, then alarms began to sound everywhere and the screaming started.

Lying on the ground, Collins put her hand to

her head and felt something warm and wet alongside something jagged and sharp. A small shard of glass was caught up in the top of her scalp. Instinctively she reached up to pull at it. It came out easily, tangled up in nothing more than a few ragged strands of her hair. There was blood on her face, to be sure, but not all of it was her own.

Burning banknotes were fluttering down from the sky like some kind of strange tickertape parade, and the air was heavy with the smell of burning petrol...

The blast had caused devastation everywhere, and the man was screaming in agony, one of his legs bleeding badly. She could see his broken body lying on the ground in front of her, twitching slowly as spasms of pain shot through him. But during the blast Collins had seen something else. As she had flown backwards through the air, she had seen the reaction of those around her. Shock, horror, terror in hundreds of faces.

All except one.

There had been one man to the far right in her field of vision, just on the edge of the blast zone, who had not seemed to react when the blast went off. While everyone else turned, pointed or stopped in their tracks, he had simply carried on walking at a steady pace, his hands tucked deeply into the pockets of his light jacket. He hadn't even turned around to see what was going on.

There were two possible explanations. Either the man was as deaf as a post and blind as a bat – though that was unlikely, as even a deaf person would have felt the shock wave of the blast – or

304

he was the man who had set off the explosion. It was Jenkins. And he was getting away.

Collins dragged herself to her feet. Woods was kneeling beside a woman with a badly cut face. There were other people who were hurt, but it was more important to get Jenkins and, ultimately, Michael. Dozens of uniformed and plain-clothes officers were flooding into the area, convinced that the one man who could tell them where Michael was lay mortally injured on the street. She alone knew the truth, and there wasn't a second to waste.

For all she knew, Jenkins was on his way to kill Michael at that very moment.

She called out to Woods and pointed at the man leaving the scene. 'That's him – that's Jenkins.' Woods responded with a look of confusion. She had no time to explain, so she shook the dust and debris from her clothes, took a deep breath and started to run after Jenkins.

52

Collins had just turned into Regent Street when she saw Jenkins turn the corner of a road that was a few streets up on her left. She increased her pace, ignoring the pain that was now shooting through her body.

By the time she reached the corner she had gained on him considerably. The sound of her footsteps was being muffled by the wailing sirens of the fire engines, the ambulances and the scores of police cars converging on the scene a few streets away.

It wasn't until she was within fifty feet of him that he turned, and saw her bearing down on him.

He began to run, his gait heavy and awkward, his breath coming in huge, urgent gasps. Collins was almost close enough to grab him. He reached into the bag that was swinging loose at his shoulder and pulled out something small, metallic and shiny, something that fitted into the palm of his hand.

And then he turned.

His face was sweaty and red with exertion. 'If you take one more step,' he gasped, 'the boy dies.'

Collins stared hard at Jenkins's hand, which was now raised up in the air, rising and falling in time with his breathing. 'I mean it,' he continued. 'I'll do it. I've killed before, and I'm not afraid to do it again. Back off or Michael Dawney dies this instant.'

There was no way to see exactly what it was that Jenkins was holding, no way to be sure if the device truly had the power to kill the hostage at a distance. One thing was certain, though: during the execution of his two kidnaps, Jenkins had displayed an expert knowledge of the latest technology. If anyone could manufacture a hand-held device that could deal out death in an instant, it would be Duncan Jenkins.

Collins backed off.

'Give it up, Jenkins,' she said, speaking between deep breaths of her own. 'There's a cordon round here. The whole place is surrounded. You've got

306

nowhere to go. Just give it up. It's over.'

'How do you know it's over?' he asked. 'You don't know the first thing about my plans, about what I've been through. This could just be the beginning, for all you know.'

'I know that you went through a lot of pain as a child.'

'You don't know shit about what I went through.'

'I know the pain of revenge.'

'What do you know about it?'

'I watched my father half beaten to death and crippled for life. Every time I see him, I want revenge – I understand that.' She began moving closer to him. 'I know how that can shape you, can affect you. Please, Duncan, none of what happened to you is Michael's fault – you need to tell me where he is.'

For a second, Collins believed she might have got through. There seemed to be a softening of Jenkins's expression, an acceptance that everything he had done had ultimately been a waste of time, that his evil actions hurt no one more than they had hurt him. But it was only fleeting. Almost as quickly as they had appeared, the vulnerabilities vanished again.

'I told you once and I won't tell you again,' he hissed, holding the device higher still. 'Back off.'

Jenkins started to move slowly backwards along the street, his eyes fixed on Collins. When he reached the corner, more than thirty feet away, he glanced to one side and then began to run. Almost immediately he bumped into a pedestrian coming the other way, and both men were sent sprawling.

When Jenkins hit the ground, the hand containing the device sprang open. There, on the corner, Collins saw it clearly for the first time: it was a tiny silver cigarette lighter. He had been bluffing all along.

Moments after he hit the ground, Jenkins was up again and on the move.

So far as Blackwell's team were concerned, Duncan Jenkins had been critically injured in the blast, and they would be doing their best to save him in order to find out where Michael was being held. Only she knew the truth, only she knew the tramp had been nothing but a decoy. That meant that she was Michael's only hope. If she lost Jenkins, the boy would almost certainly lose his life.

Collins made her way round the corner and saw Jenkins running towards the Marylebone Road. She went after him at full sprint.

Jenkins arrived at Regent's Park tube station and disappeared inside, with Collins following close behind. With some difficulty he vaulted the ticket barrier and raced for the platforms; Collins did the same.

'Jenkins!'

His face was a picture of alarm. He turned and glanced at Collins, then began to hurry towards the open mouth of the tunnel. Within seconds Collins was on top of him. He was cornered. Nowhere to go. She had him exactly where she wanted him.

'Give it up, Duncan,' she said, trying to sound as sympathetic as she could. 'Give it up. I know you've been through some hard times, I know you've had your troubles. But it's all over now. You've nowhere left to go. Give it up and tell me where Michael is.'

Jenkins only smiled and looked back over his shoulder into the gaping mouth of the tunnel beside him. He turned to look at Collins, sighed and then put down his bag. Collins felt an enormous sense of relief sweep over her. She took a step forward, but his words stopped her dead in her tracks.

'Do you know anything about military miniatures?'

Collins frowned. 'You mean the toy soldiers? I saw the ones you have in your home.'

Jenkins shook his head slowly. 'Toy soldiers are the things that children play with. Pre-packaged pieces of plastic that are ready straight out of the box. I'm talking about military miniatures, detailed metal figurines that require painting and hours of preparation.'

'The only thing I care about right now is finding Michael—'

'It was H.G. Wells, the author, the man who wrote *The Time Machine* and *War of the Worlds*, who first popularized them. He wrote a book called *Little Wars*, which was the first time anyone had drawn up a set of rules about how the campaigns should be fought. We call it wargaming.

'You see, Wells was a pacifist. He believed that fighting battles with miniature figures was a cathartic experience. That it could help to ease man's natural aggression. Wells believed that if everyone fought battles with military miniatures, real wars in the future might be prevented.'

Again Collins frowned. 'I don't understand–'

'That's what I was trying to do. I was trying to get rid of my aggression, the anger and the hurt that I felt because of what had happened, what Peter Dawney had done to me. But it was no good. It was always there. And then it got much worse. When I was fifteen the doctors told me I'd never have children. I guess it didn't matter too much back then. I was too young and didn't really understand what it meant. And, as I got older, I knew no woman would ever want to be with me, not in that way.

'But then I read a story about Peter, about how well he was doing. I discovered that he was living a lie and that he'd been having an affair. And then I found out he had another child he didn't even know about. I wanted him to suffer, I wanted him to feel the pain that I did. I wanted him to know about losing everything. So I decided to take his children away from him.'

While he'd been speaking, Jenkins had been moving closer and closer to the platform edge. Wind from an oncoming train began to blast out from the tunnel. 'I've done that, and now that my mother is gone, there is nothing left for me in this world. Nothing left for me at all. It's time for my mother and I to be together again.' Collins realized what was going on: he was making his peace.

'Listen, Duncan, whatever you're thinking, you need to stop and ... for God's sake you need to tell me where Michael is. There will be no peace for you unless you spare the life of this innocent

310

little boy. You can't punish the child for the sins of the father. He's just a little boy, he's just a little–'

Jenkins held up a hand to silence her, his eyes lifting towards the heavens. 'Isn't God the most inspired architect of all? Every single person is a work of pure genius. So what on earth did I do to deserve to be turned into this abomination?' He returned his gaze to Collins, his eyes burning into her. 'You're too late,' he said. 'You're much too late.'

She watched in horror as Duncan grabbed the sides of his shirt and ripped it open, exposing the flesh of his chest and belly. Like some grotesque tattoo, the skin was a patchwork of ragged shapes and colours, the result of dozens of grafting operations. There was no belly button, no hair, just a mass of ridges and scars.

A sudden gust of wind pushed a cloud of dust from the mouth of the tunnel and up into her eyes. She raised her hand to clear them, and, as she did so, saw Duncan's shirt-tails flapping in the air as he leaped from the platform edge and into the path of the moving train.

The sound of screams. The horrified face of the driver. The too-late squeal of brakes, and the sickening thud and rumble of human flesh hitting hard steel.

The train continued to make its way into the station, and Duncan's body slipped underneath its front wheels, crushed and broken.

Duncan Jenkins was dead!

53

Collins felt sick to her stomach. It was a combination of the horrific sight she had just seen and the sudden and awful realization that she now had no way of finding out where Michael Dawney was being held. The moment Duncan Jenkins had thrown himself under that train, he had in effect taken two lives.

Her entire career was in the balance because of the death of Duncan Jenkins, even though he had actually taken his own life. Everyone would blame her. She couldn't face her colleagues, and she couldn't face Peter Dawney.

But, if Collins had learned one thing and one thing alone during the course of the investigation, it was that Duncan Jenkins was the kind of man who never did anything without putting a great deal of thought into it. Everything had a meaning, everything had a purpose. Everything was a piece of the puzzle. The trouble was, only Duncan Jenkins knew what the entire picture actually looked like, and now he was dead.

She tried to get inside the dead man's mind, to imagine the rage and frustration that drove him to commit such acts in the first place. To catch a killer, you had to become a killer. She hadn't actually taken a life herself, but when she'd backed Jenkins into a corner, she'd given him no choice.

He'd been rushing, rushing to get on the train.

Rushing to get somewhere. Rushing to get to Michael in order to finish him off? Was it really too late, or was that just wishful thinking on Duncan's part? Surely it was too late only because she didn't know where Michael was being held. If she could solve that one mystery, there was still a chance she could save the boy's life.

The echo of the squealing brakes of the tube train, the screams of the commuters as they ran from the platform and the sound of the station alarm were ringing in her ears as she took a few steps forward in order to retrieve the bag that Jenkins had been carrying, now lying at the entrance to the tunnel.

It seemed pointless to look in it now. Everything seemed pointless. She felt the weight of failure and defeat pressing down on her shoulders. He himself had told her it was too late. She picked up the bag and rummaged through its contents. No need for gloves now. Jenkins was dead, and so was the enquiry.

Yet a part of Collins refused to give up all hope. There was a chance, there had to be. Jenkins had been at the scene in order to set off the explosion, to destroy the money. He wouldn't have risked killing Michael beforehand in case something went wrong. If his aim had been to make Peter Dawney suffer for as long as possible, he would have waited. And there was one more thing, something he'd said earlier, that was bugging her.

The bag contained an old Bible and a mobile phone. She called up the phone's list of recently dialled numbers, hoping it might give her some clue as to Michael's whereabouts. There were three numbers listed: the first one belonged to Blackwell's mobile; the second was the number of the phone she had collected at the jewellery shop; the third she didn't recognize at all. She thought about dialling it but was too far underground to get a signal.

Collins made her way along the platform to the front of the train, passing members of the London Underground staff who were in the process of escorting passengers away from the scene. One casually dressed man caught her attention: he was standing over Duncan Jenkins and using his mobile phone to record a clip of his mangled body.

It instantly made her see red, and she grabbed him by the scruff of the neck. 'What the fuck are you doing?' he squealed, dropping the phone, which flew over the edge of the platform and on to the tracks below. Collins pulled him towards her until he was only an inch away from her face. 'Get the fuck out of here,' she hissed.

'You lost me my phone!'

She gritted her teeth and spoke slowly, her voice full of anger. 'Leave before I have you nicked, you sick fuck.' When she let go of him, the man turned and skulked away.

As she looked up at the entrance to the platform, she noticed Woods and a group of uniformed and plain-clothes officers rushing down towards her.

'What's happened? Blackwell's been following you on CCTV ever since he realized the tramp was a decoy.' He was breathing hard, having run all the way there. 'Where's Jenkins?'

'He jumped.'

'Fuck. What about Michael? Did he say anything?'

Collins shook her head. 'Nothing. Just that it was too late.'

Tube staff were gathering around them, and she glanced at them anxiously. 'Listen, Tony, I don't have time for this. We need to get out of here.'

Woods looked concerned. 'You've got to be kidding. Blackwell's throwing a fit. He's ordered half the teams to make their way here. You've got to stay. They're going to want to know exactly what happened.'

'The whole thing's been caught on CCTV. That will have to do for now.' She pulled him to one side. 'Listen, something's been bugging me. Do you remember what we talked about at Jenkins's house?'

'What are you on about?'

'Think, Tony. When we were searching it, what did we talk about?'

'I dunno. All sorts. It isn't the time for this.'

'Yes, it is. What did we talk about? I need you to remember. Did we talk about Sophie?'

Woods frowned in concentration. 'Yes, at the end when we went back into the lounge. I asked how you two were getting on now after she ran away.'

Collins nodded. 'We've got to get back to the house.'

'Why?'

'Because he was there.'

'Who?'

'Jenkins. He heard our conversation. He must have been there the whole time.'

54

Martha Day turned left off the Purley Way on the edge of Croydon and headed to the back of a large warehouse at the end of an industrial estate. She parked and opened the boot, helping an exhausted Peter Dawney to climb out.

'Shall I call the police?' she asked.

'No. He said not to. You shouldn't even be here. You'd better go, in case he's watching. I need to do this alone.'

'But Peter—'

'Promise me you won't tell the police. If you do, he'll kill Michael.'

'I won't. I promise.'

Peter reached into his pocket and pulled out Martha's mobile. 'You'd better take this. He told me not to take a phone with me.'

'Why don't you try to hide it somewhere?'

'I need to do what he says if I'm going to get Michael back.'

She took the phone, climbed back into the car and drove away. He looked around. In front of him was a disused industrial building surrounded by high metal fences, just as Jenkins had described. He walked towards the main gates and saw that the padlock had been cut. He pushed them open and went inside.

His breathing quickened as he strode up the short path, a growing sense of anxiety building up inside him. He hoped the nightmare would soon be over.

The heavy front door opened with a gentle push. The inside of the building was in semi-darkness, with light filtering in from holes in the derelict roof.

He moved forward gingerly. In the distance, somewhere in the bowels of the property, he thought he heard a noise: the sound of water running and the occasional muffled sob of a terrified child.

'Michael? Are you there? Michael? It's Daddy.'

The reply was hard to make out. It seemed to be Michael, but Peter couldn't work out what he was saying. The sound was coming from behind a door at the far end of the building. He hurried towards it.

And that was when a blast knocked him off his feet.

For a few seconds the shock of the impact kept him free of pain, but then the most searing, agonizing burning sensations began to travel through his body, and at once he understood exactly what had happened. He had been shot in the legs.

Screaming in agony and with his face contorted by pain, he twisted around and saw that a shotgun had been attached to a trip wire.

The blast covered his lower back, buttocks, and the backs and sides of his legs. He clenched his fists as tears of sheer agony began to roll down his cheeks. He could feel blood seeping out of him. He reached down to feel the mass of raw flesh where the skin on the back of his right leg had been torn away.

All around him small white rocks were strewn across the floor. A regular clay-pigeon shooter, he realized that the cartridges had been filled with rock salt. Duncan Jenkins could have easily killed him with a booby trap if he had wanted to. A shotgun filled with regular pellets and aimed at his head or neck would have proved instantly fatal. The man obviously had some darker plan in mind.

The muffled cries were getting louder. 'Michael, I'm coming, Michael.'

Using his arms, he dragged himself along the filthy ground towards the door, towards the place where the muffled screams were coming from.

He knew that if he stopped fighting, if he tried to block out the pain and let his body's natural painkillers take over, that he would simply slip away into unconsciousness. He couldn't let that happen. He had to keep fighting, no matter how much it hurt. He had to save his son. He had to get to him.

And then he brought himself to a sudden stop, his arms stretched out in front of him as if he were swimming the front crawl. Jenkins had already placed one booby trap in the building. What if there were more in place? What if every inch that Peter crawled towards his son brought him an inch closer to his own death?

Peter dismissed the thoughts from his mind. At last he was beginning to see how Jenkins's mind worked. He wanted him to suffer. He wanted his son to suffer. And he wanted Peter to be there to see his son die. But whatever horrors awaited him at the end of this short journey, he would be sure to stick to the path. He was certain of that. And, holding that firmly in his mind, he resumed his crawl.

55

With the exception of the uniformed officer on guard outside, Duncan Jenkins's house was pretty much as Collins and Woods had left it earlier in the day.

Collins moved through the rooms slowly and deliberately. The clues were here, she was sure of it; she just wasn't looking properly. She had only spoken about Sophie in the front room, so Jenkins must have been hiding close by to have heard them.

'Are you sure he was here, guv?' asked Tony. 'He could have found out about Sophie some other way.'

'How?'

Woods shrugged. He had no answer.

Collins shook her head. 'No, what he said was specific. It was exactly what we'd been talking about when we were here.'

Collins walked towards the old sideboard and picked up a photograph of Duncan and his mother in a loving embrace.

'There's nothing here, boss. Blackwell's going mental trying to get hold of you on the radio. We really need to get back to him.' Woods's voice was becoming tense with impatience. Collins felt it too. Yet somehow she knew the answer simply had to be here.

'Fuck Blackwell. I know Jenkins was here listening. And if he was here, then Michael might be here too.'

It was all too clear that the kidnap and murder of Daniel Eliot and the subsequent kidnap of Michael Dawney had taken a great deal of privacy. If not here, then where had Jenkins carried it out?

Then Collins saw something that her mind instantly registered as out of place. 'How many televisions are there in the house?' she asked.

Woods scratched his head in an effort of memory. 'Just the one, in here.' He pointed to it. 'Why, do you want to put the news on?'

Collins ignored him and continued. 'If there's only one television in the house, then what's that cable for?'

Woods looked up to where Collins was now pointing, and their eyes followed the line of the thin white cable that had been tacked into the corner. The two stepped almost in unison up to the wall, where the cable vanished into a small dark hole.

'What's on the other side of that wall?'

'The kitchen.'

They walked through the hallway and into the kitchen, turning to face the door of the small pantry. 'It must come out behind there,' said Woods.

Collins opened the door and looked inside. It was a typical larder, full of tinned and dried goods neatly stacked on shelves on three sides. She crouched down and examined the far wall. The cable came through from the other side of the wall and passed down into the floorboards. She hammered on the lino-covered floor with her fist. It sounded hollow.

'There's something down there.'

She pulled at the lino. It felt heavy and Collins quickly realized that it had been stuck on to a hatch door that was opening at the same time. She threw back the door and looked down at a dark narrow staircase.

She opened her mouth to ask for a torch, but Woods had already taken one from the larder shelf. She switched it on, gripped it firmly and began to descend into the darkness.

'Careful: this might be a trap, just like the money.'

Collins shone the torch beam on the walls of the stairs and the steps in front of her. There was nothing except bare plaster. With Collins leading the way, they headed cautiously down.

When they reached the bottom of the stairs, Collins found a light switch. As she flicked the bulb into life, she gasped in astonishment.

Every inch of wall space in the rectangular room in which she now found herself had been covered with photographs, newspaper clippings and drawings.

Leading off from the main room was a smaller blocked-off area, accessed through a door that was now ajar. Collins headed towards it and shone her torch into the room beyond. At first she did not quite take in what she was seeing, but after a few moments she knew she was looking at the cell that had been used to hold the kidnapped children.

There was congealed blood on the mattress and floor. It was here that Daniel Eliot had been tortured and killed.

She walked back into the main room and looked around. Directly opposite was a small desk on which sat a computer and dozens of folders. Behind that was a small television with a digital video camera sitting on top and a pile of tapes.

One wall was full of photographs of the Dawney family spanning many years. There were pictures of Peter Dawney in his university days, distance snapshots of his marriage and press cuttings chronicling his rise in the corporate world. There were even shots of him learning to drive.

Collins scanned the images around her, and suddenly one of the biggest mysteries of the case was solved. How had Jenkins known that Daniel Eliot was Peter Dawney's child when Dawney himself hadn't known?

A long sequence of photographs at the bottom of the wall appeared to have been taken with a telephoto lens. They showed a couple kissing passionately on a park bench, and the same couple going in and out of hotels.

Collins recognized them at once, though they were at least ten years younger in the photos. They were Peter Dawney and Christina Rogers, as she was known back then.

Duncan had been obsessed with Peter and had followed him for years; he had done this so well that he had even stumbled across the fact that he had been having an affair. There were photographs of Christina going to ante-natal classes and then meeting up with a friend at a wine bar.

Jenkins had written a scruffy note on the wall next to the print: *Told friend that Peter Dawney is father of baby!*

Then there were pictures of Michael and Daniel growing up, going to school, playing and visiting friends.

Collins's eyes continued around the room. Another wall was a testament to the years of torment that Jenkins had suffered, with many of his innermost thoughts sketched on the wall. There were crude pictures of men whom Collins presumed to be Peter Dawney with their throats cut open and blood pouring out.

As she stared intently at the pictures, she began to truly understand Jenkins's torment and his desire for revenge. She thought back to her father and to the fact that, for many years, not a day had passed without her wishing harm on his attackers. But his need for revenge had been way beyond any desire of hers.

A chill ran down her spine as she found herself staring at a drawing that was horribly familiar. It depicted a child hanging from the rafters of a building. The position of the body, the angle of the rope and the position of the windows – it was an exact replica of the scene she had encountered when she found Daniel Eliot's body at St Andrew's.

'Tony, come and have a look at this.'

Woods walked over and stood beside her. She pointed at the drawing. 'It's Daniel Eliot. He drew it just the way it happened.'

Woods nodded towards the drawing beside it. It was a crude sketch of a cylinder and a simple circuit diagram. 'This must be how he blew up the money at Oxford Circus.'

They studied the next two drawings in the sequence. The first showed a boy in a pool of water. The second showed a woman with her stomach slit open and the contents pouring out.

Collins touched the first drawing with her finger. 'If that's Michael–'

'Then that must be Alice Dawney.'

56

Peter Dawney's arms and lungs burned like fire with the effort of trying to drag himself along towards his son.

The entire bottom half of his body was soaked in blood, and it formed a slick slug-like trail behind him. He had no idea how much blood he had lost but was acutely aware that he was starting to feel light-headed and dizzy. He needed to get to Michael soon. He couldn't give up, he couldn't stop.

It seemed to take an eternity for him to reach the door, and then a massive effort was required to reach up and grab the handle before pushing it open. Any last remaining hope that Michael's torment was at an end quickly faded away.

Peter found himself staring into a small dark room. The sound of fast-running water was much louder here, as were the sounds of muffled cries. Peter tried to call out his son's name, but his throat was dry. He swallowed hard, forcing down what little saliva remained in his mouth, and tried again.

'Michael, are you in here? Michael?'

A whimper was the only reply.

Something bright glinted in front of him. As Peter's eyes slowly became accustomed to the light, he found himself looking at bands of razor wire, running in a spiral around what appeared to be a square hole in the middle of the floor. He blinked a few times and stared hard in front of him, willing the images to become clearer.

Using all his strength, he raised himself up on his arms so that he could look down at exactly what was ahead of him. The centre of the room was occupied by a square inspection well, the kind you could drive cars and other vehicles over in order to inspect their undersides. Michael was in the middle of the well, strapped to a chair with thick ropes that seemed to wind up and down his body like an endless snake. A thick piece of silver tape had been stretched across his mouth, and there was a look of absolute terror in his eyes.

But what scared Peter the most was the large piece of plastic pipe sticking out just behind where Michael was sitting: water was gushing through it and into the well at a furious rate. It was already high enough to cover Michael's knees, and it was only a matter of time before it covered him completely.

The sight of his son in such peril gave him new strength, and Peter pulled himself quickly towards the middle of the room. The razor wire completely surrounded the well, and there was no way to go round it. Disregarding what the blades would do to him, Peter surged forward.

One sliced through the back of his hand, another caught on the belt of his trousers, yet another hooked into the skin on the back of his neck. Every new movement not only left him in more pain but caused more of his body to be caught up in the blades. After a few moments Peter was trapped, completely unable to move.

He looked over at Michael, the boy's face silently pleading for help, but there was nothing Peter could do.

Michael seemed to be indicating at something with his eyes, and Peter shifted his gaze to the right. There, in the centre of the bands of razor wire, was a small cassette recorder. Peter was only barely able to reach it with his one free hand.

He hit the play button. 'Hello, Peter. So sorry I can't be there to share your agony, but I'm on my way to your house to kill your wife. You took everything away from me: my childhood and any chance of my having a family of my own. I've spent many years thinking about how best to show you what it's like to have everything in your life that means something snatched away from you. You never knew about Daniel until I killed him. How does it feel to be responsible for the death of a child you knew nothing about? The money's gone. I blew it up. You'll leave this place alive but spend the rest of your days tormented by what's happened over the past few days, as I've been tormented from the day you took my life away. Enjoy your life, Peter. I'm leaving you with nothing. No money, no children, no wife, nothing at all. It's no more than you deserve. Enjoy the show.'

The tape clicked off, and Peter Dawney looked back over at Michael, who had also heard Jenkins's words. The boys eyes blinked furiously in terror at the sight of his father, who lay helplessly tangled up in the razor wire. His strength was fading fast.

He had no choice but to do exactly what Duncan Jenkins had wanted him to do: sit back and watch his last remaining son die a slow and horrible death.

57

'We got a problem, boss, a big problem.' The voice of Tony Woods echoed down from the room above.

'What is it?'

Woods made his way down into the basement. 'Alice Dawney is fine, but Peter's gone missing.'

'Since when?'

'Fifteen minutes before the money-drop.'

'Shit, it has to be Jenkins. He must have made contact with him before the money-drop.'

'How? Blackwell's monitoring all communications in and out of the house.'

Collins shook her head in frustration. 'I don't know. I really don't know.' She stared again at the drawings on the wall. Did one of them hold the clue she was looking for?

Then she remembered the phone. The phone

she had taken from Jenkins's bag after he had killed himself. She pulled it out and quickly made her way upstairs in order to get a signal.

The minute she got one, she hit the redial button. A woman's voice, tinged with panic, answered almost immediately.

'Peter? Is Michael all right?'

'Who is this?' barked Collins.

The voice on the other end of the line immediately fell silent.

'This is Detective Inspector Stacey Collins of the Metropolitan Police. I want to know who I'm speaking to.'

'How do I know you are who you say you are?' said the woman's voice, still timid and unsure.

'For fuck's sake,' said Collins. 'I don't have time for this shit. I'm working the Michael Dawney case. This number is the last one dialled on a phone that was in the possession of the kidnapper. Unless you want to be charged as an accomplice, I suggest you start talking.'

Collins could hear the woman swallow hard and knew her threat had got through.

'My name is Martha Day.'

'And how do you know Duncan Jenkins?'

'I don't. I don't know anyone by that name.'

'And how do you know Peter and Michael?'

'I'm Peter's secretary.'

It was slowly starting to make sense. Jenkins clearly knew enough about police procedure to know that Peter's own phones would have been monitored, so he had got round this by calling his secretary.

'Do you know where Peter is right now?'

There was a hesitant silence on the other end of the line.

'For God's sake, woman, I'm trying to save a boy's life. Tell me where Peter Dawney is.'

'He ... he said if I told the police, he'd kill Michael.'

Collins wanted to reach down the phone line, grab the woman by the neck and shake her until she told her what she wanted to know, but she understood that the only way to get anything out of her was to do her best to be sympathetic. 'Martha,' she said softly, 'I know how frightening this must be for you, but you have to trust me. The man who took Michael and called you is dead. People like that, they always make threats about what they're going to do if the police are called, but the truth is that there is no one better placed than the police to rescue the victims in cases like this.'

Collins heard the woman take a sharp intake of breath. 'I could never live with myself if Michael died like Daniel. For all I know you could be working with the kidnapper, and this could be some kind of test.' The woman was crying now. 'I promised I wouldn't tell. I just can't.'

Martha Day ended the call. Collins immediately dialled her number again, but this time she was greeted by the answering machine. 'Shit,' she said in frustration. Then she looked at the keypad and began to dial a new number. This time the voice that answered belonged to a young man with a South London accent.

'Khan? It's Stacey Collins here.'

'Where are you? The whole world's trying to

track you down.'

'That's not important right now. Khan, I need a favour.'

The tone of her voice told him she was deadly serious and that his questions would have to wait for another time.

'What can I do for you?'

'I've got the number of a mobile that belongs to Peter Dawney's secretary. I need to know everywhere that it's been since midday until now.'

'I can make the call, but it's going to take–'

'No, Khan. There isn't time to do this officially. I don't care what you have to do, whose system you have to hack into. I need the information as quickly as possible. And you have to call me back on Woods's phone; I don't have mine with me.'

'What's the number, boss?'

Collins returned downstairs to find Woods scrutinizing the pile of video tapes next to the camera.

'He made the videos here too,' he said. 'He must have spent years putting this place together. I doubt even his mother knew what was going on down here.'

Collins had no time to respond. She went to the wall where the drawings were pinned up and began to pull them down.

Woods stood up, alarmed at what seemed to be his boss's irrational behaviour. 'What you doing, guv?'

'Let's get out of here,' she said.

'Sure,' he said hesitantly. 'Where are we going?'

She held up a drawing of the boy in the pool of water. 'Here.'

58

Collins had only just got into Woods's car when Khan called back with a list of locations for the mobile phone.

'It's registered to a Martha Day,' he began, and read through the list of masts that had picked up the phone's signal since noon. 'She was at Dawney's office until 12.20, then she went over to his house. Then they went to an area just off the Purley Way in Croydon, and the phone is still in that area. It's on the main road, just off Five-ways corner.'

'Do you know what she drives?'

She heard Khan tapping away at the computer. 'A red Suzuki Vitara.' He proceeded to give her the registration number as Woods started up the car and headed towards Croydon.

They were there in less than twenty minutes and spotted Martha Day's car in a lay-by. Woods pulled up directly in front of her. 'I haven't got my warrant card,' said Collins; 'you'd better show her yours.'

The two officers jumped out and went to the driver's side of the vehicle. Martha Day looked scared as the officers approached. Woods held up his warrant card. 'I'm Detective Sergeant Tony Woods and this is my colleague Detective Inspector Stacey Collins. Please get out of the car.'

She stepped out cautiously as Collins led her

on to the pavement.

'Martha, please listen. You know I'm a police officer now. What I told you on the phone was the truth. Duncan Jenkins, the man who kidnapped Michael, is dead. Please tell me where Peter is now. He and his son are in great danger. We don't have time to wait.'

'He said he would kill them both if I contacted the police.'

Collins placed her hand gently on the woman's shoulder. 'Please, Martha, you're the only person who knows where they are. You're the only one who can save them.'

Tears of panic and emotion began to fall from her eyes as she began to explain the sequence of events that had brought her to Croydon.

Collins pushed open the heavy front door, stepped into the derelict building and looked around the empty space in front of her, which was illuminated by beams of light from several large holes in the roof.

An acrid odour hung in the air. 'Shotgun residue,' said Collins to Woods, who was following behind her. 'You'd better call an ambulance, and some back-up.' She continued on into the building and soon spotted a shotgun on her right, tied to a post and with wire attached to the trigger. A trail of glistening blood led through the room to a door at the far end. She could hear the sound of running water coming from beyond the door and ran towards it.

She pushed the door open and instantly saw the motionless body of Peter Dawney in a pool of blood, tangled up in a four-foot-high roll of razor wire. Just in Peter's view was Michael Dawney, tied up in a pit of water. The child's eyes showed that he was petrified.

She reached through a gap in the wire and took Peter's pulse. It was weak. He was alive but only just.

In an instant Collins had taken in the situation. There was no way through the wire, no way to help Michael. The water was above his neck. He was screaming through the gag, desperately trying to suck in the air he needed to stay alive through his nose.

She circled the room, moving around the razor wire, looking for some way to turn the water off. She was still looking when Woods entered the room.

'Tony, we've got to get the water switched off.'

'How?'

'Call the fire brigade, call the Water Board. Call anybody who can turn it off. And fast. Try the other units, see if anyone can help.'

Woods rushed out, and Collins turned back to Michael. 'It's going to be okay, Michael. Help is on the way.'

But the look in the boy's eyes, and the fact that the water had already risen while she had been there, told her that help would not arrive in time. The water was above the boy's upper lip, and his nostrils were almost submerged. If Michael was going to be saved from drowning, it had to be now.

She took off her shoes and stepped back so that she was flat against the wall. Taking a deep breath, she ran as fast as she could towards the wire and jumped over it into the water. She felt her left foot rip as it caught one of the blades, but she landed safely in the water and quickly stood up. She removed the gag from Michael's mouth, but he couldn't talk because the water level was too high.

The water reached just below her chest. She tried to lift the cast-iron chair that Michael was tied to, but it was far too heavy to budge. She could feel where the flow of water was coming from, so she took off her jacket and plunged under the water, trying to block the pipe. It was useless. The water flowed just as quickly as ever.

She went back to the chair, standing behind it and planting her bare feet firmly on the ground. She gripped the bottom of the seat and tried to lift it with all her might. The chair rose a few inches into the air, just high enough for Michael's mouth to be out of the water. She heard him suck in a lungful of air and then begin to scream with panic.

The muscles in her arms and shoulders began to burn. She knew she couldn't hold the chair up for much longer. Her voice was strained as she spoke. 'Michael, I can't hold you up for long. You're gonna have to take a deep breath. I've got to put you back down.'

'No, please, please, no.'

Collins had to ignore the boy's screams. 'Take a deep breath, Michael, now,' she shouted as the chair sank back down, taking the boy's mouth and nose under the water. She shook her arms and lifted him back up again, knowing she wouldn't be able to keep doing this for long. Within a matter of minutes the water level would be too high for her to lift him above it.

The door burst open, and Woods entered with three men, one of whom immediately began to slice through the razor wire with a pair of bolt cutters. Michael's screams again filled the room.

'Quickly,' gasped Collins. 'I can't hold him.'

Woods didn't wait for the wire to be cut. He jumped over it and helped her lift the boy higher, until the three volunteers were able to get through and carry the boy out.

Within minutes the room was filled with police, paramedics and fire fighters, who untied Michael's bonds and conveyed him and his father into waiting ambulances.

Collins sat alone in a corner of the room, struggling to dry herself with a towel because of her exhaustion. Suddenly a familiar face entered the room; she stood up, and he went straight over to her.

'Listen, Collins, just because you were right this time, doesn't mean you'll always be.'

Blackwell turned and headed towards the door, pausing as he reached it and looking back at her with a half-smile on his face. 'But well done.'

Monday

59

In place of an opening hymn, there was music by some semi-obscure boy band. Collins couldn't name the song, but she recognized the tune, having heard it blasting out of Sophie's room dozens of times in recent months.

She was in a pew of the chapel right behind family and friends, at Higgins's insistence. If the choice had been her own, she would have sat much further back. But he had wanted the police to be highly visible at the funeral. Although they had failed to save Daniel Eliot, Collins had managed to rescue Michael Dawney in the nick of time. Higgins wanted the press and the public to know that the police had done their best.

From where she sat, Collins could see Christina and David Eliot sitting in the front row. Their faces were full of tears. Christina's brother and sister sat on one side of her, while David was on the other. His face was full of redness, betraying the fact that he was still drinking as heavily as ever. For once Collins couldn't blame him. The family liaison officer had told her that David Eliot now knew he wasn't Daniel's biological father.

Looking along the pew, Collins saw the usher make a gesture. Everyone rose to their feet as the tiny coffin was carried up the aisle. By the time it reached the top, the song was only a little more than halfway through.

The service that followed was heartbreaking. 'What can you say when a life ends at such a young and tender age?' the priest began. 'We'll never know the man that Daniel Eliot would have become, but we know that he was a kind and considerate boy with a gentle and generous nature that his parents were rightly proud of.

'These days we hear a lot about evil. We read about evil tyrants and dictators in obscure parts of the world, we read about evil figures from history, but few of us ever come face to face with evil. Daniel Eliot did just that. The thing that took his innocence away from this world, the thing that cut short his bright and beautiful life, was the worst kind of evil that any of us will ever know. But the ultimate justice, the justice handed out by God himself, awaits the man who did this.

'Daniel's laughter, smile and love of life will always be missed in our community.'

The congregation stood for the final hymn as the curtains opened and the coffin was conveyed away for cremation. Collins found her eyes filled with unstoppable tears.

As she left the crowded chapel, she saw someone whom she hadn't expected to be there. Peter Dawney rolled towards her in his wheelchair, his eyes bloodshot, his face weak and tired.

'Peter,' she said. 'I didn't think you'd be ... well, I suppose...'

He held up a hand to silence her. 'I know, I wasn't sure whether I should come. The doctors said I wasn't strong enough. I certainly don't think Christina and David wanted me to be here, but I had to do it for Daniel. Poor little kid never had a chance, I wasn't there for him. Perhaps if I had been, none of this would ever have happened.'

There was nothing Collins could say. In her heart she knew it was a waste of time to worry about things that could no longer be changed.

Their eyes followed Christina as she was led away from the chapel by family and friends. Christina met Peter's gaze, but the sad expression on her face did not change. David followed closely behind, staring at the ground in front of him.

Peter watched Christina vanish into a parked car. 'Still hasn't spoken to me,' he said.

'What is there for her to say?' said Collins. They stood in silence.

Peter Dawney's marriage was in tatters – the revelation that he had been having an affair at a time when his wife thought they were at their happiest had been devastating. But at least for them there was hope of a reconciliation. Christina Eliot was seeking a divorce from her husband. The pain of the loss they were feeling was simply too great for either of them to bear.

'Tell me something, Stacey. What's your take on all of this? How could she not tell me? Keep something like that hidden for so long? And now he's not here any more. My own flesh and blood, and I never even knew him. How can it be right for a child to grow up not knowing who their real father is?'

'She had her reasons,' said Collins gently.

'I guess. But it's still not right. How would you

feel if you never knew your real father? Every child deserves to know who their father is. I mean, it's just a fundamental right. Don't you think?'

Collins said nothing. Her thoughts were of Sophie. There was nothing she could possibly say to Peter. Not under the circumstances.

Epilogue

When DCS Higgins received an urgent request to meet with the Area Commander, he assumed it would be to discuss the Duncan Jenkins case. Jenkins's desire for publicity had ensured that far too much information about the workings of the unit had gone into the public domain. If the police were to remain one step ahead of kidnappers in the future, a radical upheaval and redrafting of all their procedures would have to take place. Never again would they be able to get away with simply providing a small portion of whatever ransom had been requested, along with a note from the family of the victim asking for more time. The tactic was now far too well known – every kidnapper would be expecting it.

'Excuse me, sir,' said the constable at the desk beside him. 'The Area Commander is ready to see you now.'

Higgins sat down on the leather chair opposite, but he could instantly tell that this was not an informal meeting.

'Do you know this man?' Assistant Commander

Patterson laid the glossy black-and-white photograph on the desk directly in front of DCS Higgins, who leaned forward and studied it closely. It showed a dark-haired, rugged-looking man in a black leather jacket standing next to what looked like a low brick wall.

Higgins waited a few seconds before he spoke. 'No.'

Patterson nodded, got up from his chair and began to pace around the room. 'His name's Stanley. Jack Stanley. We've been after him for years. He's linked to drugs and organized crime on a bunch of estates throughout South London. In particular the Blenheim Estate. He's always managed to stay one step ahead of any investigation that's been launched against him. Earlier this year his file was passed on to SOCA.'

Higgins scratched his head. 'I'm sorry, sir, but I don't quite see how the work of the Serious and Organized Crime Agency is relevant to...'

Patterson moved back towards his desk and slapped another photograph down over the first. It showed the same man, but this time speaking to a woman whom Higgins knew only too well. A woman he thought that he knew, a woman he thought he could trust: Stacey Collins.

Higgins's face became red with anger.

'I know about her role in the Eliot and Dawney cases, but what is she up to at the moment?' asked Patterson.

'She's a team leader and has just been assigned to the case involving that young kid stabbed to death on the Blenheim Estate. There must be an explanation for this, sir. Although sometimes she can be a bit a maverick, she's a good officer.'

'She grew up on the Blenheim Estate, didn't she?'

'I think so.'

'Has anything happened to make you think that she might be corrupt – any cause for suspicion of any kind?'

Higgins curled his brow as he thought hard. His mind wandered back to the information Collins had provided about the first drop site. There had been rumours about her connections with some dangerous underworld figures.

'Not that I can think of.'

Patterson sat back and rubbed his chin. 'I want you to sideline her on her current investigation. I need to make sure that she no longer has access to anything sensitive. She's now the target of an internal investigation.'

'But if I do that suddenly, she's going to become incredibly suspicious. Surely we should just continue as if nothing has happened but keep her under close watch?'

'Okay – but keep her on a tight lead. Is there anyone you can trust, anyone you can put on to her team?'

'There is one person I could bring into this.'

'Who do you have in mind?'

'A DI by the name of Yvonne Drabble.'

They had driven in absolute silence for the best part of an hour, but for once Stacey didn't mind. Despite her best efforts she was unable to engage in any kind of conversation with her daughter.

At least Sophie was sitting in the front – things

had improved enough for her to make that one small concession towards the two of them having a proper mother–daughter relationship. It had given Stacey the first inkling of hope that one day things might be the way they should be: laughing and joking, talking about their boyfriends, going shopping and even sharing their clothes.

The car slowly passed a large park on the right. From there it began to climb up a gentle slope, passing a series of large gated houses with extensive grounds. The road continued until it reached a dead end. The way ahead was closed off by a large metal gate with signs that read NO TRESPASSING and BEWARE OF GUARD DOGS.

Stacey pulled forward slowly, wound down her window and pressed a button on the gate's intercom. A gruff voice she did not recognize answered.

'Who is it?'

'It's Stacey.'

'You got an appointment?'

'Just tell him it's Stacey.'

There was a long pause, then a squeal and grinding of metal against metal as the large gate began to roll back.

A circular gravel driveway, with a fountain at its centre, led to a huge mock-Arts-and-Crafts house. The man whom she'd come to see was waiting for her at the front door, a bemused look on his face.

'What the hell are you doing here, Princess?' he asked. 'It's not safe–'

Stacey placed a finger on her lips to silence him.

'What is this?'

'Please, for once just listen. I came because there is something I need...' She had run through this many times in her mind, but now she was unable to make the words come out right.

'I mean, I've come here because there is someone you need to meet.'

Jack Stanley looked past her shoulder and into the car. 'Who?'

Stacey turned and followed his gaze. Sophie was still in the passenger seat, but now she was looking up, staring intently at the two sets of eyes that were fixed on her. Sophie hadn't heard what had been said, but she sensed something was happening. She recognized the man who had brought her to her grandparents' flat after she'd spent the night away from home. She thought she was getting into trouble. Stacey opened the door, and Sophie got out, looking at the two of them.

Stacey held her daughter's hand and led her closer to Jack Stanley. 'Sophie, this is your father.'

Acknowledgements

My deepest thanks to DCS Kieron Sharp of the City police and DCI Ian Horrocks of the Met's Kidnapping and Extortion Unit, whose time, effort and knowledge are always appreciated. Enjoy your retirement. To Tony Thompson for his intimate knowledge of London's gang culture. A long overdue thank you must go to my editor, Alex Clark, for his invaluable guidance and objective readings. Also to the rest of the team at Penguin for their continued support, especially Louise Moore for her belief and understanding from the beginning.

A special thank you to Peter Horton and Barry Bush for their friendship and encouragement in the darkest times of *Fallen Angel*. My agent, Barbara Levy, for her honesty.

As always, to my loving wife, Jackie, without whom none of this would ever have happened, and my children, Charlotte and Nathan, for being the best kids a dad could ever have.

Cheers Everyone
Kx

The publishers hope that this book has given you enjoyable reading. Large Print Books are especially designed to be as easy to see and hold as possible. If you wish a complete list of our books please ask at your local library or write directly to:

Magna Large Print Books
Magna House, Long Preston,
Skipton, North Yorkshire.
BD23 4ND

This Large Print Book for the partially sighted, who cannot read normal print, is published under the auspices of

THE ULVERSCROFT FOUNDATION